W9-BMU-925

A BAD DAY'S WORK

A NOVEL

Nora McFarland

A TOUCHSTONE BOOK
Published by Simon & Schuster
New York London Toronto Sydney

Touchstone
A Division of Simon & Schuster, Inc.
1230 Avenue of the Americas
New York, NY 10020

This book is a work of fiction. Names, characters, places, and incidents either are products of the author's imagination or are used fictitiously. Any resemblance to actual events or locales or persons, living or dead, is entirely coincidental.

First Touchstone trade paperback edition August 2010

Designed by Renata Di Biase

Manufactured in the United States of America

10 9 8 7 6 5 4 3 2 1

Library of Congress Cataloging-in-Publication Data

McFarland, Nora.
A bad day's work / by Nora McFarland
p. cm.
"A Touchstone Book"
1. Photojournalists—United States—Fiction. I. Title.
PS3613.C4395B33 2010
813'.6—dc22

2009051129

ISBN 978-1-4391-5548-6
ISBN 978-1-4391-7233-9 (ebook)

For Jeff

A BAD DAY'S WORK

ONE

The pager woke me.

In the dark, my hand reached for the nightstand and found the small, shrieking device. I was the on-call shooter that night, but not every page was something worth photographing.

I pushed my tangled curls out of the way and focused on the flashing display panel.

Possible 187. Valley Farms. Weedpatch HWY. Sheriff's Dept. on scene.

"Crap." My hand darted for the light switch.

I grabbed my jeans from the floor and slammed into them. No sign of my red shirt with the TV station logo. I threw on something from the hamper and ran down the hall to the living room.

Boots? Not under the coffee table. Not by the door.

I put on my blue coat and unzipped one of the bulging pockets. From the mess of batteries, antacids, mic cables, and who knows what else, I pulled out a large rubber band. I jammed my hair into a ponytail and searched for the hiking boots I wear to work.

A cell phone rang. I flew to my canvas gear bag at the front door. I grabbed the cell phone, and found the boots hiding underneath the bag.

I shoved a bare foot into the already tied boot while cradling the phone between my ear and shoulder. "I got the page. I'm on my way."

"It's a 187. Do you understand? Am I being clear? A 187."

Walter Trent, my station's news director, was in his early

thirties, upwardly mobile, and just doing time in Bakersfield on his way to a better job in a bigger city. He had a habit of making a statement and then asking, in the most condescending way possible, if it had been understood.

"Yes," I said. "I understand. I'm on top of it."

"Because David's ready if you can't handle it."

I almost dropped the phone. "You called David? Do you know how that makes me look?"

"This story is more important than how you look. There's only two more nights of sweeps and we're in position to take back the number one spot from Channel 19. Do you know what that means?"

It meant Trent would get a bonus and the rest of us would share a pizza, but I didn't say so. "We all want to be number one, but that's no reason to second-guess me."

His voice abruptly softened. "You've covered a lot of shifts this week. Haven't you earned a break?"

He was right. I'd worked nine days straight, one of them Thanksgiving, and felt way past fried. But this was a question of professional pride. "You know I won't be able to show my face in the newsroom if you send David out on my night."

"It's not that simple." He paused in a rare moment of indecision. "You've been screwing up a lot lately."

There it was. I knew the talk of the watercooler was my descent from dependable pro to unreliable screwup, but until now the talk had stayed behind my back.

"It's been bad luck, not screwing up." My second foot was stuck half in its boot so I kicked against the wall. The leather refused to give way. "And my luck is due to change."

A sharp exhale cut through the phone line. "Lilly, if you take this call and don't come back with an amazing story, you'll be looking for another job. Understand?"

"I can do it." I raised my knee and kicked harder. My foot went through and landed in the boot. The boot also went through and landed in the wall.

"Then get off the phone and get down to Arvin. Am I being clear?"

I pulled my foot out of the wall and shook off the plaster. "Crystal."

The line went dead.

I hauled my bag outside, pausing only to lock the front door. I turned quickly, anticipating a sprint to the news van parked at the end of the walk, but instead stopped cold.

No walkway. No palm trees. No neat row of fifties-era bungalows. Even the neon lights from the top of the Golden State Hotel had vanished. All of downtown Bakersfield had been eaten by the tule fog.

A parade of bloody images flashed through my mind. Every winter the tule fog creeps into California's Central Valley and kills motorists stupid enough to drive in its pea-soup conditions. I'd photographed enough of the gruesome wrecks to know.

My hand made a furtive move to the gear bag, but stopped midway. Calling Trent back was the smart thing. No shooter would be stupid enough to go out in this, not even a testosterone-fueled alpha male like David, but I wasn't just any shooter. I was the only woman in town who did this for a living, and plenty of jerks quietly thought I wasn't up to it. If a rival station got a shooter down to Arvin, they'd get a scoop during sweeps and I'd be the wimpy girl who chickened out.

And Trent was right, things hadn't been going well for me—mics not working, taking home the wrong pager—and this wouldn't help.

I found the news van and tossed the gear bag in the back next to my emergency stash of Mountain Dew and the already loaded camera.

I drove slowly and listened out the open window for traffic. On Highway 58 I trailed a truck in the slow lane. I followed his lights east, then exited at Weedpatch Highway.

The fog thinned as I sped past miles of Kern County farmland immortalized by Steinbeck in *The Grapes of Wrath*. In the seventy years since my grandparents had made that desperate journey from the Dust Bowl, billions of crops had been planted, grown, and harvested, and the towns of Lamont and Arvin had become small but thriving Latino communities. Agriculture had remained, along with pockets of shocking poverty, but now there were subdivisions and SUVs as well.

I had no trouble finding the right place despite the fog and the way the orchards bled into one another. A Sheriff's Department cruiser, its lights flashing alternately red and white, guarded a dirt road from behind sawhorses and police tape. Farther into the orchard, where the dirt road began to fall into darkness, a Valsec Security car held two rent-a-cops. One was older and talking on a cell phone while his younger female partner slept.

An officer jumped out of the police cruiser as I cut the engine. I took the camera from the back of the van and went to meet him at the barricade.

"I'm a shooter from KJAY. We got an automated page about a 187 at this location."

His arm swung up and pointed a blinding flashlight in my face. This wasn't the plastic kind you buy at the supermarket for $5.99. This was in the hard-core, let-there-be-light, professional-law-enforcement category.

"No statements and nobody's getting in," he said.

I raised my free hand to shield my eyes. "No statements at all?"

The officer ran the light up and down my body and settled the brightest part on my chest. "Did you say you were a reporter?"

I'm a petite woman and I've been told my dark, curly hair and big green eyes are pretty. I don't fit the mold for a typical shooter, and this wasn't the first time someone had doubted my profession. It shouldn't annoy me anymore, but it does. "No, I'm a shooter," I said. "Reporters aren't on call in the middle of the night."

"Really? You're a shooter?" He tilted his head as though it might change what he was seeing. "We're talking about the same thing, right? A news photographer? 'Cause those guys are usually pretty big and—"

"Yes, we're talking about the same thing," I interrupted. "I shoot video for KJAY's local news. Can you at least confirm there's been a murder?"

He didn't answer. His attention had been sucked back to my chest.

I was ready to reach out and smack him, cop or not, when something sparkly on my shirt caught my eye. With dawning horror I recognized the metallic decal. I was wearing my Care Bears T-shirt. I'd bought it as a joke. It depicted Care-A-Lot, the magical cloud city where the Care Bears did their best caring and sharing. I'd hoped it would look innocently sexy if I ever found the time for a social life.

This was not the time or place to look innocently sexy.

"You don't look like a shooter," the officer said.

I set the camera down in the dirt and tried to zip up my coat. "We usually have shirts with the station logo, but I dressed in a hurry." The small metal tongue fit into the zipper and I quickly pulled up. "Wanted to be first on the scene, you know, scoop the competition."

He ran the light up and down my five-foot-four-inch frame. "How do you carry all that equipment?"

I reached down and picked up the camera. "Like this."

The officer was silent behind his flashlight.

I smiled. "So, you got a dead body in there, or what?"

"I'm not authorized to comment."

My smile disappeared. "You must at least know if someone's dead."

"No comment."

"It's off-the-record."

"No comment."

"This is crazy. We always get something." I paused and took a deep breath. "Okay. You can't comment, but when will someone be here who can?"

He shook his head. "No one is giving any statements. You can take it up with the department's information officer in the morning."

Part of me knew it was a mistake to lose my temper, but it wasn't the part of me that was talking. "I want to take it up with you, right now. Do you have a body in there?"

His eyes collapsed into thin slits. "Step back onto the highway. You're trespassing."

Technically he was right. The road leading into the orchard was private property, but I doubted the owners would mind if I stood on their dirt. "I'm four feet from the public road."

He leaned forward over the barricade and raised the flashlight so it shone directly in my face. "I said step back."

I took two large steps backward onto the asphalt. "Yes, sir."

He kept the light on me as I took my tripod, called sticks by most shooters, from the back of the van. After making a few minor adjustments I attached the camera and checked its settings. When I was ready to record, the officer retreated to the darkness of his vehicle so I couldn't photograph him.

At least there were flashing police lights. They can make a grandma knitting look sinister. As if cued to my thoughts, the cruiser lights abruptly stopped. A dim bulb lit a VALLEY FARMS sign, but I knew it wasn't enough for video. I turned on the small light attached to the top of my camera and iris'd up, but a quick look in the viewfinder confirmed I'd need more light.

"I'm so fired," I mumbled.

At minimum, a VO/SOT would be required for a story this big. A VO is video that the anchor speaks over, and a SOT is a sound bite taken from an interview. I had neither.

I took a deep breath, and for the first time the familiar smells of earth and fertilizer registered. I'd spent my early childhood on a farm, and this smell, part growing, part decomposing, was almost comforting.

My eyes fell on the security car where I'd seen the man and the woman. Without the flashing lights from the police cruiser I couldn't see inside, but I knew they were there.

I raised my arms and waved back and forth. Nothing happened so I picked up a pebble and threw it at the hood of their car. The driver's door opened and the light came on inside the vehicle. The male guard pointed a questioning finger at himself.

"Yes," I said. "Please, can you come over here for a second?"

He reached for one of two identical uniform caps sitting on the dashboard while saying something to the female guard. She nodded and went back to sleep.

He ran a hand through his hair and put on the hat. It gave him a more formal air, and when he tugged on the plastic brim, it reminded me of a TV cop. As he walked to the barricade, I looked him over. He appeared to be in his fifties with salt-and-pepper hair and a comfortable spare tire. He didn't wear a jacket over his khaki-colored uniform even though it was cool enough to see our breaths.

"You're persistent, aren't you?" the man asked. The words could have been hostile, but his tone conveyed reluctance, not aggression.

"Can I interview you? It'll be real quick."

The man's mouth twisted into a sheepish frown as he shook his head. "Wish I could help, but the boss doesn't like us talking to the press. I shouldn't even be out of the car."

I didn't pause to feel disappointed. "How about off-camera? Is there anything you can tell me about what happened?"

"Not much." He gestured behind him to the cruiser. "Me and my partner were doing rounds when we got a call from the cops. They let us know about 911 calls on properties we patrol." He shrugged. "Thought it was a prank, but we headed over anyway. Cops got here right after we did."

"What time?"

"A couple hours ago. Near midnight."

I looked past him. The fog and darkness combined to hide everything beyond the security car. "How far is the crime scene?"

"A ways in. I think it's one of the spots where they load up trucks during the harvest."

"Did the victim work here?"

He rubbed his arms to fight the cold and I knew he was

regretting not wearing a jacket. "Nobody does right now. These orange trees won't yield for another year."

"Then what was he doing here?"

"There's an empty truck with the body. Looked to me like maybe a trucker got hijacked and they needed an out-of-the way spot to unload the cargo."

He stepped back as a prelude to leaving so I rushed in with another question. "Can you describe the victim?"

He shook his head. "Nah. The cops asked us to have a look, but, well . . . my partner took it kind of bad. The EMT gave her something to calm down." He looked at his shoes. "We don't usually handle this kind of thing. The most trouble we get out here is kids drinking or sweethearts using the secluded areas."

My voice softened. "Finding a body would be awful."

"It's not a good thing, that's for sure. Truth is, I'm a bit shook up myself."

"There'd be something wrong if you weren't."

He nodded and rubbed his arms again.

"Is there anything else you can tell me?" I asked. "You didn't see anyone when you got here?"

"Nope. Place was deserted. The cops said to wait out here and that's what we've been doing."

"Frank?" His partner had got out of the security car and leaned against the hood. She wore a zipped-up Valsec Security jacket over her khaki pants. "When can we go home?"

"I don't think it'll be much longer," he said over his shoulder. "Why don't you get back in the car and rest. I'll try and find out."

She nodded and got back in.

"I better get back. I have a couple more calls to make to my supervisors." He shook his head. "You have no idea the amount of paperwork something like this is going to generate."

I stepped back to the camera. "Thanks for your help and I'll keep it off-the-record."

"Sorry it has to be like that, but my boss is kind of a jerk."

"So is mine. That's why I'm worried. He wants pictures of the crime scene and they won't let me in." I looked back at the news van. "I'll try putting my headlights on and shooting here. If I'm lucky, there'll be enough light."

The security guard looked around, eyed the cop in his cruiser, then leaned toward me. "On the south side of the orchard," he whispered. "There's a dirt road that runs the edge of the property. You can get in from there."

I managed to suppress my excitement in case the cop was watching. "Thanks."

Frank smiled. "If anybody asks, you didn't find out from me."

He returned to his car and I rolled off some shots of the entrance. It was still too dark for the camera to work, but my suddenly rushing off might have made the cop suspicious. After a minute or two I casually packed up my equipment.

I sped down Weedpatch Highway as the fog poured in like cotton batting. The dirt road was small and, in the fog, would have escaped my notice without the tip. I slowed the van and left the main road. Visibility was back to a couple feet, and there was a real danger of driving into an irrigation canal.

A flashing red light broke through the fog. I slammed on the brakes and narrowly avoided a police car.

I jumped out and spotted what looked like another dirt road cutting into the orchard. The police cruiser, a circling stream of red and white light shooting from its roof, blocked the road. I had my camera out, gear bag strapped across my chest, and the sticks up on my shoulder before the two cops could get out of their cruiser and stop me.

The female officer took the lead. Her partner was a younger Latino man with dark patches on his face I guessed were acne. He hung a few feet back but smiled in a friendly way. Both wore the brown uniform of the Kern County Sheriff's Department.

"This is a crime scene," the female officer said. "Turn your vehicle around and return to the highway." Her voice was matter-of-fact. She held a flashlight, but was careful to keep it out of my face.

"All I need is a statement and a couple pictures of your car with the lights going."

She shook her head. "Not tonight. We've got a complete media blackout in effect. Order came down from the top."

I glanced toward the dirt road. Visibility lasted about three feet beyond the police cruiser, but somewhere down there was the crime scene. Was my job worth making a run for it?

I turned my body away from the dirt road. "I guess the crime scene is in the orchard anyway."

"It's down that road, but we're . . ."

I ran straight for the trees. "I'm so sorry," I yelled.

Considering all the equipment I was carrying, they should've been able to stop me. I think it was simple shock that held them back.

"Sorry about what? Where are you going?" she shouted. "I said the crime scene is off-limits."

"I have to get some shots." My voice echoed as I disappeared into the fog. "I'll be real careful."

The last thing I heard was the male officer's quiet lament "Tell me that didn't just happen."

I went in the direction I thought the road would be. I'd gone a couple feet when I hit a tree. The sticks, balanced on my shoulder and jutting out in front of me, took the hit. I readjusted and stumbled on an irrigation hose.

I pushed forward, reasoning that if I moved in the opposite direction from the police lights, I'd travel directly down the dirt road. Before long, even those tiny flashes were smothered, and I was plunged into complete darkness. I could have used my camera light, but if one of the officers followed me, I'd be a sitting duck.

"His head looks like the inside of a watermelon." The man's voice came from my right.

I dropped the sticks and flipped on the camera light. Tree limbs poked out of the fog. Small white flower buds dotted the dark foliage.

"More like sloppy joes," a second voice teased from behind me. "You know, with extra sauce."

I swung the camera around. Nobody was there.

"Show some respect for the dead, you jackass," the first voice scolded.

I did a 360-degree turn, confirming I was alone, and switched off the light. Fog can do strange things to sound. The men could have been a few feet away or a mile.

"Oh, and I suppose your watermelon crack was respectful?" They both laughed.

I knelt down onto the rock-hard dirt and thought about my options. I could keep moving forward, hoping I was going toward the crime scene, or I could turn around and try to find my way back to the van. The latter might end with Trent firing me.

A breeze came though the trees, turning the beads of sweat accumulating around my hairline into icy pinpricks. It must also have cleared some fog because, for an instant, a dull flash broke through.

I lifted the sticks back onto my shoulder and carried the camera with my other hand.

Another flash of light. I followed.

Some distance later I emerged, unseen, at the edge of a large clearing in the heart of the orchard. Water particles danced in the beams of a powerful work light and made the air appear dense and alive. On one end of the clearing a series of official vehicles stretched down a dirt road into the darkness. At the opposite end sat a large, white, unmarked tractor-trailer. Through the open side door I saw two men with the Technical Investigations logo on their jackets. They took photos inside the semi's empty cavern while a female TI appeared to be taking fingerprints from the open cab door. At various places around the clearing numbered, yellow plastic markers were placed in the dirt.

On the ground, in the middle of all this, two plainclothes officers squatted next to a blue tarp. I recognized their laughter.

A crash of metal startled me and I turned to see two attendants pulling a stretcher from the back of the coroner's wagon. "Hey, are we clear?" the first one asked.

One of the officers stood up. He wore a badge on a chain around his neck identifying him as Arvin PD. "You're fine. They got photos and did a grid search."

"For all the good it's going to do." The second officer stood and watched the attendants wheel over the stretcher. "I know you're upset we missed jurisdiction by two miles, but I'm glad the Sheriff's Department is stuck with this case. Who knows how many footprints and tire tracks those security guards destroyed driving through here."

Still unobserved, I opened my sticks and attached the camera.

"You're right, but I still don't like getting cut out of a murder case this close to Arvin."

My fingers fumbled for the record button. My eye looked through the viewfinder. I cranked up the iris and the grainy black-and-white scene sprang to life.

Behind me I heard soft steps in the dirt. "There you are." I recognized the voice of the young male officer I'd run away from. "You're not supposed to be here."

I ignored him and focused on my shots. Close-up of the word MORGUE. Medium shot of the blue tarp. Close-up of a shell casing next to a numbered, yellow marker. Wide shot of the clearing. Every extra second it took to get me out of there was another shot I could take back to the station.

A walkie-talkie crackled and then I heard the young officer say, "I found her. We're on our way back."

"Ten-four," the female officer's voice replied through static.

"Okay," he said to me. "Time to go."

I kept my eye glued to the viewfinder. "Just another minute."

"You could contaminate the crime scene, jeopardize evidence."

"I promise I'll stay right here."

The two gloved attendants lowered the stretcher and knelt next to the blue tarp. I knew the shot of the night was about to play itself out. The wheeling of the body into a morgue van would be the perfect five-second distillation of an unfathomable tragedy, easily conveyed to the morning TV audience over their oatmeal. Without that shot all my little close-ups were worthless.

The morgue attendants lifted the blue tarp off the ground.

Sloppy joes.

My stomach did a somersault and I tasted burnt metal at the back of my throat. The two Arvin PD officers walked away and disappeared behind the truck. Behind me the male officer took several deep breaths.

I continued to record as the attendants carefully bagged the victim's hands, then lifted the body into a black bag on the stretcher.

The officer behind me took a final deep breath and said, "Time to go. I really mean it."

"Just another minute."

"No. If you don't come with me right now, I'll tell one of the detectives in charge and you'll be arrested for trespassing and tampering with evidence."

Cops don't arrest the media. It's bad PR. If you misbehave, they usually complain to your news director or even the station's general manager. Even so, I was pushing it and I knew I should leave. Not just because I didn't want to go to jail, but because I didn't want to jeopardize their investigation.

But the shot was seconds from playing itself out. I think my staying had more to do with that, the compulsive need to get it right, than trying to please Trent.

The officer took a few steps back and called to someone off-camera. "Detective? We have a situation over here."

My finger gently pressed on the zoom as the attendants wheeled the body to the morgue van. The picture grew in size and panned in exact synchronization. It was textbook smooth. I was in the zone. As the van doors closed a hand covered my lens.

"Turn it off," said a voice featured prominently in my fantasies.

TWO

I hit the off button and pulled away from the viewfinder.

The man standing next to my camera exuded confidence. His good looks stood out even in generic slacks, cop buzz-cut, and Sheriff's Department jacket.

I tilted my head up and tried to look him straight in the eye, but chickened out and focused on the bridge of his nose. "I'm sorry."

"No, you're not."

One night at a gang shooting, the story went, a reporter had called him Handsome Homicide. It had stuck, but only the very brave or very stupid used the nickname to his face.

"I don't think you're the least bit sorry." Handsome turned to watch the morgue van pull out. "This area is restricted to the press. We could arrest you right now." He turned back to me as the van disappeared into the fog. "I may still do it if you've destroyed evidence stumbling around here."

We both looked down at my feet. I told you earlier I was small. That's not exactly true. There's one part of me that's huge. I'm five-four and I wear size-ten shoes.

Handsome eyed my giant, muddy, masculine boots, then looked at the younger officer's name tag. "Soto, we'd better confiscate those boots for comparison."

Soto lit up. "Yes, sir. I'll get an evidence bag."

He disappeared and I was left alone with one of Bakersfield's most eligible bachelors. I hadn't got past the first date with a guy in two years. I don't know why. Evenings always began well, but ended with the guy mumbling an awkward "We should do this again, sometime," then the screech of tires on asphalt.

Desperation compelled me to attempt small talk with Handsome. "Your job must be very challenging."

He managed a diffident shrug.

"But very rewarding too," I continued. "The harder things are, the more you get from them, right?"

Handsome ignored me and looked longingly after Soto.

So much for small talk. I stopped sucking in my stomach and glanced around the crime scene. The female TI had begun taking photos of the ground where the body had lain. One of the two men working inside the truck called her to the open side door.

"Looks like he found something," I said.

Handsome's head whipped around in time to see the male TI raise several small, transparent packages in his gloved hands.

I stepped toward the semi trying to get a better look. "Is that what's left of the cargo? What was the driver hauling?"

Handsome stepped in front of me. "We're not waiting here so you can ask questions. You may have contaminated evidence in a murder investigation."

I smiled. "So it is a murder?"

His entire body tensed as he realized what he'd done. "That was off-the-record."

I shook my head. "No, it wasn't. You have to ask before you start talking." I barely paused. "What time did the murder take place?"

"No comment."

"Any suspects?"

"No comment."

"Why aren't you making a statement for the press?"

"No comment."

"The cop out at the road said the order had come down from the top."

Handsome was spared having to repeat "No comment" by Soto's return.

He carried an evidence bag and a pair of blue bootees. "Shall I bag them here, sir?"

Handsome nodded. "Yes, then get her out of here."

Soto knelt and reached for my shoelace.

"Hold on," I said, and jerked my foot out of his reach.

Handsome took a deep breath and spoke in a controlled monotone. "What now?"

"If I'm giving up my shoes, I want a statement."

"This isn't a trade. I can arrest you for tampering with a crime scene. Is some lousy story worth getting arrested for?"

"It isn't only for the story." My raised voice drew the attention of the TIs. The two Arvin PD officers, now drinking coffee down where the cruisers were parked, also looked in our direction. "My news director says if I don't come back with something fantastic, he's going to fire me. And nobody's going to believe that no cop on this entire case would give me a statement."

Handsome didn't move. Whatever he was thinking, he kept it to himself.

"Come on," I said. "I'm a damsel in distress."

"You don't strike me as the kind of person who needs rescuing."

I paused, then nodded. "Okay. Like I said, I'm sorry for causing all this trouble." I indicated to Soto that he could remove my shoe, and once he'd knelt down, I leaned into Handsome as though I needed help balancing. He frowned, but supported my arm. The TIs went back to their work.

"But here's the deal," I whispered. "You already told me it's a murder. I'm going to quote you on the air. You can't control that now."

Soto removed the first boot and placed it in an evidence bag. He slipped a blue bootee over my bare foot and continued with the next boot.

"Now you have to decide how you want it to look." I kept my voice in a whisper and my head bent in toward his chest. "Did you deliberately disobey orders and talk to the press, or were you an incompetent ass who got tricked into saying something he shouldn't have?" I gestured to the Arvin officers. "And they're mad the Sheriff's Department got jurisdiction on this case. They'd love to tell every law enforcement agency in the county you got suckered by a girl shooter."

A smile crept in at the corners of Handsome's mouth. "Like I said, you don't look like someone who needs rescuing."

Soto put the bootee on my second foot and I let go of Handsome.

He gestured to the evidence bag in Soto's hands. "That isn't big enough for both her shoes. Go get another one and bag them separately."

"Yes, sir." Soto darted away.

Handsome turned to me. "I'll give you a brief statement, now."

I didn't waste time thanking him. I raised my sticks to Handsome's height and hit record. "Say and spell your name for me."

He complied and I checked the sound levels and adjusted the shot. Without the boots I was even shorter than usual. I had to stand up on the tips of my toes to see through the viewfinder.

"All right." Handsome pulled out a notepad and flipped the pages. "I'm going to make a statement on behalf of the Kern County Sheriff's Department."

He took a deep breath. "At approximately eleven thirty p.m. a 911 call was received stating that a man had been shot in the Valley Farms orange grove on Weedpatch Highway. A patrol unit was dispatched and the orchard's private-security firm was notified. The deceased is a black male. He was pronounced dead on the scene. Preliminary evidence suggests foul play, and we ask members of the public who might have information to come forward."

Handsome consulted the notebook and then looked up. "That's it."

"Who called 911?" I asked.

"Get out of here before the detective sergeant gets back and I arrest you."

• • •

I cursed the old, cantankerous gate as I waited for its ancient machinery to let me into the KJAY parking lot. At the first possible second I nosed the van into the slowly widening gap. That early in the morning the lot was mostly empty, and I had no trouble finding a space near the rear door of the station.

My paper bootees made a loud swishing sound against the industrial-tile floor as I entered the newsroom from the back hallway. Rows of desks, their surfaces crowded with old PCs, filled the room. A series of sliding glass doors extended down the wall on my left. Inside each was a small alcove with editing equipment. Most of the edit bays were empty, and only a handful of the newsroom desks were occupied, but in a few hours the place would be a madhouse.

I placed my tape inside the large basket hanging on the wall by the first edit bay. "I'm back from the murder," I called over to our assignment manager.

Callum's tired, jowly, old newshound face looked down at me from the raised platform where he reigned over the room. The assignment desk rose only two steps above the newsroom floor, but it had a view of almost everything. A long wall about five feet high ran along the front edge of the platform with a counter behind it that served as Callum's desk. Behind him a bank of monitors screened satellite news feeds while scanners on each side blasted the city and county emergency frequencies.

He pulled phones from each side of his head, revealing the tufts of gray hair that grew from his ears. "How'd it go?"

I waited to reply until I was standing directly in front of him. "A complete scoop. I even got the body being loaded into the morgue van."

Callum's black-and-gray unibrow parted and a small hairless strip of skin emerged above the bridge of his nose. "No kidding?"

"No kidding." I grinned. "And when I left, the other stations were parked out front with nothing."

"Lilly, you're gold." His face lit up as he hung up one of the phones. "I knew you'd break out of your slump. Won't be long before all the reporters are begging for you to shoot their stuff again."

I must have made a face because Callum shook his head. "Not that you've turned into a pariah or anything. Rod still asks for you, and he's the best we've got."

I rolled my eyes. "Rod's not our best, despite those cheesy ads Trent's been running." They were truly awful. A voice-over promised honesty and trust while an off-camera wind machine caressed our star reporter and the American flag behind him.

"Are you kidding me?" Callum scolded. "He's the hottest thing we've had in years."

I absentmindedly reached for my jacket's zipper. "I know he has a fancy doctorate in communications, but he's only been here for six months and this is his first reporter job." I lowered the zipper several inches, remembered the Care Bears shirt, and immediately reversed direction. "And out in the field he sits in the van fixing his hair while I do all the setup. Last time he was out there for thirty minutes."

"TV is a visual medium, kiddo. That's why you don't see me in front of the camera." Callum laughed, and his large, round middle jiggled. "The problem is, Lilly, you charge like a pit bull. When that works, it's great, but sometimes stories need a softer touch. Sometimes you've got to finesse it. You could learn a lot from Rod."

I made a halfhearted attempt to sound reasonable. "But he's dishonest. Once he faked interest in *Star Wars* genealogy to butter up an interview. Another time it was Dungeons and Dragons. He pretends to like people so he can use them to get what he wants. Even his name is fake."

"Rod Strong?" Callum laughed. "You think Edward R. Murrow would have done as well if he'd gone by Egbert?"

"Is that even a name?"

"I guess his parents thought so." Callum waved his hand holding the phone. "Anyway, right now Rod's the only reporter who asks for you, so maybe cut him some slack."

"He used to be the only one asking for me, but as of today, my slump is officially over."

"What's the story with the 187?" Callum put the phone back to his ear, listened for a moment, then hung up. "Do they have any leads?"

I filled him in on what I knew.

"I'm only going to say this once." Callum used a tone usually reserved for shooters who broke cameras or crashed vans. "We do not pull those kinds of stunts around here, okay? You do not disobey the cops like that."

"I know. I've never done anything like that before, but Trent said . . . let's just say he made it clear I couldn't come back empty-handed."

"He didn't mean you should break the law."

I nodded.

Callum relaxed a little bit into his chair. "But it's good you got a statement. I've hit a brick wall working my sources."

"You'd think for a hijacking they'd want publicity to flush out witnesses."

"It may still come to that, but for now I'm guessing Leland Warner is clamping down on publicity. He's big into control."

"Who?" I asked.

"Leland Warner." Callum paused, and when I didn't react, he explained, "Warner Land Holdings owns most of the unincorporated land along Weedpatch Highway and another big chunk south of Arvin."

"But the orchard was called Valley Farms."

"That's just a subsidiary. Most of the old man's businesses are set up that way. He's into everything from agriculture to sports franchises to real estate—and not just in Bakersfield."

"Then why haven't I ever heard of him?"

"He's into privacy. He's always the guy standing behind the guy getting attention."

"And you think he can give orders to the police?"

"No, but he can ask for favors. He's got a lot of sway in

Sacramento." Callum shook his head. "But it doesn't sound like the murder has anything to do with him. The thieves needed a secluded spot to transfer the cargo, right?"

I nodded. "And the orchard was perfect. They must have scouted it out in advance." I had an idea. "We haven't covered any other hijackings lately, have we?"

"No, but I can check press releases and news stories from the rest of the state." He reached for the computer mouse. "Maybe a group working the northern end of the valley has come south."

I left Callum to do his search and took a seat at an empty desk. I turned on the computer and searched the KJAY video library for Leland Warner. Nothing came up.

I returned to the assignment desk. "How come there are no hits for Warner in the archives?"

Callum didn't take his eyes off the computer monitor. "I told you. He likes his privacy. The man knows how to stay out of the news."

"You mean we've never done any kind of story about him, ever?"

"I think Leanore was going to do something a couple years ago, a profile maybe, for one of her local-history pieces. But then it got canceled."

Leanore had been the historical reporter, but had left the station a year earlier when Trent made cutbacks.

Callum glanced at the clock. "The morning show's starting soon. Where's our anchor?"

I looked around the newsroom for Marcie, but didn't see her. "She's probably getting ready."

"She spends way too much time in makeup before her shows. She's an anchor/producer. She's responsible for more than just how she looks."

My voice rose. "That's not fair. Everyone agrees the morning show has gotten sharper lately."

"Oh, and I suppose you think that's her doing?"

My reply was stifled by the arrival of Marcie herself. Her

elegant red pants suit set off the highlights in her long, strawberry-blond hair. She saw me and came straight to the assignment desk. As she approached, I noticed she'd swapped out her usual American-flag lapel pin for a sparkly snowman.

"What happened with the 187? Did you get . . ." She trailed off as she saw the blue bootees on my feet.

"I had to give up my shoes to the cops in exchange for an exclusive."

Her cheeks flushed underneath the artificial blush she'd applied for television. "A scoop during sweeps? This could make us number one again."

Callum picked up a ringing phone and started shouting into it, so Marcie pulled me a few steps from the assignment desk and lowered her voice. "And being an anchor at the number one station in town makes me a lot more attractive to bigger markets."

"Are you up for something?"

"Don't say anything, but I think Sacramento's going to make me an offer."

"Good luck," I said, trying to sound happy and failing. "It's going to be hard to replace you."

She shook her head. "Trent knew my contract was coming up and he's had Rod shadowing me. Rod doesn't know it, but I think he's a shoo-in for my job."

"Lilly?" Callum's voice interrupted the string of expletives going off in my head. "I'm coming up with zilch on other hijackings."

I returned to the desk with Marcie behind me. "Nothing at all?"

"No. The only thing even close happened last month. Almond distributors in Visalia and Hanford had loaded trucks stolen in the middle of the night."

A distant voice called from the phone in Callum's hand. He raised it to his ear, consulted a grainy monitor behind him, and barked into the receiver, "Teddy, that's awful. Your bars are barely coming in. Tilt the dish to the right. . . . I said the right!" He covered the mouthpiece with his free hand. "Some days I think Teddy couldn't shoot his butt with a Polaroid camera."

I couldn't help smirking. "I heard he managed to do it once with Freddy's help."

"Yeah, the Wonder Twins." Callum paused while Marcie and I laughed. "But this is a new low. I think Teddy may have found a way to get his head even farther up his butt."

"Go mellow on the Tedster." The three of us turned and saw Freddy standing just inside the doorway with a slice of pizza in his hand. He wore a pair of Bermuda shorts and his red logo shirt. A thick mass of bleached curls bobbed on his head, revealing dark roots. I assumed that Teddy, out on his live shot, was similarly attired. They weren't actually twins, or even related, but they were hard to tell apart. I didn't know how much of our conversation Freddy had overheard, but I doubted our comments would bother him. As far as I could tell, he wasn't bothered by much.

"We had a rager last night," Freddy explained. "Somebody spaced on putting water in the punch. It was like Kool-Aid mix and straight vodka. He's pretty fried."

Callum sighed. "I don't know enough curse words to do justice to everything stupid in that story." He glanced at the grainy monitor behind him, then took his hand off the phone's mouthpiece. "Teddy that looks worse than before. . . . Don't *dude* me, dude. I'm not your dude."

Freddy spoke to me while chewing pizza. "I heard you totally bagged a murder last night."

"She got us an exclusive," Marcie said.

"Awesome."

"Totally," I replied.

"Totally, righteous," he added.

I cocked a finger like a gun. "Right back at you."

"Freddy," Callum interrupted. "Why aren't the Christmas decorations up? You and Teddy were supposed to . . ." Callum took his first good look at Freddy and slammed the phone down. "Freddy, you know you can't wear shorts to work. What if I had to send you to court for a story?"

"Dude, I got pants in the van."

Callum turned red. "How about we wait until Trent gets in and see if he fires you this time?"

"You won't have to wait long." Walter Trent, our station news director, passed the assignment desk on his way to his office. He carried a leather Coach briefcase in one hand and what was almost certainly a latte in the other.

"Hey, you're in early, boss man." Freddy said.

Trent entered his office and set down his things. His lack of a response felt more ominous than if he'd yelled at Freddy.

Marcie glanced nervously at her watch. "We're getting close to air. I should go check the rundown."

"Don't stress. He totally won't fire me," Freddy told her. "Teddy and I work cheap. It's awesome job security."

She laughed, but made a quick exit.

Trent returned to the assignment desk. "Freddy, if I see you in shorts again, you're fired."

"Right-o, boss man. Like I said, I got pants in the van." Freddy turned and exited out the back.

Trent carefully avoided looking at me and addressed Callum. "What did we get on the murder?"

Trent's early-morning presence at the station was unusual, and I was sure he was there to check up on me. That made it all the more enjoyable to say, "It's a scoop."

"Seriously?" His face brightened. "How big a scoop?"

"Huge," Callum told him. "She got exclusive video of the body and a bite from the Sheriff's Department. We should get on the phone with promotion and run a proof-of-performance spot. Ratings are going to be great."

"Exclusive video. Do you two know what this means?" Trent took quick strides to the basket and picked the tape out. "I need to see this."

I heard movement inside the first edit bay, then my least favorite shooter appeared. David and I had never got along, but things completely deteriorated when Jake, our chief photographer, left for a better job in Las Vegas. Without a chief to keep them in line, the jerks like David were free to be, well, jerks.

"I'm done in here, if you want a deck." David's muscles bulged from under his red polo shirt as he leaned against the open sliding-glass door. "And if you don't mind, I'd like to watch Lilly's video with you."

I've heard that in large television markets a shooter works with the same reporter every day. At small stations, we have to be much more flexible. My main job is to shoot video, but sometimes I'm drafted to edit or even run teleprompter for a show. When there's no reporter available, a frequent occurrence in our understaffed newsroom, I conduct interviews and handle the newsgathering myself. Just about the only thing I don't do is write or produce, and you'll never see or hear me on the air.

So it wasn't unthinkable that David might help out with some editing. The bizarre thing was his being at the station at all, considering he worked the 10:00 a.m. to 8:00 p.m. shift. Also, it infuriated me that he'd been in the edit bay the whole time—almost certainly eavesdropping.

"What are you doing editing?" I asked. "And at this time of day?"

He returned the raw tapes he'd been using to the basket and set the edited video on a small shelf for the producer to take to playback. "Callum was short editors so I offered to work some overtime."

"You just got the urge?" I said.

David glanced at Trent, then turned his ugly smile on me. "I got an upsetting call from Trent in the middle of the night. I was so worried we were about to blow a huge story, I couldn't sleep."

"Sounds like some kind of anxiety disorder. You should see a shrink. They can do amazing things with medication nowadays."

"Okay, okay. That's enough, you two." Trent glanced at his watch and then David. "Watch the video with us and then cut a quick VO/SOT for the morning show. We'll need to lead with this story."

"Do you mind watching on one of my decks?" Callum hung up the phone he'd been using to talk to Teddy and gestured to the bank of monitors behind him. "I need to see the video so I can decide how much to use on the website."

Trent agreed and took him the tape. Callum swiveled around in his chair and inserted it into an unseen deck.

"You'll need to rewind," I told him. "All the way to the top."

He pushed a button, then reached for one of the scanners. "In honor of our scooping everybody else in town, I'll even turn down the county line."

In the five years I'd worked at KJAY, I'd never seen or heard of Callum turning down a scanner. He even had a portable one he took with him to the bathroom.

I glanced at David, hoping to catch him in a jealous sulk, but instead chanced to see a female writer in the newsroom look up from her computer. What the writer saw made her tired and cranky face melt into a dewy half-smile. Without seeing him I knew Rod had entered the room.

"Lilly?" he called to me, somehow managing to shout tactfully. "You're in early."

He took short, graceful strides and joined us at the assignment desk. It wasn't that he was handsome, because he wasn't. His face was too thin and his nose too pointy. And he was small. Not as small as me, but standing near David he looked short. What made the girls in the newsroom swoon, what made him so attractive on television, was the incomparable packaging job that was Rod Strong.

My eyes swept over his creamy brown suit and matching vest, and I couldn't help but appreciate the cut and drape of the rich fabric. A blue-striped tie coordinated with a handkerchief discreetly peeking out from the jacket pocket. They both set off the flawless blue of his eyes. On top, golden waves of silken hair crowned his head, and when he smiled, rows of perfect ivory gleamed from his mouth. I didn't know how much it cost to keep him in that style, but it had to be more than he was making at KJAY.

He exchanged greetings with David and Trent, then turned to me. "Are you available?"

"Not if you want me to shoot something. We're about to watch the video I shot at last night's homicide."

"I'm sorry, I didn't mean to interrupt." As he stepped back, he saw my feet and giggled. This undulating laugh that he never failed to produce when we worked together felt like fingernails on a chalkboard.

At that moment it annoyed me even more because I knew it was at my expense. "The police confiscated my shoes at the crime scene."

Callum cut off Rod's response. "It's done rewinding." He turned the jog wheel to scan through the black at the top of the tape. "Is this thing going to be bloody?"

"Just in the beginning," I said. "But then I did a perfect pullout as they wheeled the body bag into the coroner's wagon."

"The coroner's wagon." Trent repeated my words like a child naming his favorite candy.

"I'm scanning pretty far into the tape." Callum said. "Why didn't you start recording at the top?"

For a moment all I could feel was a dull pain in my chest as all my muscles tensed. "I did start at the top."

Callum turned the jog wheel all the way to the right. The machine revved up and wavy lines danced all over the black screen. No picture appeared. Finally, the machine grunted and stopped.

David's voice broke the silence. "End of tape."

THREE

Freddy returned wearing a pair of cargo pants and drinking a Coke through a child's curly straw. "Keepin' it real with pants." We all ignored him and stared at the black screen.

"Maybe the monitor is bad," Rod offered.

"No." David lowered his head and squeezed the ridge between his closed eyes. "You could see the tape forwarding through black."

Callum reversed the jog wheel and scanned backward through the tape. "He's right. The tape itself is black."

Black is a setting on the camera used to recycle tapes. Black video is recorded over old images to prevent them from bleeding into new ones. It's rarely used, but I always check the button before I shoot, just in case it's inadvertently been switched on.

David started to laugh. "Lilly had her camera in black."

"It can't be that." Callum shook his head. "Not even Teddy and Freddy are that stupid."

Freddy opened his mouth and let the curly straw fall back into the can. "Dude, I'm like standing right here."

"You're wrong," I told David. "That's a rookie mistake."

"Maybe it's the wrong tape?" Rod suggested.

Callum hit the eject button, glanced at the tape, then handed it to me.

Printed on the label, in my own handwriting, was *Weedpatch 187*. "No, this is it."

"Let me get this straight," Callum said. "We got nothing on a murder? Not even a cell-phone picture? We're going to be laughingstocks." Callum turned the scanners back up and reached for a phone. "We have to get somebody down to Weedpatch, ASAP."

That's when I remembered Trent. The crease between his eyebrows looked like the Grand Canyon. "David, you and Rod go turn a package on the murder."

"Nothing against David." Rod smiled in his superficially friendly way. "But since Lilly already has a handle on the story, maybe she should go with me."

"No." Trent turned and walked toward his office. "Lilly, I'd like a word."

I started to follow him in, but stopped at the doorway. "Can I check my camera first? It'll only take a minute."

"Not now."

"But it could be broken." I began to back away. "I could take it to engineering."

"No." His voice rose. "Come in and sit down."

I entered, but didn't sit. "I don't know what could have happened. I'm so careful."

"I know." He closed the door and carefully lowered the blinds on his window looking out on the newsroom. He passed the row of muted TVs tuned to cable news and took a seat behind his desk. "How old are you?"

I hesitated. Trent and I were the same age, and it wasn't fun to be reminded. "Thirty-one."

He nodded. "And how long have you worked here?"

"Five years. Are you firing me?"

He gestured to one of the empty chairs in front of his desk. "Take your coat off and have a seat? We need to have a serious talk."

I sat down without unzipping my jacket. I was sweating like a pig, but didn't think flashing the Care Bears would help me hold on to my job. "Are you firing me?"

He shook his head. "Don't be silly."

"But last night you said . . ."

"Forget last night." He picked up the latest management stress toy and squeezed the gooey ball. "You take better pictures and work more overtime than anybody else, but the last six months has been one disaster after another. You have to get your act together. I don't care what it takes. Am I being clear?"

"Yes," I said out of habit.

"Before Jake left, you were my best shooter and I hope you will be again." Trent switched the ball to his other hand and leaned back in his chair. "You won't, however, be our new chief photographer."

My eyes whipped up from the floor, where they'd been appropriately downcast. "Chief photog? What are you talking about? You're hiring from outside."

"We've gotten by with a crew of six since Jake left. If we don't hire a seventh shooter, we can pay for equipment upgrades with money saved on payroll. Before your recent problems, you were a leading contender."

"But I could never replace Jake. Nobody here could."

"I've already interviewed an internal candidate. He's been here almost as long as you and wants more responsibility."

My breath caught. Only one shooter fit that description. "Not David."

"I'm waiting for approval from upstairs before I offer it to him."

"Are you crazy?"

"Next to you he's the best I've got, and people respect him."

I stiffened. "Are you saying people don't respect me?"

"Aside from your recent sloppy work—"

"I'm not sloppy. It's been bad luck."

"You have other issues too. The chief has to be someone the other photogs will listen to, someone who can coach them and referee disputes. David can do that."

"There has to be someone else. What about that new guy on nights?"

Trent sprang forward. "He's been here for three months and you don't even know his name. Right there is half the reason you can't be chief. You make no effort to have any kind of relationship with the other shooters. When your buddy Jake was here, it was okay, he smoothed the way, but now you have to get by on your own—and you're doing a lousy job of it. Am I being clear?"

I shook my head. "I'm not running for Miss Congeniality and I never asked to be chief photog."

"And that's the other half. You've got no ambition. The minute Jake gave notice, you should have been beating down my door trying to get the job. You've been here longer than anybody else and you're the best shooter."

"What happened to nobody respecting me?" I yelled, not caring who heard.

"Respect is the other half."

I jumped out of the chair. "That's one hundred and fifty percent of why I can't get a job I don't want!" I stormed out and slammed the door behind me.

I took large, quick steps out of the newsroom. I walked straight to my van and ripped open the back door. My camera rested between two sandbags. I flipped it over. All my anger vanished. The camera was set to black. After staring at it for several moments, I flipped the switch back to normal.

I spent the next several hours posting video to the station website and editing tape off the national feeds. It allowed me to hide in an edit bay while being productive.

Eventually I heard the sliding-glass door open and looked up to see Marcie. "How was your show?" I asked.

"Fine." She pointed to my feet and smiled. "No more blue bootees?"

"I keep an extra pair of boots in my locker." Along with the station-logo shirt I was now wearing.

She paused. "You okay? About this morning?"

"Sure."

"If you need to talk or something . . ."

"I'm good, but thanks for the offer."

She nodded and slid the door back into place. Marcie was the closest thing I had to a friend and I should probably have confided in her. But talking about it was the last thing I wanted to do.

An hour later, one of Callum's desk assistants banged on the glass and said they needed me. I finished the piece I was working on and left the safety of the edit bay. The newsroom was busy now. Most of the desks were taken and people were working. No one looked at me or acknowledged my early-morning disgrace, but they all knew.

At the assignment desk, one of the Wonder Twins stood next to a female reporter while the other one—I had no idea which was which—hung back watching.

They both chomped on cookies from Smith's Bakery. The one in back saw me and held out the bag. My longing for one of the sun-shaped butter cookies, with yellow icing and a brown smiley face, reminded me that I'd skipped breakfast. But I shook my head and stepped up to the assignment desk.

"I thought we weren't doing the sick kid's stories anymore." The other Wonder Twin spoke while still chewing. "The mom is, like, from hell, okay? I mean, I can get bossed at from my own mom. I don't need it from her."

The reporter rolled her eyes. "It doesn't matter, Freddy. You're coming with me to shoot my crime-on-the-rise package." She glanced at her watch. "And we're late for the first interview." She grabbed Freddy by the arm and they exited.

Callum picked up a piece of paper and offered it to me. "And you get over to the ballpark. Shoot some B-roll and a couple sound bites."

I took the paper. It was a press release from the local baseball team about their hosting a little sick kid. I glanced over my shoulder, then lowered my voice. "I'm shooting a puffy D-block feature story and Freddy is shooting the hard-news piece? Reporters would actually rather work with Freddy?"

Callum shuffled some papers and avoided looking at me. "What can I say?"

I threw the press release back on his desk and raised my voice. "I thought the little boy went into remission?"

Teddy, oblivious of the tension, stepped forward while brushing cookie crumbs off his shirt. "He did. This one's the little blind girl. She's way cuter."

"The kid's throwing out the first pitch at practice today," Callum explained. "The team is making a donation so the kid can get . . . stuff that blind kids need. It's going to be a 'KJAY Cares' piece."

"If she's blind, how's she throwing out the first pitch?" I asked.

Callum raised his voice in frustration. "She's not actually blind. She's going blind."

"But, like," Teddy stammered, "she's totally cute. The sugar-and-spice quotient is so ginormous, it makes up for her not being, like, you know, totally blind."

"Get out of here, Teddy," Callum ordered. "They want a live shot from the murder scene in the noon show. I already texted Valley Farm's address to your cell phone. And I don't want a repeat of this morning. Get me a good, clean signal."

"Yes, sir." Teddy exited.

Callum handed the baseball fax back to me. "If you get a chance out at the ballpark, there is something you can shoot for the crime-on-the-rise package."

"What? Some kind of community outrage/reaction thing?"

"Not exactly. The package is about criminals using foreclosed or secluded properties without the owner's permission—like the orchard last night. Ideally we'd have a sound bite from Valley Farms." One of his phones started ringing and he reached for it, but didn't answer. "But of course Valley Farms won't comment because Leland Warner likes his privacy."

Callum took an extra second to shake his head in disgust at people who like privacy, then answered the phone. "KJAY, we're on your side." He listened, then glanced at Trent working in his office. "Yes, he does. May I ask who's calling? . . . How big is the leak?" Callum listened, then frowned. "I'll tell him. . . . I'm sure he'll come right home."

Callum hung up the phone. I started to ask a question, but he cut me off. "So here's the deal, Warner also owns the baseball team. While you're there shooting the little sick kid, make sure you interview someone from management. The higher up the better. In the middle of all the 'we love charity, we love kids,' ask about the murder. Just get somebody from management to say crime is bad and they're all upset it happened on company property, yada yada yada. It might earn you some goodwill around here." Callum got up and started walking toward Trent's office. "And get me a nice VO/SOT about the little sick kid. Make it heartwarming and here by noon."

I turned off the road at Drillers' Park—the home of the Bakersfield Drillers for the last sixty years. The modest ballpark has a large concrete grandstand with two smaller stands running down each baseline. An abundance of trees and shrubs around the structures, and the emptiness of the parking lot that day, made it look like an oasis in the center of an asphalt desert.

A few cars were parked near the entrance, and I recognized a Valsec Security car similar to the one at the orchard entrance. What I did not see were other news vans. This was bad for the little sick girl. At the height of tearjerkers' celebrity, every news organization in Bakersfield would turn out to watch them pick their nose. Clearly this kid's star was fading.

I sound cynical, I know. My first little sick kid died. The whole town went into mourning. Reporters walked around the newsroom crying. Hundreds of people, most of them strangers, turned out for the funeral. All that raw human emotion was genuine. I've never had the least doubt of that. But in the midst of all that genuine emotion people had time to primp for the cameras and angle themselves so they'd be in the background of my shots. The tears are always real and the grief is always real, but people want their tears and grief to be seen. They want to get credit for it.

I parked next to a giant inflatable Santa awkwardly placed near a palm tree and got out. The morning sun had chased off the last of the fog, but a chill still hung in the air. After double-checking every button, setting, and connection on my equipment, I locked the van and entered the ballpark through an unmanned turnstile.

I turned into the passageway leading to the field and passed a security guard. He wore the same tan uniform as the man I'd met at the orchard entrance, but was much younger. He saw my camera and smiled. "I'll let them know you're here."

"Thanks."

I continued and emerged in the stands on the third-base side. Even on that December day, with the grass brown and the temperature low, I felt a rush of nostalgia seeing the men warming up in the outfield. Our ballpark is authentic—the tickets are cheap, the mustard is bright yellow, and the field is close enough to see the players' faces. When God created baseball, this is what he intended.

I quickly carried my gear down to the seats behind home plate where the sick girl's mother stood videotaping the players in the field. Her daughter, in a sweet yellow dress, devoured an ice cream cone nearby.

"I don't know if you remember me," I said to the mother. "My name's Lilly. I'm from KJAY."

She put down the video camera. Her hot-pink Jackie O ensemble stood out against the blue stadium seats and complimented her platinum blond hair. "You came to our house when Stenson's donated that wonderful new TV, right? So my baby could hear the special video descriptions."

I glanced at the little sick girl. Her thick, black glasses, pink ribbons, and general aura of adorableness hadn't changed. "That's right. About two months ago."

"I remember." The woman folded up the video camera and placed it in her purse. "The new TV has been such a help."

"That's a nice-looking camera."

"Isn't it? The people at Camera Barn donated it." She looked down at her daughter, then back up at me. "My baby's touched so many people's hearts."

I started to ask how an expensive camera would help her daughter, but was interrupted by the arrival of two men.

"Howdy there," the younger one said, and waved the cowboy hat he carried in his hand. He wore a dark brown suit with white piping around the edges, a gaudy bolo tie in the shape of a horse and rider, and a ridiculous belt buckle with the words REMEMBER THE ALAMO. Despite the good-old-boy greeting I hadn't detected an accent.

The second man, about fifteen years his senior, followed in conventional slacks and dress shirt. I recognized him from previous shoots as the general manager of the team. I offered my hand to him. "I'm Lilly Hawkins from KJAY."

The would-be cowboy intercepted me and vigorously shook my hand. "I'm Tom Sinclair, general manager of the Drillers." He gestured dismissively to the other man. "And this is my assistant Bob."

A ghost of a frown shot across Bob's face.

Sinclair's palm was damp and clammy so I tried to withdraw my hand. He responded by bringing his other hand up and locking me in. He made eye contact and leaned in. "The Drillers love the press. You guys at"—he looked at the logo on my camera—"you guys at KJAY are my favorite station. I watch you all the time."

"That's very kind, Mr. Sinclair."

"Please call me Tom."

I gave a strong tug and freed my hand. "So what's the plan for today? This is only a training session, right?"

"That's right. The league isn't playing this time of year." He gestured to the little girl. "This precious angel will throw out the first pitch and then we can move on to the important part of the story—the part where I make a generous donation to her care."

"Do you mind if we go ahead and start." I glanced at my watch. "I'm on a tight deadline."

"Shouldn't we wait for the other stations?" the mother asked. After a few moments of uncomfortable silence her perkiness faded. "Unless you don't think they're coming."

"Sometimes signals get crossed," I explained. "Stories fall through the cracks."

Sinclair scanned the empty grandstands. "I thought some fans would come out today, but I can't really blame them for not showing. The Drillers are boring." He turned to me. "But that's all going to change. I've been brought in as a fix-it man to get us back on track."

Bob stared daggers at him, but remained silent.

"But it isn't just today," the mother said with growing outrage. "More and more, the press is ignoring my baby. The public must be so disappointed. My baby is in the hearts and prayers of the entire community."

Sinclair ignored her and continued on his own topic. "I'm really going to shake things up around here and bring in a younger crowd."

The mother jumped toward me. "I know! How about your station does a special just about my baby?"

"Let's head down to the field." I picked up my gear and didn't wait for anyone to agree. I stepped onto the field and made a beeline for the players in the outfield.

Sinclair followed at my elbow. "We're going to turn this place around. I'm putting in a sports bar and—"

"That's just in the idea stage right now." Bob rushed to my other elbow. "Please don't put that on TV."

"And we're going to have a million-dollar raffle at the end of the season," Sinclair continued. "The more games you attend, the more times your name goes in the pot."

Bob's face turned red. "Oh, please don't put that on TV. That's really, really in the idea stage."

The mother came from behind and pushed through the gap between Bob and my elbow. "Maybe the special could air after the news. It could be an hour of local interest."

"Those time slots are spoken for," I said. "We have contracts."

Sinclair jumped out ahead and stepped in front of me. "The Drillers could sure use the media's help getting the word out."

The mother took my arm. "The community is desperate for news of my baby. She's a precious part of Bakersfield that won't be forgotten."

As if a lightbulb turned on over our heads, we simultaneously turned around. The little sick girl stood where we'd left her, still eating her ice cream cone in the stands.

The mother laughed nervously before hurrying back for her daughter. "Baby. We're throwing the ball now."

Sinclair placed a clammy hand on my shoulder. "So anyway, I'd like to partner with the media and get the word out."

I escaped his grasp by bending over to set down my equipment. "Which player is going to catch the girl's throw? I should probably interview him."

Sinclair and Bob exchanged nervous glances.

I took my first good look at the players. Suspicious strands of gray peeked out from under several Drillers caps, and some of the men sported unusually large guts. "Those don't look like professional ballplayers."

Sinclair passed his cowboy hat from one hand to the other, crushing it. "Sure they are."

I looked at Bob. "What's going on?"

Sinclair didn't let him answer. "Okay, okay. You got me. It's December and the team isn't here."

"Then who are those men?"

"Amateur enthusiasts," Sinclair said proudly. "They play every week for their company softball team."

I stared at him without speaking.

"This is the season of giving," he continued. "It's much more appropriate to do something like this now than in the middle of the summer."

I still didn't say anything.

Sinclair dropped his hat and his air of confidence. "Okay, okay. I thought we could do something nice for the kid and get the team some publicity. Is that so wrong?"

"But these aren't the Drillers," I yelled. "You lied to us."

"You have to do the story." Sinclair looked over his shoulder. The mother and little girl had reached the field and were quickly approaching. "Think how disappointed the kid will be. You'll break her heart and she has that awful disease."

His mouth contorted into an over-the-top grin as he hurried to meet the mother and the daughter. "Are you ready to play some baseball?"

Bob picked up Sinclair's hat, but didn't follow him.

"Why is he dressed like a cowboy?" I asked.

"When Mr. Sinclair got here two weeks ago, he saw a forty-year-old picture of Jim Ensley, the original owner, in my . . . I mean, *his* office. Jim was a Texan and proud of it. Tom seems to think dressing like the picture is part of being general manager."

I watched as Sinclair put an arm around the mother and took the little girl's hand. "How exactly did he get this job?"

When Bob didn't answer, I said, "Off-the-record."

"From what I can tell, he made one heck of a first-class mess in his last position. The powers that be wanted him transferred fast, and I got stuck with him."

"Why keep him around if he's a screwup?"

"Nepotism." Bob sighed. "He's pretty much unfireable."

Nepotism? If Leland Warner's family tree was filled with idiots like Sinclair, then I understood why the man valued his privacy.

Bob continued, "They probably figured Tom couldn't do much damage here, during the off-season."

"They were wrong."

Bob looked from Sinclair in the distance to me. "The Drillers have a long history of charitable works. We care about kids—really care about them. I've been doing fund-raisers for CASA and the Boys and Girls Clubs for years."

"I know. I've covered them and I know you do a lot of things privately, without any publicity."

Sinclair was now only a few yards away with the mother and child in tow. "Please," Bob begged. "Please try and remember that, if this goes badly."

"I think you mean *when,* not *if.*"

Sinclair came to a stop and bent down to the little sick girl. "Tell the nice lady how excited and happy you are. Tell her how much fun it's going to be when you throw out the first pitch."

The little girl looked down at her patent-leather shoes.

"Would you like to interview me?" the mother asked. "I have a lot to say about how blessed my baby feels."

"I don't think we'll need to record you today," I said. Her smile vanished. "I'm going to concentrate on your daughter. Get her perspective."

"Fantastic." Sinclair tossed his hand backward and struck Bob in the chest. "See, I told you. The players don't matter."

I lowered the sticks to the girl's height and attached the camera. Her glasses were outrageously thick, but her gaze followed me as I moved to clip the mic on her dress.

"Hi there. Do you remember me?"

She looked in my direction and nodded her head. I crouched down next to the camera, and the girl's head followed my movement.

"How old are you?"

She didn't say anything. She looked at her mother, then back at the camera. She lifted a finger to her nose and reached inside.

"Baby!" The mother grabbed her hand. "Now tell the nice lady how old you are."

"Four," she said in a small voice.

"You're a big girl," I told her. "Do you like baseball?"

She didn't answer.

"I love baseball," I said. "My whole family used to come to games."

No reaction.

"How about sports? Do you like sports?"

She shrugged her shoulders.

"Can you say in your own words how you feel about sports?"

She looked at her mother, then back at me.

I tried to give her a reassuring smile. "How does it make you feel to be here today?"

No answer.

"She's shy." The mother took the video camera out of her purse and walked behind me. "Baby, pretend it's you and me. I'm the one taking the pictures, okay? Don't be nervous because it's just you and me."

"How does it make you feel to be here today?" I asked again.

She thought for a moment, looked past me to her mother, then said, "I like ice cream."

"Can you talk about that a little bit?"

"It's good."

I waited for her to continue, but nothing happened.

From a sound-bite standpoint, "It's good" doesn't cut it. At the very least I needed "Ice cream is good at the ballpark," and even that wouldn't make it on the air.

I took a deep breath and tried again. "In your own words tell me if you like ice cream at the ballpark?"

She looked at me. She looked at her mom. She didn't say a word.

Sometimes when a kid won't talk, it helps to play a game. It can loosen them up. At least you get video of a happy kid having fun. I picked up a softball from the grass and tossed it at her. "Catch."

The ball hit her in the chest like a cannonball. She fell backward and for a few seconds the field was silent. Then the most gut-wrenching wail I've ever heard erupted from her prostrate little body.

FOUR

"Baby." The mother ran past me and dropped to the ground. Bob followed.

"I'm so sorry," I said, then turned to Sinclair. "I don't understand. She didn't even try to catch it."

"You know she's blind, right?"

"She's not blind, she's going blind."

"Who told you that?" He laughed. "She's blinder than a bat."

"She is?"

"Of course. Everyone knows that."

The players wasted no time responding to the emergency. Soon a mini-mob surrounded the mother and child. "What happened?" someone asked over the child's cries.

Another man in the crowd answered, "Somebody threw a baseball at the little blind girl."

I started packing up gear in case the mob turned.

Sinclair raised his hands in the air and adopted what he probably thought was a statesmanlike demeanor. "Now, now. I'm sure doing violence to the guilty party would make us all feel a lot better—"

"No, no, I'm sure it wouldn't." Bob broke free from the crowd. "It was an accident. Remember that everyone. An accident."

"Yes, as I was getting to before you interrupted me." Sinclair glared at Bob, then continued, "No matter how good we might feel punishing the person who did this, and I'm sure it would feel very, very good . . ."

The crowd grunted its agreement. I wondered how fast I cold make it to the van carrying all my equipment.

"We have to remember, it truly was an accident and we have to keep things in perspective." Sinclair gave Bob a superior smirk, then lowered his hands. Several men rushed in to ask questions.

"Bob?" I stepped to his side and tried to keep my voice level and calm. "Is the kid okay?"

He started to answer, but kept pausing to look at the potential catastrophe of Sinclair fielding questions from angry players. "Ah . . . she's . . ."

The crowd parted and the mother charged at me. She cradled the girl in her arms. "How dare you assault my child like this?"

All eyes turned to me, and a frightening quiet descended on the field.

"I'm so sorry," I said to the mother. "Of course your daughter won't want to continue with the interview. Maybe if you're not too busy caring for her I could interview you instead?" Don't judge me. It was an extreme situation.

She tilted her head slightly. "I thought you didn't want to interview me?"

"That was before this unfortunate accident."

She looked at her daughter, who had stopped crying. The girl squirmed and contorted her body so the mother was forced to set her down.

"I think if she has another ice cream, everything will be fine." The mother reached down and adjusted a ribbon in her daughter's hair. "And after all, it was an accident. I certainly don't blame you."

The girl jumped up and down. "I want strawberry."

The girl's show of strength appeased the players, who drifted back to the outfield while Bob took the girl to get the promised treat. When I'd finished interviewing the mother, a player led the little girl to the pitcher's mound and helped her toss the ball toward the catcher. Everyone cheered. Then, just like that, the photo op was over.

Sinclair pushed his way out of the dugout as players streamed in. "That was just great," he said, and turned to gloat at Bob, who was carrying a box behind him.

The mother took the little girl's hand. "Oh, yes. She loved it, didn't you, sweetie?" The mother didn't wait for a response. "Sports are so important to children and I feel terrible that she won't . . ." She paused as if struck by an idea. "By the way, do you have something for me?"

Bob removed an envelope from his back pocket and extended it to the mother. "Here's the—"

Sinclair snatched the envelope. "It's my place to make the presentation, not you." He straightened his jacket, then held out the crushed envelope to the mother. "Please accept this generous check on behalf of the entire Drillers team and myself personally."

The mother took the envelope and tore into it. The contents made her smile.

Sinclair gestured to the box in Bob's hands and asked, "Are those the items we talked about?"

Bob glanced at me before stepping closer to Sinclair and saying in a low voice, "Sir, I'm not sure—"

"Are they or are they not?" Sinclair cut him off.

"They are, but this may not be the best—"

Sinclair took the box and extended it to the mother. "In addition, please accept this selection of Drillers merchandise."

Sinclair paused to smile at the little girl, and I thought he might not be that bad of a guy. The thought only lasted a moment.

He looked back up at the mother. "Merchandise which, I remind you, your daughter is contractually obligated to wear at various events for which there will be media coverage."

"What?" I interrupted.

Bob groaned and placed a hand over his eyes.

My voice rose. "You signed an endorsement deal with a little sick kid?"

"It's a very common practice," Sinclair explained. "Tiger Woods wears Nike gear to all of his tournaments."

I grabbed a Drillers cap from the box. "Is she contractually obligated to wear this at the doctor's office?"

"Don't be silly." Sinclair laughed. "Nobody would see her there."

Bob groaned again.

Sinclair extended the box to the mother, and this time she took it. "If any of it doesn't fit or you need replacements, don't hesitate to call us. You have my direct line because I'm taking charge of this project personally."

"Thank you. You've been very kind. A true gentleman." She took the cap from my hand, then looked down at her daughter. "You want to take some ice cream home?"

The little girl giggled.

"I'm sure we can arrange that," Bob said. "If you'll follow me . . ."

I wanted to stop him from going. An interview with Bob would be straightforward and to the point. He'd speak in nice sound-bite-ready sentences. Sinclair would be a disjointed, self-involved nightmare. But if I was going to sandbag one of them with a question about Valley Farms, Bob was much more likely to keep his head and not comment.

I let him leave with the girl and her mother, then held out a lapel mic to Sinclair. "May I interview you?"

"Of course." He leaped toward my outstretched hand. "I'm only too happy to help."

My cell phone rang as I was getting him miked up.

I checked the caller ID and let it go to voice mail.

It wasn't that I didn't like my uncle Bud. When I was a kid, I used to love when my father's much older brother rolled into town. Bud never failed to stop by for a home-cooked meal between escapades and misadventures. He was mischievous, slightly seedy, delighted in provoking my straitlaced mother, and had no problem getting down on the ground to play with his little nieces. He was old enough to be my grandpa, but in his way seemed younger and more alive than my quiet and deliberate father.

But despite the occasional voice-mail messages we exchanged around holidays, and despite our being the only two members of the family left in Bakersfield, I hadn't seen him in twelve years. I assumed this message would tell me how sorry he was we hadn't connected for Thanksgiving. He'd go on to suggest, in a vague way, that we do something for Christmas. Later in the day, I'd call him and leave a similar message. At Christmas we'd repeat the whole thing.

I didn't know how we had got into this loop. Probably it started after my father's death, when neither of us wanted to be reminded of the loss, and then became a kind of self-fulfilling prophecy. I didn't know what I'd say if I actually had to talk to him. I think he felt the same way. My calls to him always went to voice mail too.

I raised the sticks to Sinclair's height and began triple-checking the camera settings. "This will only take a second," I told him.

"How on earth did you end up in a job like this? You're much too pretty to be carrying all this equipment around."

His oily tone made me want to give him a nasty put-down and head back to the station, but I hadn't even tried to get the Valley Farms sound bite. "I needed a job and an old friend was the chief photographer at the station. He got me on part-time, but I did well and moved to the regular crew."

"Is your boyfriend still around?"

I stayed focused on the camera and didn't look at him. "If you mean my friend the chief photographer, he's working in Las Vegas now."

"If you ever want to get together for a drink, let me know." He followed my gaze to his wedding ring. "It would be strictly business, of course. I'd love to discuss my plans for the team."

"I'm sure you have all kinds of plans," I said before I could stop myself.

Luckily, Sinclair didn't appear to notice the sarcasm. "Tons and tons. I'm going to whip this place into shape."

I began the camera recording and asked him some basic

questions. He spoke in run-on sentences about children being the future and the team's commitment to charity. Once that was out of the way, he quickly resumed talking about his own accomplishments and plans for the Drillers.

Finally he paused to catch his breath. I jumped in with a question I hoped would set me up to ask about Valley Farms. "Where were you working before you came to the Drillers?"

"That was a very different business. But my role there was similar. See, I look for big ideas and—"

Fearing another monologue, I interrupted. "Bob mentioned you were transferred from somewhere else in the same company."

"That's right. One of our wineries, but I've also worked in real estate and construction." Sinclair smiled. "Actually, I'm being groomed to take over. That's why I move around so much. I'm getting a good overview of all the different aspects of the business."

"It's terrible about the murder last night at Valley Farms."

He didn't say anything. In retrospect, that should have been a sign something was wrong. I didn't notice, though.

"It must be upsetting for something so gruesome to happen on company property," I continued. "I was actually there last night taking pictures. Some of the things I photographed should never be seen on television. It must be very unpleasant for you to be connected to a crime like that."

This was where he was supposed to smile and tell me everyone felt terrible and hoped the criminals were caught and prosecuted.

Instead, I watched in shock as Sinclair turned and ran for the dugout.

Chaos spiraled around the now packed newsroom. An intern sprinted between desks, then exited toward the control room. An editor burst from his edit bay just as I placed my tape in the raw-video basket, and almost ran into me.

I stopped one of Callum's desk assistants as she prepared to run a handful of tapes to Playback. "Everything okay?"

"Noon's crashing," she said. "Marcie got way behind without

Rod, but it's okay. He's back now." She turned to go, but stopped. "I thought you went home?"

"No. I've been shooting the little blind girl."

"Oh, right." She looked confused, but continued on her way.

I walked to the assignment desk, now decked out in festive garlands, and pinched Callum on the shoulder.

He noticed me for the first time and pulled the phones away from his ears. "How'd it go?"

"Video's in the basket. I got the kid throwing out the first pitch and an interview with the mom. It's cued up." I was crossing my fingers nobody decided to rewind the tape. Throwing a ball at a little blind kid was not the way to revive my reputation. "Anything new on the murder?"

"Rod and David are back. They got enough for a package."

I shook my head. "No, I mean new information."

"Oh, sure, didn't anybody tell you? It's solved." He smiled sweetly. "It was Miss Scarlet with the lead pipe."

"I'm serious." I stepped up onto the platform and sat on the edge of Callum's desk. "Something weird happened at the ballpark."

He hung up one of the phones. "Something newsworthy weird or something I'm-wasting-Callum's-time weird?" Before I could answer, he leaned around me and shouted, "Carl."

An editor appeared in an edit-bay doorway. "What? I'm crashing the second package."

"We need you to edit the sick-kid VO/SOT for the noon."

"I just told you I'm crashing the second package."

"Lilly, you're back." Rod was doing a walk-and-talk across the newsroom while juggling scripts and wire copy. "I'm producing the noon for Marcie."

The editor took advantage of the momentary distraction to retreat into the edit bay.

"How was the shoot at the ballpark?" Rod's voice carried an air of confidence and authority I hadn't heard before. "Anything I need to know?"

"Usual stuff," I said. "The kid throwing the ball and an interview with the mother. It's in the basket, all cued up."

The sports reporter stepped backward into Rod's path while attempting a trash-can free throw, but Rod deftly maneuvered around him and stopped at a writer's desk. "Did you hear that?" Rod asked her. "Can you handle the script?"

She looked up from her keyboard with a dreamy smile. "Whatever you say, Rod."

"It doesn't matter," Callum said. "We don't have an editor."

"I'll find someone." Rod started toward the door.

"Remember, it's cued up," I said. "No need to rewind."

He stopped suddenly and turned back to me. "I'm a little pressed now, but I need to talk to you. Come find me before you go home."

I shook my head. "I'm not going home."

"Right . . . um . . ." He produced his annoying giggle. "I mean if you have to leave for some reason, come find me so we can talk."

"What about?"

"It's not a big deal." He looked around as though he didn't want to be overheard. "It's about the chief-photographer job."

"I already know David's probably getting it."

"Right, but you were in the running, early on."

"Did everybody at the station know that but me?"

He shrugged. "It was common knowledge."

"Well, after all my equipment problems, I'm definitely not in the running anymore."

Rod took another look around to make sure we weren't being listened to. "That's kind of my point."

"What do you mean?"

"Rod," the control room TD called from the doorway. "The director needs to see you, like five minutes ago."

"I'm coming." Rod turned back to me. "I'm sorry, I have to go, but find me before you leave."

"I'm not leaving," I said loudly.

"Right. Sorry." He flashed his perfect teeth before exiting.

Callum had disappeared into the copy room and I followed him. "I need to talk to you about this guy Sinclair."

He took some pages off the copier and began leafing through them. "Who?"

"Tom Sinclair. He's the new Drillers' GM and I think he's related to Warner."

"So?"

"I asked him about the murder last night."

"Good." He looked at me. "Did you get a sound bite for the crime-on-the-rise package?"

"No. He ran away and wouldn't talk to me."

He sighed and turned his attention back to the copies. "Okay. I guess we'll try something else."

"You don't get it." I stepped farther into the room. "He literally ran away—like I was chasing him with a cleaver."

Callum's unibrow raised and he chuckled. "What?"

"I know. I've never had an interview end that weird." I couldn't help smiling as I pictured Sinclair. "He was still miked up. If I hadn't grabbed the camera, he would have knocked the whole thing over and dragged it into the dugout."

Callum's amusement faded. "You think Valley Farms has something to hide?"

"It would explain why they're not talking. Have you heard anything more from the Sheriff's Department?"

"No. They haven't released the name of the victim or the trucking company or even what he was hauling. . . . Maybe the dead guy was an employee."

One of the Wonder Twins walked in, saw us, and froze with a corn chip halfway to his mouth. "Oh, dude. Are you, like, telling her? I'm totally sorry. I wouldn't have come in."

Callum glared at him. "Close the door on your way out, Teddy."

"For sure." He started to leave, but dropped his bag of chips. He nervously bent to pick them up. "Sorry," he stammered, then exited.

"Telling me what," I asked.

Callum took a deep breath as though girding himself. "I don't like having to be the one to do this. Trent went home for the day, which is fine except now he's called and dumped this all on me."

"Just tell me."

"You're going to be formally reprimanded for this morning. Trent says the suits upstairs are pushing for it."

"What kind of reprimand?"

"It's not a big deal."

"What kind of reprimand?" I repeated with more urgency.

Callum paused. "An official write-up in your file and a two-day suspension."

Shooters who used news vans to transport kegs of beer were suspended. That's the league I was in. "Starting when?" I finally asked.

"Now." He glanced quickly at me, then away. "Trent said to collect your cell phone and van keys and send you home."

The door opened, and one of the Wonder Twins stuck his head in. "Dude, Teddy told me you two were in here." He looked at me. "I'm full on commiserating with you, Lilly. Looks like you and me are in the same club. We both been suspended." He laughed. "I think it's a pretty sweet deal. I mean, you screw up and then get time off. How awesome is that?"

Callum rolled his eyes. "Now is not the time, Freddy."

"But, like my mistake was superboring. Chronic lateness. How lame is that?" Freddy pointed at me. "But, dude, you're, like, in the record books. People will be talking about this forever. You're going to be legend."

"Close the door on your way out," Callum ordered.

"Dude, you've been hanging in this business forever," Freddy said to him. "Isn't this, like, the most? Won't people be talking about this forever?"

Callum looked down at his copies. "I said, shut the door behind you."

"Later." Freddy withdrew and the door closed.

As soon as we were alone, I spoke. "Thanks for jumping to my defense."

"He's right. It was the most boneheaded thing I've ever seen. You should be thanking me for not saying so in front of him."

"Wow, thanks."

He shook his head. "I won't pat your hand and tell you it's okay, because it's not."

I gestured to the closed door. "What about those two idiots? A day doesn't go by where Teddy and Freddy don't lock themselves inside something."

"They're jokes." His eyes focused on me with a rare directness. "You are so much better than them. You've got so much talent, but you never step up. You never put yourself out there, and it really pisses me off."

I started to leave.

"Wait," he ordered. "I'm not the enemy here."

"You don't sound like a friend."

I left without turning in my equipment or van and made the short drive home through downtown. Major retailers abandoned the city center decades ago, but I've always preferred its fifties architecture and funky local shops to the cookie-cutter strip malls in the suburbs. The area even has extra sparkle in December from holiday banners and decorations. But on that drive home, all I saw were boarded-up storefronts and homeless crouched in doorways.

I parked the van at the curb and checked my camera settings. I loaded a fresh tape and replaced the camera battery. I wasn't on call, I wasn't even supposed to have the camera, but I was operating on autopilot and followed my usual routine.

I passed Mrs. Harris's bungalow and stopped to pull her reindeer from where it had fallen into the manger scene. Inside my bungalow the lights were on, a result of my hasty departure, and that, along with the smell of last night's fast-food dinner, highlighted the state of grubby clutter I lived in. When I was younger, I'd foolishly run up large credit-card debts. In the last five years I'd steadily paid them down by living cheaply. That meant only owning thrift-store furniture or other people's castoffs. Books were the only things I allowed myself to spend money on.

I walked down the hallway to my bedroom. Stacks of books sat on most surfaces, including the floor. I dropped out of junior college when my dad died. He never had the opportunity to get any kind of real education and wanted more for me and my sister. Back then, young and stupid and impatient for my life to start, I didn't see the value in it. I only went because he forced me.

By the time I became a shooter, I felt different about dropping out—maybe even a little ashamed. To make up for it, I began reading everything I could get my hands on. In five years I'd worked my way through the classics of English and American literature, as well as philosophy, history, and a healthy dose of pulp fiction.

Suddenly the sight of the books made me feel small and cheap and stupid.

"Lilly Hawkins?" a strange voice asked.

I spun around. Two men stood in the living room.

"We'd like a word with you," the first man said. He had a massive gut hanging over his belt and spoke with the Bakersfield twang my generation had abandoned. "If you cooperate, we'll be out of here in a jiffy."

"You can't walk right in here," I shouted. "Even if the landlord sent you, you still have to knock."

"We're not here for the landlord." The one with the belly laughed, and they both started down the hallway.

I felt fear for the first time and instinctively backed farther into my bedroom. "What do you want?"

The second man was skinny and had no accent. "You shouldn't leave your front door unlocked. It's not safe."

They stopped at the entrance to my bedroom and blocked the doorway.

"Get out or I'm calling the police."

Belly looked at Skinny. "I was hopin' we'd be able to handle this the easy way, but she looks determined to make trouble. Why don't you show the little lady the hard way?"

FIVE

The tall, skinny man wore slacks and a gray windbreaker. "If you say so."

His hands darted for me. I dived across my bed for the Mace in the nightstand. I didn't make it.

"Calm down." Skinny grabbed my legs and flipped me over.

Belly laughed. "She's obviously not a listener."

"Obviously," Skinny answered.

My cell phone rang in my coat pocket. I jerked trying to get to it.

"I'm not going to tell you again. Calm down." Skinny raised a fist and slammed it into my face.

Everything stopped except pain. It radiated outward from my head, spreading to my arms and my stomach.

Skinny reached into my pocket and removed the phone. Then he climbed off the bed and glanced at the small screen. "Looks like we're in the right place. The call is coming from KJAY."

I touched my face and felt liquid. I thought it was blood until I looked down and saw the clear tears on my hand.

The one with the belly took a seat on the end of the bed. "I'm sure they'll leave a message." Like Skinny, he wore slacks and a dress shirt, but instead of the windbreaker he had on a brown sports jacket and a bolo tie with a modest turquoise stone. "Now that you're calmed down, we can have a nice friendly talk."

The phone stopped ringing and Skinny set it down on a stack of books.

"We're all professionals here," Belly continued. "You have something of value and we want it."

"I don't have any money."

He looked around the room and laughed. "That's obvious. Good for you that's not what we're after." He handed me a handkerchief. The polka-dot kind my dad used to keep in his back pocket.

I wiped my face. "Then what are you after?"

"First, let me help you get the lay of the land," Belly said. "There's two ways this can go. You can give us what we want, and we're happy to pay you for it, or you can be difficult and we'll have to give you more of the rough stuff."

Skinny flipped through the pages of one of my books. "A job's a job."

"We get paid either way." Belly picked up a framed photo from my nightstand. In the old, brown-and-green image, my mother and father held my older, blonder sister, Clementine, while Uncle Bud carried a dark-haired toddler on his shoulders. "I'm guessin' this cutie-pie ridin' the old fella is you."

I nodded.

"What a nice picture full of nice people." Belly leaned in and I instinctively recoiled. "You wouldn't like it if something bad happened to any of them, right? You wouldn't want me and my partner to pay them a visit?"

"No," I mumbled even though my father was at Oleander Cemetery and my mother and sister had moved away ten years ago.

"Good." Belly replaced the photo. "Then all you got to do is answer one simple question and then me and my friend will give you a pile of money and nobody gets hurt. Do you think you can answer a question?"

I quickly nodded.

"Where's the tape you made last night?" He flashed a wide good-old-boy grin at me. "The one out at the orchard."

I rubbed my head where Skinny had hit me, as if my brain had been damaged. "What?"

Belly's grin melted into a flat line. He spoke slowly this time, focusing on each word in turn. "Where—is—the—tape?"

I took a gulp of air and tried to think.

"Makin' me wait for an answer isn't very respectful."

"But there isn't any tape," I blurted out.

"Now, missy . . ."

"I swear. It was black." The words tumbled out of me. "I messed up the camera and nothing recorded."

"I know that's what you told those suckers back where you work, but I'm not so stupid."

The skinny one glanced up from the book. "Neither am I."

"You don't understand," I explained. "I've been having a lot of bad luck."

Belly's forehead creased and he leaned in. "You expect me to believe you're that bad at your job?"

I flinched, not from fear, but wounded pride. "Why would I lie about it?"

"You saw an opportunity and decided to take advantage. I respect that and we're willin' to pay you."

I shook my head. "What opportunity?"

"Wherever you planned on peddlin' that tape, they're not payin' like us, and there's the added bonus of us not killin' you."

In an instant Belly's right hand grabbed my throat. His fat fingers smelled like tobacco and gasoline. "Where's the tape?"

"There's no tape," I said while trying to breath. "I swear."

"Do I have to hurt you?"

"No, please, I'll do anything you want."

"I want the tape."

"Then I'll get you the tape," I lied.

"Where is it?"

I hesitated.

He squeezed harder. "Where is it?"

"It's not here, but I can get it. I need a little time." Time to call 911. "If you come back later, I'll have it for you."

Suddenly a high-pitched shrieking filled the room. My body

involuntarily jumped, but the fat one's giant hand held me in place. Skinny removed a cell phone from his belt and glanced at the screen.

"They want us," he said, and clipped the phone back on his belt.

Belly nodded and turned back to me. "How's about we meet back here in two hours?"

"Whatever you want," I said.

He let go. "How much money you askin' for, anyway?"

I rubbed my neck and sat up a little. "How much can you pay?"

Belly laughed. "That's the spirit. Twenty grand sound okay?"

I stared at him. He was serious.

He grinned and showed me a set of yellow teeth. "Give us what we want and everybody wins." His smile disappeared. "But if you work a double cross or breathe a word about this to the police or your mama or your long-lost pen pal in China, we won't just kill you, we'll go after everybody you ever met." Belly stood up. "We'll see you back here at two, and remember, if you're not home, we're goin' to make some house calls to your friends and family."

They started to leave, but at my bedroom door Skinny stopped. He held up a paperback mystery. "Mind if I borrow it? I haven't read this one."

They both chuckled, then Belly said, "Anybody asks about your face, just tell 'em your boyfriend promised not to do it again."

They laughed at me. I heard it echoing down the hallway as they walked out of my house.

I've been told I have a temper. At that moment, temper didn't even begin to describe what I had.

I grabbed the Mace and jumped out the bathroom window into the alley behind the bungalows. A part of me reasoned I'd be able to get their license-plate number, but mostly I wanted to jump out of the bushes and Mace them back to the Stone Age. My bare feet sprinted down the alley jumping over broken glass and who knows what else. At the last bungalow I crouched down in the bushes and waited.

I heard the skinny one's voice first. "I thought she was going to pee in her pants."

"Me too. I'm thinkin' she'd never been hit before."

Their laughter echoed down the pavement and mingled with their footsteps. I clutched the Mace in anticipation.

"You think someone got to her?" Skinny asked. "I thought we made good time over here."

"Nah. She's workin' on her own. Saw a chance to make a buck and went for it."

Peeking through the bushes, I could see a white sedan parked at the curb. It was generic except for the large antenna coming off the back. I knew it didn't belong to anyone in my complex.

"I bet you could have gotten the tape for nothing," Skinny said.

"Probably, but since it's not my money, I'm not too worried about it."

Something about the white sedan bothered me. Even though it had never been parked there before, it felt familiar—and the clean white was too perfect, too institutional.

"Too bad we can't be that rough all the time." Skinny laughed. "We'd get a lot more results."

My body froze as I recognized the car, or rather the type. I'd done several ride-alongs in similar unmarked vehicles for stories.

Skinny and Belly passed inches from the bush. I didn't move. They got in their police car and drove away.

Calling 911 was no longer an option.

I could hear my cell phone ringing in the bedroom. I ignored it and went straight to the kitchen. "Focus on one problem at a time." I opened the freezer. No ice. I opened the refrigerator. A six-pack of Mountain Dew and some maraschino cherries sat on the otherwise empty shelves. I popped the top on a soda, took a sip, then placed the can to my eye.

What did Skinny and Belly think was on that tape? Everything I'd shot had been in plain sight, and the Technical Investigations team had thoroughly documented the scene with their own cameras. I refused to believe dozens of Sheriff's Department personnel were colluding in a massive conspiracy. As a shooter I'd seen Bakersfield's law enforcement community up close. They worked long hours under the constant threat of violence for the sole purpose of keeping the rest of us safe.

Of course every group had its bad apples. Was it possible the crime scene had been tampered with? If my camera hadn't been in black, would I have photographed something that proved it?

I opened the jar and removed the remaining two cherries. They burned slightly going down and I checked the label. Eight months past expired.

Calling the police was out. Skinny and Belly would find out I'd talked, and not knowing who else was involved, I could do little to protect myself. Even Handsome Homicide was suspect. Who better to tamper with a crime scene than the detective running it?

I put the empty jar on the counter. There was no way around it. I couldn't call the police, but I had to call someone. Trent was the only person who came to mind.

Callum answered on the thirteenth ring. "KJAY, we're on your side."

"It's Lilly. I have to talk to Trent."

"Hallelujah! Did you get my messages? I'm sorry things got tense earlier, but we need you out on assignment."

"No."

"You can start the suspension later," Callum said as though he hadn't heard me. "All the other shooters are busy or unavailable and we've got a hot lead. The murder victim's cousin wants to do an exclusive sit-down interview."

"I don't care if Jimmy Hoffa called. This is an emergency and I need to talk to Trent."

"He's not here." A burst of scanner noise filled the background. I heard a loud thud and knew Callum had dropped the phone. A few seconds later he picked up again. "Sorry. False alarm on the county line. Anyway, I texted the address to your cell phone. I don't have a free reporter, so go to the family's house and get some

B-roll. I'll send Rod over for the interview as soon as he's done with the noon."

"I'm not going anywhere. You need to call Trent at home."

He paused. "Lilly, you're not going to quit or anything? Because I know this has been a rough morning, but—"

"You have no idea how rough." I gently probed under my eye where Skinny had hit me. The flesh felt tender and slightly puffy. "I need Trent."

"He specifically told me to handle your suspension. He's taking the rest of the day off, and I'm not allowed to bother him unless the station burns down."

"Then give me his number and I'll call him."

"You know employee information is private. You wouldn't like it if I gave out your home phone number." Callum paused. "Tell me what's on your mind. If it's that serious, I'll figure something out."

He was right about our information being private, and it highlighted something I should have realized before. Skinny and Belly not only knew details about my tape being black, but they also knew where I lived and that I'd be at home when I'd normally be working. That kind of information could only have come from someone inside KJAY. Someone like Callum.

"No offense, but I have to talk to Trent."

Wind noise filled the phone line as Callum let out a long, deep breath directly into his receiver. "Get me this story and I'll accidentally page out Trent's home phone number." He chuckled. "But you better not tell him how you got it."

I stopped before getting in the news van and scanned the street for Skinny and Belly's cruiser. That they were still here, and prepared to follow wherever I led, was a terrifying possibility. But despite the risk, I'd decided to accept Callum's offer and shoot the interview. I reasoned that Trent was the only person with experience and contacts outside Bakersfield to know what to do in this extreme situation. Add to that my suspicion that someone at the station had sold me out, and there seemed to be little choice.

If I'd dug a little deeper, I would have found an additional reason—I don't like being in the dark. I'd been threatened by two nameless dirty cops because an unknown person or persons thought I'd photographed an unknown something at the scene of an unknown man's murder. I wanted facts. I wanted to get out in front instead of trailing behind. What better place to get information than the murder victim's family?

The address Callum texted me sat on a residential street off Union Avenue. Back in the golden age, Union Avenue had been the main road from L.A. to San Francisco. Movie stars and moguls had all passed by and stayed in the swank hotels along the way. By the time I was born, the motels were charging by the hour. Most of the stories I'd covered there were about drug addicts who'd wandered into traffic. It's called an auto-versus-pedestrian.

I passed the new supermarket, but not even its clean and bright construction could shake my sense of crossing into the bad part of town. I expected my destination would be a sad street with parked cars on dead lawns and pit bulls chained behind dilapidated fences. I was surprised when I turned onto a nice block of pretty, well-tended houses. The address belonged to a lovely white cottage with flowers flowing from manicured beds and several mature trees shading the house.

I carried my gear onto the porch and rang the bell. While waiting for an answer I casually looked down the street and saw a white, unmarked police car.

For a moment I couldn't breathe. Then it registered that the car was empty, and I began breathing too much. I frantically looked in every direction. Where were they? I dropped my gear and dug into my coat pockets. A year ago I'd tossed a tiny key-chain Mace in there, never dreaming I'd actually need it.

Footsteps taunted me from the other side of the door. It was a trap. They were inside waiting. I considered running for it, leaving the gear and the expensive camera and getting out of there. Instead, I dug farther into my pockets.

My right hand connected with something metal and cylindrical just as the doorknob turned. I shoved the Mace into the widening doorway. My trigger finger shook. All of me shook.

He didn't panic or flinch. His face was the picture of control. His hand casually passed into his navy blue suit jacket, revealing the silver badge at his waist, and rested on what was probably his gun.

I said it before I had the chance to censor myself, "Handsome?"

SIX

He recoiled as if the word were a blow.

From inside the house a strange voice teased, "Handsome? This guy is butt ugly." Behind Handsome a middle-aged Latino man in a dark brown suit joyfully bounced down the interior hallway. "Everybody knows I'm the good-looking one."

I returned the Mace to my pocket. "I'm sorry. I was expecting . . . I mean, I wasn't . . . I'm from KJAY."

Handsome withdrew his hand from inside the jacket. His face remained an unexpressive blank slate.

I didn't have his physical control. My blush was so strong you could probably have fried an egg on the side of my face. "The family called the station. I'm from KJAY."

The man with Handsome ran a hand over his neatly trimmed goatee. "Are things so bad you reporters have to shoot your own stuff?"

I began picking up my gear. "I'm a shooter, not a reporter. Lilly Hawkins from KJAY." I realized, seconds too late, that it was the third time I'd said the name of the station.

"This is Detective Lucero." Handsome sounded detached and unemotional as he gestured to the other man. "He's working with me on last night's homicide."

Lucero smiled. If he'd been wearing a hat, he'd have tipped it. "A pleasure to meet you, Lilly Hawkins from KJAY." He turned to Handsome with a wicked grin. "It's good to know you're on such intimate terms with the media."

Handsome gave him a dirty look, which only widened Lucero's grin.

"We got a call from one of the victim's family members," I said, trying to change the subject. "Can I come in or do I need to wait until you're through?"

Handsome joined me on the front porch. "We're leaving. The family is understandably upset."

"Are they ever. I don't envy you guys in Homicide," Lucero said. "You only meet people on the worst day of their lives."

Lucero and Handsome had felt out of sync from the beginning, but it wasn't until now that I realized the significance of it. "Then you're not in Homicide?" I asked Lucero. "What part of the Sheriff's Department do you work for?"

"The RCIU out of Lamont."

The Rural Crimes division was charged with investigating crime, usually thefts, at the many farms and oil fields in the county. "Are you on the case because the crime scene was an orchard? Because I didn't think the RCIU worked homicides."

Handsome interrupted before Lucero could answer. "All inquiries should be directed to the department's information officer. Excuse us, we have an appointment."

Lucero shrugged and started to leave.

"Any chance you'll give me the victim's name?" I asked. "Or any information about him?"

"Sorry," Lucero replied. "But there should be a press release this afternoon."

"We need to be going," Handsome said behind me.

"Couldn't you tell me now?" I kept my eyes on Lucero and ignored Handsome. "If it's coming out, you wouldn't be doing anything wrong."

"We need to be going," Handsome repeated with rising frustration.

"Okay, okay." Lucero stepped around me. "He gets testy if his blood sugar drops."

The two men walked down the short steps. "So, Handsome,

have you been doing some outreach to the press? Improving our PR and all that?" Lucero turned around and winked at me.

I cringed. In addition to almost macing Bakersfield's resident dreamboat, I'd embarrassed him in front of a colleague. Maybe next time I could get him fired or throw up all over him.

I turned my back on yet another romantic disaster and entered the house. "Hello?" No one answered, so I left the front door open and stayed near the threshold. "Hello?" I repeated.

The house felt warm and inviting. The living room was furnished with older but well made furniture in attractive earth tones. The simple and clutter-free room felt more comfortable than anywhere I'd ever lived. The only formal touch was a large oil painting of Jesus looking down from above the fireplace.

"Can I help you, miss?" I turned in the direction of the voice. An African-American man walked down the hallway from the rear of the house. He wore a white dress shirt, black tie, black slacks, and in his hands he carried a black book.

My grief-sensing radar, finely honed by countless assignments, told me he wasn't upset enough to be a family member.

"I'm from KJAY," I explained. "My name is Lilly Hawkins. The family is expecting me."

"I don't believe they are." He looked at my camera with obvious dislike. "I don't think any of the family wants to be on TV at a time like this."

If I'd learned anything in my five years on the job, it's that everyone wants to be on TV all the time. "Why don't we ask? Everybody grieves differently."

I silently prayed for a bereaved mother to be there. She is the "get" interview after a tragedy, and I'd already decided to ignore Callum's instructions and start without Rod. The clock was ticking on Skinny and Belly's deadline, and I was in too much of a hurry to wait. I also hoped to avoid the spectacle of Rod fawning all over the grieving family. I couldn't stomach that explosion of bogus sympathy today.

"This is a very difficult time for everyone." The man had

finished coming down the hall and was standing a few feet from me. I identified the black book in his hands as a Bible. "You should leave these people to shed their tears in private."

The tears sounded figurative, but if they were literal, I'd hit the jackpot. "Are you a family member, sir?"

"No. I'm Reverend Phillips. Mrs. Boyle is a member of our congregation, and several of us are here offering our condolences."

"Of course, but since a family member did call and invite me, don't you think we should at least go ask?" I pushed past him and walked quickly down the hallway. "Are they in the back of the house?"

"Yes, but I'm not sure . . ." He started to follow me, but had to pause to shut the front door.

I didn't wait for him. The door at the end of the hallway was open and I walked into a large family room filled with about a dozen African-American men and women. Some held coffee mugs while others held Bibles. The conversation died the minute I entered. The only remaining sound was of two women crying.

The first was young and pretty. Maybe not even eighteen yet. Her shoulder-length hair had been carefully straightened and dyed with blond streaks. She cried loud, wet sobs onto the shoulder of a young man wearing jeans and a basketball jersey. The girl's showy, over-the-top grief would play well on TV, but I knew it was basically self-centered emotion. She wanted attention and was getting it.

The young man comforting her also looked like a good bet. He was now eyeing my camera with barely concealed lust.

The other crying woman was older, probably in her forties, and sat on a couch being comforted by what looked like a friend. The crying woman's hair was cut close to her head, and she wore slacks and a flowery sweater. She didn't sob or make a lot of noise and, in contrast to the girl, had an aura of quiet bewilderment. She seemed only vaguely aware of what was going on, or maybe she didn't care. This was either the grieving wife or mother. Given her age, I guessed wife.

From behind me Reverend Phillips cleared his throat. "Did someone call the TV station?"

They all looked at each other, but no one confessed. I didn't blame them. Reverend Phillips's tone had made it clear what he thought of people who call TV stations.

The reverend, thinking I was leaving, relaxed into a kindly demeanor. "As you can see, no one here made that call. Thank you for coming, but now is not the appropriate time."

If I got kicked out of the house, I'd have to wait for Rod and then endure one of his schmoozefests as he tried to regain entry. I didn't have that much time to waste. "Someone in this room invited me here." I set down my equipment. "They're obviously afraid to say so because they don't want you to disapprove. If you truly want to help them grieve, you'll let it be on their terms and not your own."

I thought my disrespect might upset him, but he made no change in his tone or demeanor. "As I said before, the press is not wanted here. In fact, you're trespassing on private property."

"That's a good point." I turned away from him and toward the rest of the room. "Whose house is this?"

No one said anything. Several of the faces were openly hostile. The woman I thought was the wife hadn't even looked at me.

The crying girl's face peeked up from where it was buried in the chest of the young man. "It's Diana's." She glanced at Reverend Phillips, saw his reaction to her statement, and immediately lowered her head. The boy comforted her, and then, when no one was looking, nodded his head in the direction of the lady on the other couch.

I stepped toward her. "Are you related to the victim in last night's tragedy?"

Her head remained bent over. She took a long, ragged breath, then exhaled.

The room was collectively frozen. It felt as though even the tiniest movement, taking a breath or adjusting my weight, would make a thundering sound.

"Was he your husband?" I asked.

Her head slowly tilted up, but her eyes remained down. "He's my son." She pointed, without looking, to the wall where a group of photographs depicted two boys at various stages of youth. The poses were stereotypical with the largest showing the two boys around age ten. It was the last picture of them together. The teenage years of one of the boys was chronicled through a series of school pictures culminating in a graduation photo, but the other boy was absent.

"Is that him in the cap and gown?" I said, using the present tense for the first time. "He's very handsome."

Her eyes slowly rose. "Thank you."

I knelt down in front of her. "I work for the TV station. We want to do a story about your son. About who he was and what he was like. May I videotape those pictures of him you have on the wall?"

She nodded.

"Is there one in particular that you like? That you want us to use when we talk about him?"

"His graduation photo. I want people to see him like that."

"Would you be interested in talking to me a little bit about him, on-camera? To give people a better idea of who he was?"

Her head lowered back down.

After a moment Reverend Phillips came and stood next to her and placed a hand on her shoulder. He looked at me. "Mrs. Boyle needs to be with family and friends now. This is not an appropriate time for an interview."

I ignored him and scooted closer to her bent head. "Is there something you want people to know about your son? Isn't there something that you want to explain or make people understand about who he was?"

She didn't say anything.

"Right now is your chance. In a day or two everyone will begin to forget. They'll get caught back up in their lives, and we'll be doing other stories and life will go on. Right now, this is your chance to tell people about your son, and right now, they're going to listen."

She didn't say anything.

I stood back up and found myself facing Reverend Phillips.

"She gave you permission to videotape that picture." He pointed to the graduation photo. "Please do so and then go."

"Val wasn't in a gang." Mrs. Boyle's voice was small compared to Reverend Phillips's, but it got the whole room's attention. "Everyone is thinking that. I know they are." Tears flooded her eyes. "I told the police and I know they don't believe me."

A woman on the other side of the room shook her head. "We all know the truth."

"Yes, we do," a man added. "I'm always saying I wish my boys were more like Val."

The room jumped to life as everyone quickly agreed, then almost as quickly fell back into silence.

"Mrs. Boyle," I began.

"Call me Diana. Mr. Boyle has been gone a long time."

I nodded. "Diana, we have so many viewers. You can tell all of them about Val. Not what the police think, but what you know."

"He had a good job and was saving for college. That's all I wanted, my whole life."

"It would only take a few minutes."

She nodded her head. "I don't want people thinking he was in a gang."

I knelt down again and placed a hand on her arm. I knew I had her. "You can tell them."

"I don't think—" Reverend Phillips started, but was interrupted by the doorbell.

"Maybe Reverend Phillips can get that for you?" I said in what I considered a brilliant strategic move.

Her teary brown eyes looked up at him. "Would you mind?"

"Of course not." He frowned at me and left.

"Should I go ahead and set up my equipment?"

She nodded and I went to work. I moved slowly so I wouldn't

frighten her. The rest of the room fell into clusters of whispered conversation.

"You want to interview me too?" The young man had released his hold on the girl and was sitting forward on the couch. His eyes focused on my camera, and he appeared unaware of the disdainful looks coming from some of the other mourners.

I locked down the tripod and attached the camera. "What's your name?"

"Gideon. Val was my cousin, but really he was like my big brother." He gestured to the wall of photos. "That's us together before I went back to live with my mom. I have great stories. You definitely should interview me."

The girl suddenly stopped crying and sat up. "Me too. Val was the love of my life and now I'm all alone."

Gideon rubbed her back. "You're not alone."

"Let me get Mrs. Boyle on tape first and then we'll see." I didn't see their reactions, but I heard the girl resume her sobbing.

I checked the camera settings and made sure the battery was good. I rolled off forty seconds of the graduation photo and some insurance shots of the other pictures. "When was the graduation portrait taken?"

"It will be two years next June," Diana answered. "I was so proud of him."

I uncoiled the mic and clipped it on her sweater. "He couldn't have been very old. How long had Val been driving a truck?"

A ripple of dissent flowed through the room. Diana shook her head. "Never."

I stopped what I was doing. "Maybe I confused some of the details. Your son was the one killed last night in an orchard in Weedpatch?"

"Yes. He said he had to stay late at the winery where he works." Her face compressed as she tried to squeeze her eyes shut. "I don't understand how this happened. It makes no sense."

I went back to setting up the camera, more confused than ever.

"Do the police know what happened to his car? Did he leave it at work?"

"He didn't have a car. We were saving for college." She started to cry. "But he said he had a ride home. He said not to wait up."

The women sitting next to Diana moved closer and murmured comforting words. After a few moments I asked, "What's the name of the winery?"

When she didn't answer, a man across the room said, "Dewey Ridge. It's south of Arvin."

"That's right." Diana raised her head. "His high school counselor referred him for an internship. We used to get up at four every morning so I could drive him, then in the evening he took the bus home." The grief that had covered Diana's face was giving way to maternal pride. "He wouldn't get back till nine at night sometimes, but he never complained. When he graduated from high school, he was offered a full-time position. We decided he could put college on hold for a year or two because it was such a good opportunity."

I nodded. "What did he do at the winery?"

"He was an executive assistant, but recently he's been filling in on special projects. The man he worked for left the company several weeks ago and he's been waiting to be reassigned." She smiled. "In Val's last performance review he was called 'indispensable.'"

"He was always a smart boy," a woman across the room said. "And he got it from you, Diana." Several people murmured their agreement.

I quickly asked something to keep Diana talking. "I didn't know there was a winery in Arvin."

"It's not like the tourist places over in Santa Barbara," she explained. "They don't invite people in. That part of their business is in Napa. Val said they do all the real work of growing the grapes and making the wine here, so he was learning all the important things. He was learning the nuts and bolts of the business."

"They make the wine here and sell it in Napa?"

She nodded. "Val said it was part of the marketing plan."

I smiled. "I take it Dewey Ridge doesn't like to talk about where the wine actually comes from."

"Val was always very careful. He said that everyone who worked there was expected to be discreet."

Instead of looking at her I focused on taking a mic level. This was delicate and I had no idea how to say it right. "Val sounds like a successful young professional man. Why do the police believe he was in a gang?"

Her posture immediately sagged. "They wouldn't tell me anything. Just kept asking the same questions over and over. Didn't even ask if Val was in a gang. They asked when he'd joined. Not if."

"I'm sorry."

"I told them over and over. He stayed away from all that violence. He wanted more for himself than that kind of life." She looked at me. "He was talking about going to Stanford and majoring in business. What would a boy like that need from a gang?"

The door opened and Reverend Phillips entered. "The police are here again. They wanted to go over some of the arrangements for Val. His remains won't be released for some time, but his personal effects will be available this afternoon."

The contrast between the life Diane had been describing and the cold reality of Val's remains lying in the morgue broke her self-control. She bent her head and muffled a sob with a tissue. Her friends whispered more comforting words, and after a moment she looked up at Reverend Phillips.

"Thank you." She wiped away some fresh tears. "It's really his watch I care about. It belonged to my father, and Gideon should have it now."

She looked at Gideon, who nodded and managed to look truly upset for the first time.

Reverend Phillips took Diana's hand. "I made an appointment to pick his things up. You don't have to worry. I'll handle it." He paused and looked at me. "The officer would also like to speak with you. He's waiting in the living room."

Clearly Reverend Phillips hoped that in my absence he could convince Diana to kick me out. "I'm happy to speak with the police. Send them back here."

His lips spread into a wide smile. "He wants to see you privately. He was very specific."

I exited, making sure to leave the door open in case Skinny and Belly had caught up with me. Halfway down the hall, I heard it shut. I hesitated, fearful of a trap, but then Handsome stepped into view.

"You needed to see me?" I quickly walked the rest of the hallway and met him in the living room.

"Lucero is waiting so I have to make this fast, and I know you're working too."

"I'm about to interview the grieving mother." I realized how that sounded and rushed to add, "I don't mean to be disrespectful. After a certain number of stories people start to fit into categories."

"Don't worry. I've worked a lot of cases too. People become very predictable. You know what they say; it's a cliché because it's true."

I smiled with relief. "What can I do for you?"

"I couldn't help noticing, your station didn't use any of that video you shot last night."

"Oh, that." I nodded, unsure of what to say. "Right."

"Of course I'll have to put it in the final report, that you snuck in, but I can spin it my own way. Do some damage control. So . . . I wanted to thank you, in person."

Any qualms I had about accepting unearned thanks, heightened by the oil painting of Jesus looking down on us, were quickly overcome by hormones. "No problem. I'm glad things worked out for you."

His usually stoic face broke into a smile, and my insides melted.

Unfortunately his smile was short-lived. "There's something else. If you're not comfortable discussing this, I understand."

"What's on your mind?"

He paused. "How did you get that black eye?"

My hand shot up and felt the puffy fold of skin. "It's black?"

"It will be, in about half an hour."

"Really?"

My skin tingled as he brushed back a strand of hair that covered the edge of the tender spot. He leaned in and looked closely at my face. "Maybe an hour."

"I'll have to cover it up with makeup."

He straightened. "If you're in trouble, I can help."

And I wanted to let him help, but a rush of paranoia overpowered me.

What did I really know about him? He made my insides melt. He was Handsome. That's not much. It wasn't as if people called him Honest Homicide or Really Trustworthy Guy Homicide. And Skinny and Belly were cops. Law enforcement was involved in this, one way or another.

"Don't worry about it," I said. "Trent, my news director, is going to handle it."

"You're sure?"

I nodded. "There is something you could clarify for me, though, off-the-record."

He pulled back. "What kind of something?"

"Mrs. Boyle says her son didn't drive trucks. If he wasn't the driver of the semi, then who was?"

Handsome glanced behind him and down the hall. "Val Boyle got his license to drive a truck last summer. He didn't tell his mother."

"So what's the deal? He had a second job?"

He shook his head. "Not that we know of."

"Then what?"

He hesitated.

I glanced down the hallway to make sure we were alone. "His mom says you think he was in a gang."

"Statistically, a black kid that age from this neighborhood dies violently, it's almost always gang-related."

"But do you have more of a reason than that?"

He shook his head. "I've already said too much."

"Please. I'm a damsel in distress, remember?"

He glanced at my black eye. "This stays off-the-record?"

I nodded.

"The 911 call came from a pay phone near an Eastside Crew hangout."

I recognized the name of one of Bakersfield's most notorious gangs, and the one whose territory we were now in. "You think the Eastside Crew hijacked that truck and stole the cargo?"

"I'm not saying anything for sure, and this is completely off-the-record."

Out the window, I saw Lucero getting out of the cruiser and knew my time was running short. "Of course."

"The truck found with the body was untraceable. Its serial numbers and registration were all bogus." Handsome must have recognized my confusion because he added, "It's the kind of vehicle you'd use to transport stolen merchandise."

"And you think Val was driving it?"

"The only fingerprints on the steering wheel belonged to him."

It was hard to reconcile what Handsome was telling me and the picture Mrs. Boyle had painted of her son. "And you think a member of the Eastside Crew killed him, came back to Bakersfield, and made the 911 call?"

He nodded.

"Where's the gang hangout—the one near the pay phone where the call came from?"

"Oh, no." His voice rose. "Don't you even think about going over there and snooping around."

"I wasn't—"

"Yes, you were. It's written all over your face." He shook his head. "Stay away from the Eastside Crew. There's a new guy in charge and he's about as dangerous as they come. He's brazen and crosses lines most gang members wouldn't go near."

"Like what?"

"We think he murdered a cop's wife in Fresno. That's why he came to Bakersfield. Things got too hot for him up there."

The doorbell rang. We each jumped backward and landed about five feet apart.

Handsome walked to the door. Before disappearing into the entryway, he stopped. He took a business card from his wallet and handed it to me. "If you need help, about the eye, call me. Okay? Anytime. My private cell is on there."

I felt my cheeks getting hot again. "Thanks."

A knock sounded from the door and I jumped into the corner. "I'll stand over here so Lucero doesn't see me."

Handsome looked embarrassed for the first time. "Thanks. He's going to razz me enough already."

I heard the door open and then Lucero's voice. "Hey, Handsome, you working or making time with your honey?" The door closed with a loud slam.

SEVEN

Two very different portraits of Val Boyle were emerging. In his mother's eyes he was a hardworking, disciplined young man with a strong sense of right and wrong. In Handsome's, he was just another kid who got sucked into the local gang life and came to a violent end. So who was right?

Val had lied about getting a truck license, but did it follow that he was using that license to knowingly transport stolen goods? The cousin or girlfriend might know more, but I doubted either would speak honestly in front of Mrs. Boyle. I decided to finish her interview, then get each of the teenagers alone. I didn't even need to get them on-camera. All I wanted was the truth.

I started back down the hall, but before I reached the family room, the door opened and mourners poured out. I flattened myself against the wall as each passed and offered a polite thank-you or good-bye. Reverend Phillips, the last to appear, shut the door behind him and blocked my way back in.

"What's going on?" I asked.

"Mrs. Boyle has decided she needs some quiet time alone. Your interview will have to be indefinitely postponed." He watched the last of the mourners exit out the front door, then looked at his watch. "May I help carry your equipment back out to your car?"

On a normal day my heart would have sunk. To lose the "get" interview is painful, but today wasn't normal. I needed to get Trent's phone number more than I needed a flashy exclusive interview. Gideon and the girlfriend would be good enough for Callum.

"I understand," I told the reverend. "Where can I interview the two teenagers?"

He stumbled for a moment, then found his voice. "I'm asking you to have the decency to leave this family in peace."

"They're the ones who asked me here. They want to go on-camera. Diana even wanted to, before you beat her down."

"I most certainly did not beat her down."

"What's your problem anyway? You've been trying to get rid of me from the moment I got here."

He drew himself up and took on an air of importance I found far more intimidating than physical superiority. "I have a problem with people like you who come down to our neighborhood and make the rest of the world think all we do is kill each other."

"That's not fair."

"When else are you ever down here? I don't see you when something good happens, but I sure see you for the bad things."

I frantically searched my memory to come up with a positive story I'd covered on this side of town. Nothing came to mind.

"This neighborhood is full of real people trying to live good lives," he continued, "but all you're interested in are racial stereotypes."

"I've never heard a single racist thing said by anyone who works at KJAY."

"Well, none of you live here, and I'm guessing the only thing you know about this neighborhood is we're black and we have crime."

A lightbulb didn't magically appear over my head, but instead of getting angry and yelling back at him, I paused. It wasn't that I thought he was right. Instead, it was the nagging and unpleasant feeling that he could be right and I wouldn't know it.

"Okay, I understand better what this is about," I said after a moment. "I doubt we'll even say where Val Boyle was from. The murder was in Weedpatch, not here."

"That doesn't seem to matter to the police. The one who just left all but said Val was running with the Eastside Crew."

"Are you sure he wasn't?"

"Diana raised that boy all by herself. She knew every part of him, and if she says he wasn't in a gang, I believe her."

I thought about Mrs. Boyle's quiet insistence. I wanted her to be right.

He pointed to the back room. "Now kindly take your equipment and leave this house."

I shook my head. "I'm not leaving. You don't want Mrs. Boyle on-camera. You think I'll exploit her. That's fine, I promise not to ask her again, but Gideon and the girl are going to be interviewed. I could walk in there and announce I was going to exploit them and they'd shout, 'Please, please, me first.' They want the attention. Your best bet is to make a deal."

His lips opened, then closed into an angry, thin line. "What kind of deal?"

"I'll interview the teenagers, but I'll leave Mrs. Boyle out of it and I won't say anything about the neighborhood."

He took another look at his watch.

"If you have somewhere to go, don't worry. You can trust me," I promised. "And maybe when this settles down, you can talk to my news director about the way we cover this part of town."

The reverend thought about it. "We're having a memorial service for Val the day after tomorrow. I don't want your cameras there exploiting the situation."

I shook my head. "I have no control over that."

He silently shifted his weight from one leg to the other.

"I keep my promises." I fished in one of my overstuffed pockets and pulled out a creased business card with the KJAY logo. "Here's how you can reach me if you're unhappy with my work."

He took the card, examined it, and looked at the door. "I guess I don't have much choice. You're right about Rachel and Gideon."

Reverend Phillips left and I returned to the back room. Rachel once again cried her loud, lusty sobs onto Gideon's shoulder. The room felt much larger with only the four of us, and Diana looked very alone without her friends.

"Reverend Phillips said you'd changed your mind about going on TV," I said to Diana. "I completely understand."

She tried to smile at me, but it came out as a quick lifting of her head that turned into a nod.

I turned to the young woman sloppily patting her eyes with Kleenex. "Miss, are you Rachel?"

She peeked coyly from behind the tissue. "Yes."

"Rachel, would you like to talk about Val?"

Her face lit up. "Oh, yes. I want to be interviewed. I'll never get over it." As if trying to prove it, she completely broke down and buried her head in her hands.

Gideon took her into an embrace. "It's okay. I'm here." He made sure to turn his head outward so I could see his grief-stricken face.

I crossed to my camera and changed the setup from Diana to Rachel.

"You're going to interview me too, right?" Gideon asked. "Val was like a brother to me. We grew up together as kids. Then my mom got her act together and I went back home, but even then we were only ten minutes away."

Not to be outdone by the victim's almost brother, Rachel bravely wiped tears from her face. "We were engaged."

Her announcement had a dramatic effect on the two other people in the room. Diana's head jerked up and she made a loud gasp.

Gideon forgot to look sympathetic. "You were not."

At this exact moment the doorbell rang, again.

"I don't believe this." I dropped the mic I was about to clip on Rachel's shirt. "I'll get it. It's probably one of our reporters."

As I walked down the hallway, I heard Rachel's angry voice behind me. "How do you know what went on between us? Maybe we didn't want anybody to know about it."

I expected Rod, but took a quick peek out the window in case Belly and Skinny had tracked me down. What I saw made me angry, not frightened.

I jerked the door open. "What are you doing here?"

David looked up from his cell phone, where he appeared to be reading a text message. "Good to see you too." He slipped the device into a pocket and picked up his camera.

"This is my shoot." I physically blocked the doorway. "Callum and I have a deal that doesn't involve you."

He pushed past me into the entryway. "Not anymore."

"Excuse me?"

"I'm here to shoot Rod's interview with the family. I agreed to work a double shift so we'll have coverage without you this afternoon."

"Nice try, but this is my assignment."

His confidence didn't falter. "No, it's not. Callum's orders are for you to return to the station and turn in your gear. You're back on suspension."

"I don't know how you managed this, but you're not stealing my interview."

"Talk to Trent. He's the one who suspended you, not me."

"Is everything okay?" Gideon leaned out the doorway at the end of the hall. Rachel's sobs could be heard through the open door. "We heard yelling."

I turned around. "I'm sorry. Everything's fine."

"You're not leaving, are you?"

"Don't worry. I'll be right back. Why don't you check on Rachel? She sounds upset."

Gideon cast a dirty look toward the interior of the back room. "Okay." He disappeared and closed the door behind him.

I glanced onto the empty porch. "Where's Rod?"

"In the van. Said he had to fix his hair."

I took a moment to run over my options. It didn't take long because there weren't many. "I need a favor."

This unexpected request actually cracked David's aura of calm assurance more than my earlier anger. "What kind of favor?"

"I need you to walk away and leave me to shoot this." He laughed and I continued, "And I need you to take Rod with you so I can shoot it fast."

David laughed again. “You want me to give up a huge story and hand it over to a shooter on suspension for incompetence?”

That last word stung. It took all my willpower to speak calmly. “Yes. That’s what I want.” He opened his mouth, but I cut him off. “Go away, take Rod with you, and I’ll do one of your on-call nights.”

He hesitated for a moment, then licked his lips. “Eight nights, maybe.”

“Are you crazy? That’s two months’ worth.”

“You’re the one asking for the favor, not me.”

I squeezed my eyes shut and tried to block the urge to kill him. “Two nights.”

“Deal.” He picked up his gear and stepped onto the porch. “At least this way you know I won’t tell Trent to fire you.” He laughed. “Well, not for a two weeks, anyway.”

I reached for the door. “You shouldn’t have caved. I would have done it for eight.”

Rod came up the steps at that exact moment. He saw me and smiled. “Hi, Lilly.”

“Bye, Rod.” I closed the door on both of them.

I didn’t know how David would explain to Rod, and I didn’t care. I quickly returned to the room at the back of the house and finished setting up the camera. I’d asked Rachel a few questions and patiently waited through the long and overwrought answers when the doorbell rang again.

I pulled my eye away from the viewfinder and slammed my fingers onto the stop button. “I don’t believe this.” I looked at Gideon. “Can you answer that?” Gideon looked disinclined to rouse himself so I added, “I’m on a deadline and if I’m interrupted, I won’t have time to interview you.”

He leapt off the couch. “I’m on it.” He disappeared down the hallway.

I hit the record button again. “Please begin that last answer again.”

Rachel had gotten several sentences in when I heard footsteps behind me. I looked up just in time to see a man in a dark suit place his hand in front of the camera.

"Don't tell her anything," he instructed the room.

I stood. "Excuse me?"

"Immediately cease this interview and leave the premises," he ordered me. "This is private property and you have no right to be here."

Behind him a second and a third man, also wearing dark suits and carrying leather briefcases, poured through the open door with Gideon.

"They said they needed to talk to us," Gideon explained. "They said it's about our inheritance."

"You must be Mrs. Boyle." The first man approached Diana, who was now standing and looking annoyed. "Please allow me to apologize for the way we barged in. We saw the news van outside and realized the situation was urgent."

"I'm waiting for you to introduce yourself," Diana told him.

"Once again, my apologies." He withdrew a silver case from his inside coat pocket and offered her a business card. "My firm represents your son's employers, and I've come to make arrangements for the sizable death benefit your family is due to receive."

"Death benefit," Diana repeated. "Val didn't have any insurance."

"It was something he did through the winery. He wanted to make certain you'd all be taken care of if he wasn't able to be here for you."

She opened her mouth to say something, but nothing came out. Slowly she lowered herself back onto the couch. When she did finally speak, the words were choked. "He . . . he did that?"

"Yes, Mrs. Boyle. He must have loved you very much."

She began quietly crying.

"There is, however, a clause in the company's insurance program that prohibits communication with the media." He turned to Rachel and Gideon. "It will take some time to sort out who is eligible for what amounts, but giving this journalist an interview will jeopardize your settlements."

Gideon looked at me and pointed to the door. "Get out."

"I appreciate your coming," Diana said, her voice still full of emotion. "But it's probably best if you go now."

I was beat. No way round it. I packed up my gear while the lawyers produced reams of paperwork for Diana to sign. When I was ready to go, several of them escorted me to the door and locked it behind me.

The once deserted street now boasted a horde of luxury cars. BMWs were parked in front and back of my van, and across the street I recognized a Mercedes, a Lexus, and a brand-new Jaguar. I didn't see Skinny and Belly's car, but just to be safe I made sure the Mace was still in my pocket.

I loaded my gear in the back of the van and paused. No options were left. I'd have to tell Callum everything and hope he wasn't the one who'd sold me out to Skinny and Belly.

I heard a car door open across the street and turned to look. The driver's-side door of the Jaguar was slightly ajar.

"Lilly?" a voice tentatively called.

"Who's there?"

A hand appeared and gestured for me to come.

I cautiously approached. "I said, who's there?"

The door widened and Tom Sinclair's head appeared, without the cowboy hat. "It's me, Tom. Come closer."

I walked to the car. "What are you doing here?"

"Get in. We can talk in private."

I stood my ground in the street. "There is absolutely no chance I'm getting in that car with you."

He sulked, but got out of the car and joined me.

"What are you doing here?" I repeated.

"I'm acting in a supervisory capacity, even though I thought it prudent to stay outside."

I followed his gaze to the house. "Why are you supervising lawyers from a winery in Arvin?"

His hand went to his wedding ring and began twisting back and forth. "Um, we're . . . we thought . . . you see . . ."

In the time he took to hem and haw I figured it out. "This morning, at the ballpark, Bob told me you're related to Leland Warner."

"He's my father-in-law," Sinclair admitted. "But I've earned my position in the company. Leland depends on me."

"Warner owns the winery, doesn't he? Dewey Ridge, or whatever it's called."

He nodded. "I was director of production there. I made a lot of improvements to our operations, but Leland needed my help with the Drillers so I transferred."

"And Val Boyle was your assistant."

He nodded. "I mentored him. I wanted him to transfer with me to the Drillers, but things . . . circumstances—"

I cut him off. "What happened last night at the orchard?"

His wedding ring made a clinking sound as it hit the pavement. He snatched it back. "Don't pretend with me. I know all about your plan to blackmail us."

"Blackmail you?" I cried.

He replaced the ring and checked the empty street for witnesses before speaking. "You should take the money that's being offered." He stepped forward and made a lame attempt at intimidation. "Things could get very difficult for you otherwise."

I paused to calculate all the implications of his statement. Then I got very angry, very fast. "Did you send those cops to my house? Did you tell them to beat me up?"

He jumped back. "No. Of course not."

I noted his lack of surprise. "But you know about it?"

"You asked me those questions this morning, like you knew I was involved, so I called Leland. That's when I first learned about the tape."

I advanced on him and he stumbled backward. "There is no tape. The tape was black. Do you know what those goons said they'd do to me? Do you honestly think I'd hold out after that?"

He shook his head as if he didn't believe me. "It's much smarter to deal with us than to try and sell to someone else."

"I can't sell what doesn't exist."

Tires screeched on asphalt. An SUV barreled down the street followed by an old Buick. We each instinctively stepped toward our own vehicles to clear the road. When the vehicles showed no sign of slowing, I further retreated to the space between the rear of my van and the BMW.

At the last moment, the two cars stopped. Eight young African-American men got out. They weren't all dressed alike. Some wore sports jerseys. One wore a T-shirt. But dark blue was present in all their clothing. It announced their unity as clearly as a uniform.

One emerged as the leader and advanced on Sinclair. He carried anger and violence in every step. "You don't ignore me, Tommy Boy. You don't ever ignore me." Compared to this man, Skinny and Belly were mild annoyances.

Thankfully, no one appeared aware of my presence and I was very happy to stay back.

Sinclair tried to sound friendly and upbeat. "I tried calling your cell, Jason. All morning. I would never ignore you. Your network must be down."

"Funny." Jason gestured to one of the men behind him. "The man I had watching Val's place didn't have any trouble calling and telling me you were stupid enough to come here."

Sinclair put his hands up in the air. "Let's remember we're all friends."

"Where's my money?"

Sinclair dropped his fake smile. "I never had it. I swear. Whoever killed Val stole it."

Jason shook his head. "Not my problem. I jacked the Sonoran Fancy and put it on a clean truck. You owe me sixty percent of the take, plus interest, and since my truck is now sitting in the police impound lot, you're going to pay for that too."

"But it wasn't my fault."

"Not my problem. You made a tidy sum from the first two jobs by sitting back on that useless butt of yours. You can afford to pay extra."

"No, I can't. Not for six months. I sent that money overseas to launder it."

Jason smiled. "Then you better call on your old man."

"He wouldn't give me the money. He hates me."

"That I believe." Jason laughed and his men followed his lead.

When the laughter died, Sinclair made another attempt at reasoning with Jason. "You need to find out who killed Val. I know he made the delivery and was bringing the money back. Find out who killed him and you'll find the money." Jason's silence encouraged Sinclair. "And I'll give up my share. You can have it all."

Jason's slender smile faded. "Tommy Boy, do I look stupid? Is that what I look like? You think I'm just some dumb, tacked-up, little boy?" Jason turned to his remaining men. "Put him in the car."

"Don't you dare." Sinclair gestured toward the house. "I'm not alone. I have men inside. They'll come out any minute looking for me."

"And when they do, you'll be gone," Jason replied.

Like a rat on a drowning ship, Sinclair jumped back and pointed to where I was hiding at the rear of the van. "She's the one you want. She's a blackmailer."

They all turned.

"What? No," I cried.

"She says if we don't pay her, she'll put us on the news," Sinclair yelled. "She's probably recording right now."

"You're going to blackmail me?" Jason started toward me and his men followed.

That's when Sinclair saw his chance and darted for the Jaguar. They tried to stop him, but he got the power locks on too fast. I watched in horror as the car roared to life and went from zero to sixty in less than ten seconds.

Jason barely contained his rage. "Get her in the car."

EIGHT

I started to run, but Jason grabbed me. He pushed me against the side of the van and held my throat. Belly had done the same, but not like this. My hands clawed at what seemed like a vise squeezing the air from my body.

"Nobody causes me trouble." He didn't notice when my hands lowered. "Especially not a little girl like you."

My hand connected with the cool metal cylinder in my pocket just as he pulled away to yell at his gang. "Who wants to drive a news van?"

They laughed and Jason turned back to me.

The Mace hit him dead in the face. He doubled over, wheezing and crying out.

I jumped in the van and hit the power locks. His men surrounded me. They shouted threats and beat on the windows. For some reason I put my seat belt on before jamming the key in the ignition. The engine roared to life as a tire iron smashed into the driver's-side window. Small fragments of glass flew across the van. Most of the window remained in place, although now fractured and milky.

I floored it away from the curb. The Buick shot into my path and I slammed on the brakes. I heard an engine start and turned to see the SUV. I knew I had seconds before it moved to cut off the street behind me. I put the van in reverse and hit the gas.

They did the same. Metal hit metal, glass shattered, and everything spun.

Then, all at once, I wasn't moving anymore. I vaguely remember more obscenities coming from angry voices. The vehicle was a mess, but it had got around the Buick and the street ahead was clear. I put the van in drive and took off. I didn't look back. The rear window was cracked, so I wouldn't have been able to anyway.

I found the cell phone in my coat pocket. I tried to enter the familiar numbers and realized I was shaking. The alignment had lost its mind so as soon I heard a ring, I rested the cell against my shoulder and used both hands to steer.

Callum picked up on the seventh ring. "KJAY, we're on your side."

I glanced in my driver's-side mirror and didn't see anyone following me. "Callum, I need Trent's phone number."

There was an uncharacteristically long pause before he spoke. That should have warned me. Callum didn't like to waste time. "Why did you send David and Rod back? Did you get an interview?"

"Yes," I lied. "You'll love it. Now text me Trent's phone number."

Callum's voice faded as he yelled at someone in the newsroom, "Hey, get off your butt and fax these." Some papers crinkled in the background, then Callum returned to the phone.

"Text me the number," I ordered.

"No."

One of my hands jerked to the right. I quickly corrected and picked the phone up. "We had a deal. You promised."

"You're on suspension. Talking to Trent isn't going to change that, and you're acting way too erratic. You say you've got an emergency, but won't tell anyone what it is. You send David and Rod back to the station. Now you sound almost hysterical."

"I think there's another reason you don't want me to talk to Trent. I think you're taking orders from someone. Is it Leland Warner? Is he the one behind all this?"

"Forget almost hysterical. Now you're one hundred percent hysterical."

A stop sign whizzed by and I slammed on the brakes. The van narrowly missed a Volvo and came to a screeching halt in the middle of the intersection. Several cars honked at me, but I barely noticed them. "I want that number, Callum."

"Get your video back to the station," he said, ignoring me. "And then go home. You can talk to Trent in two days when your suspension is over. Hopefully you'll have calmed down by then."

I didn't think about my response. I didn't calculate what the right thing to say was. "I don't know how involved you are in this, but you give me that number or I will come back to the station, and you won't like me once I'm there."

Background static crackled. "Are you threatening me?"

"Yes."

His voice got low. "Lilly, you're out of line."

"I'm so past caring, Callum. You give me that number or else."

The line went dead. He'd hung up on me.

I drove only to put distance between myself and Jason. The shakes had leveled off, but now a weird metallic taste was in my mouth. After a few minutes, I decided to return to the station. I pulled into the KJAY lot and didn't pause to examine the damage to the van. I bypassed the newsroom and headed for the main staircase. I got halfway up to the HR office before I stopped.

When her shift ended, Marcie sometimes updated her résumé DVD if the show had gone well. I found her in the small room off Playback with the station's only digital editing computer.

She saw me as I came through the door. "Lilly, what's going on. Callum is really angry."

"I'm in a lot of trouble."

"I know. It's all over the station that you're having some kind of meltdown."

"No, you don't know. I've been beaten up and threatened and it all has to do with last night's murder."

"What? That's crazy."

"It sounds outrageous, but it's true and I need to find Trent. I'd give anything for his phone number or even an address."

"Can't you talk to someone else?" She returned to the computer and began packing up her things. "What about Callum?"

"I don't trust him. He may have given information about me to the men who beat me up, and now I think he's purposefully keeping me from Trent."

"Are you sure?"

"When has Trent ever told Callum not to call? Last time he went on vacation, they were on the phone every day."

"You're right. That is weird." She frowned. "But there must be someone else you can talk to—someone above Callum."

"I was on my way up to HR, but I got worried they won't believe me."

"They probably won't. Everyone thinks you're having a nervous breakdown over the suspension."

"I know, but I thought . . . maybe if you came along. You could vouch for me."

She paused and thought for a moment. Then all at once she smiled. "If all you need is an address, then what about those magazines Trent is always leaving in the break room?"

"What magazines?"

"The industry ones, about broadcasting and journalism. He brings them from home so his address is on the labels."

I started to run out, but stopped. "Thank you."

She smiled. "It's okay, go."

I walked quickly through the newsroom. Conversation pretty much stopped.

Callum hung up a phone and stood up. "I want that interview with the family and then turn in your—"

I ignored him and walked straight out the door to the break room. A stack of old magazines sat on the round table by the vending machine. I picked one up and looked at the label. Marcie was right.

It took me about twenty minutes to get over to the southwest side of town. The only car keys I had were to my own busted news van. I doubted Callum would give me another, so I had to drive the dented wreck. The van got a lot of stares, but nobody stopped me.

Trent lived in the Grassy Knoll planned community. The lawns were perfectly maintained and the houses adhered to a strict color palette. Some owners had decorated for the holidays, but the lighting was restrained and nothing that would attract the carloads of sightseers who cruised holiday displays this time of year.

I parked in the driveway and checked the damage to the van. A huge dent ran across the rear, and one end of the back fender was unattached and hanging down. Most of the windows were either cracked or gone. Trent wasn't going to like this, but at least the station had insurance.

I approached the large double doors and rang the bell. Almost immediately I heard a lock turn, then one of the doors opened.

"Come in," Trent invited. He wore his usual khakis, but had switched out his dress shirt for a green polo. "Callum called and told me you were on your way."

I crossed over the threshold and into warm, flowery-scented air. "How did he know?"

"Didn't say." He closed the door on the chill outside. "Just that you were very upset and coming to see me."

My thoughts about Marcie's possibly repeating our conversation were quickly obscured by the distraction of Trent's house. The entryway led into a great room with vaulted ceilings and an open kitchen. Everything was color-coordinated in hunter green and milky taupe.

Trent gestured to a seating arrangement in the great room. "Please make yourself comfortable."

I threw myself onto the oversize sofa. "I wouldn't bother you at home except it's an emergency and I don't trust Callum."

"I can see you're upset." Trent stood behind an armchair. "Can I get you something to drink?"

"Maybe in a minute. You're not going to believe everything that's happened." I sank into the couch and let the stress fall out of my body. "I don't even believe it myself."

"Is this about the suspension?"

"I wish that was my biggest problem. The real trouble started when I got home. Two men broke into my apartment and threatened me. It was horrible. They wanted the tape I made last night." I sat up and pointed to my eye. "They even hit me."

Trent shook his head. "Unbelievable. Did you give it to them?"

"How could I? There's no tape to give. It was black."

He nodded and smiled. "Right, right. Sorry."

For the first time since arriving, I gave all my attention to Trent. What jumped out at me wasn't the doubtful crease between his eyebrows or the slight smirk of his mouth. No. It was the darkening circle around his eye—like mine, but maybe an hour ahead of me in its bruising.

"What happened to your eye?" I asked.

He didn't say anything.

My exhausted brain tried to process the enormity of what that bruise meant. It tossed the revelation back and forth, rejecting and passing, but finally took it in. "I owe Callum an apology. You're the one. You sent them to my house."

He still didn't say anything.

"Answer me." I jumped up. "Or are you afraid to admit it?"

Trent's indignation propelled him forward and he grabbed the back of the chair. "I was lured home and attacked. They wanted the footage from the orchard and said they'd kill me if I didn't hand it over."

"So you told them I had it and where to find me? Way to throw me under the bus."

"Once I realized what you'd done, I didn't see any reason to protect you."

"What I'd done? I haven't done anything."

"You lied. You turned in a fake tape and held back the real one." His voice shook. "If you'd been honest, none of this would've happened. We'd have aired that video and then those thugs wouldn't have bothered either of us."

"I didn't lie."

"The company did a background check when you were hired. It's in your file. I know the kind of debt you're carrying and I know how much money you make." He shook his head and looked almost sympathetic. "I understand it must have been a huge temptation."

"Who cares how much money I owe? You've been my boss for two years. How can you think I'd do something like that? Don't you know me at all?"

"Know you? Are you crazy?" He laughed. "Nobody at KJAY knows you. That intern who left after a day had more personal relationships than you."

"Then why bother suspending me for incompetence if you don't believe the tape was black?"

But then I answered my own question. "You bastard. You only suspended me so I'd have to go home and they could ambush me."

For the first time, he managed to look a little guilty. "Honestly, I didn't think they'd hurt you. I thought you'd sell them the tape and we could all go on with our lives. I thought you'd be thrilled to have a buyer fall right in your lap."

"There is no tape. I screwed up last night. I swear."

Trent took a long, slow breath. "I don't believe you and you're fired."

"Fired," I repeated. "You can't do that."

He straightened and spoke formally. "That tape is company property. When you failed to turn it in, you were technically stealing. That's grounds for immediate termination."

"You can't fire me." I advanced on him. "I got threatened and beat up and practically strangled for this job today, and I'm not going to let you fire me. I'll take you to court for discrimination."

"You'll be in court, all right, but not suing me."

I stopped. "What's that supposed to mean?"

"Just what it sounds like."

Up until now I'd been too angry and defensive to feel fear. Trent's last statement changed that. "What did you do?"

"I called the police. I should have done it this morning, but I was afraid."

"And now you're not?"

"I made a deal. I'm being offered protection from those men in exchange for what I know."

I felt myself swaying slightly and tried to regain my balance. "And what is it that you know, exactly?"

"That at best you're conspiring to suppress evidence and at worst you're an accessory after the fact in last night's homicide. Someone's on the way. They said to try and keep you here."

"Do you know what you've done? I'm as good as dead."

"Don't be melodramatic. If you really are innocent, it will all come out if you cooperate with them."

I slowly walked around the chair. "Those two thugs, the ones you're so terrified of, are going to kill me."

Trent backed away. "In police custody you'll be safe."

"The thugs are police officers, you idiot."

He froze. "What?"

"They are the police and they're mixed up in this murder with Leland Warner and a gang who tried to kill me an hour ago. And I can identify all of them. How long do you think I'll live in police custody?"

Trent stared at me for a moment. "I don't know if you're a liar or delusional." He ran for the hallway. "And I don't care," he yelled before disappearing into another part of the house.

I focused on taking deep breaths. Was this really happening? Had everything gone completely to hell in a few hours? Then a voice inside me answered, "Yes, run for your life!"

I stumbled to the window and looked out. No SWAT team lining up. No police tape roping off the block. I ran outside and got in the news van. A few blocks from Trent's house I noticed something in my side mirrors—sparks. The trailing bumper created the bursts as it scratched along the pavement.

I pulled into the parking lot at the subdivision's swimming pool.

I tried to push the dangling end back into place, but the whole thing fell off. I threw it into the back of the van and prepared to leave. I didn't get past putting on my seat belt. An unmarked police car came to a standstill at a nearby stop sign. Handsome and Lucero didn't see me—probably because they were arguing.

I held my breath for what felt like forever. Then Handsome floored it toward Trent's house. I waited until they were out of sight, then escaped the Grassy Knoll planned community.

NINE

News vans are designed with as many bright colors and images as can fit on their frames. People are supposed to notice them. Mine was also missing a rear fender and several windows. If Handsome and Lucero got an APB out before I got the van off the street, I wouldn't last five minutes.

I took Coffee Road past the old, abandoned power plant and the suburban big-box stores. I crossed into orchards and continued until I hit Merle Haggard Drive. Merle was my ticket to Oildale.

The Dale, as my dad always called it, sprang up around 1900 as company housing for one of the nearby oil fields. As long as I can remember, it's been the rough-and-tumble place across the river from Bakersfield where hardworking blue-collar workers fight off blight and crystal meth. It's also where I grew up.

The part of Oildale I sought was a mix of valiant little old ladies trying to keep the neighborhood respectable and the seedier element that moved in when they died. I passed the big blue house my parents bought when we moved off the farm, but didn't pause or slow down.

Two blocks ahead I found the house I was looking for and stopped. It had been built by my grandfather, who died even before my father was born, and had been inherited by my uncle Bud. I didn't know if he still owned it, but I couldn't imagine him living anywhere else.

To judge from outward appearances, whoever did live here

wasn't in the respectable-little-old-lady category. Large swaths of yellow paint had peeled off the house. An old recliner and a sofa sat on the brown lawn amid a sea of beer cans, rusted scrap metal, and weird kitschy lawn ornaments. In one tableau a garden gnome appeared to be doing something obscene to a pink flamingo.

I turned into the driveway and drove all the way to the backyard.

I stepped in dog poop getting out of the van.

The back door to the house was open and I walked toward it, wiping my shoe on the grass as I went. Something creaked behind me and I swung around. "Bud?" The only structure in the yard was a crude tin shed in the corner. "Bud? Is that you? It's Lilly, your niece."

The tin door flew open. "Lilly?" Bud's dark brown, shirtless self climbed out of the darkness. He wore jagged cutoff jeans and four days' worth of gray stubble.

I instinctively ran toward him. "Uncle Bud."

His massive, tattooed arms reached out and took me into a giant bear hug. "Little Sister. I'm sorry about missin' Thanksgivin', but what're you doin' here?"

No one except Bud ever called me Little Sister, not even my actual big sister. It felt good to hear it again after all these years. "I'm sorry not to call first."

"That's okay." His happy face fell as he shot worried glances around the backyard. "Your mama's not with you, is she?"

I shook my head. "No. She's in Fresno."

He nodded. "I heard she moved up there with your sister. I'd feel sorry for Fresno, but they might try and give her back." He laughed. "You know I don't mean no offense about your mama. We were never partial to one another, is all."

"I know." I laughed nervously. "I'm sorry to show up like this when—"

Bud took hold of my face. The smell of stale beer filled my nostrils. "Who gave you that shiner?"

I laughed again. "A police officer."

Bud's hand dropped. "Crud."

"I know. I know," I said between bursts of increasingly panicked laughter. "I'm in so much trouble."

Suddenly I was crying instead of laughing. Bud put his arm around me. With his free hand he raised one of my arms and tried to blot out the tears with my sleeve. "Calm down, Little Sister. You just need somethin' to eat and a little sleep."

"You're right." I got control of myself. "Sorry."

"The cops give you those marks on your neck too?"

"No. A gang leader tried to strangle me."

"Ah, crud. Come on." He marched toward the house. "Watch where you step." He pointed to a pile of dog poop, then looked back at my big feet. "Never did grow into those things, did y'ah? Always thought you'd get a growth spurt and even out, but I guess it wasn't in the good Lord's plan."

As we climbed the steps to his back door, I glanced into the next yard. "What about the neighbors? Will they ask questions if they see my van?"

"Mrs. Foote's son might be a problem." Bud walked through the open door. "She lives across the way and I got a feud goin' with her boy. He'll cause trouble if he can."

Bud disappeared into the house and I followed. His kitchen was surprisingly clean and smelled of Pine-Sol. "What kind of feud?" I asked.

"That young punk decided he didn't like his mama havin' to look at my house on account of it needin' a coat of paint." Bud washed his hands in the sink. "So he tries to push me around, figurin' I'm an old man. Well, I showed him. I made myself a whole white-trash lawn for her to look at."

I collapsed into a seat at the yellow Formica table. "All that stuff out there, you did that on purpose?"

"Oh, yeah, I did." His grin melted. "Now first things first. You got a cell phone?"

I took it out of my pocket and placed it on the table. Bud picked it up, removed the battery, and threw it out an open window.

"Wait," I cried.

"Cell phones can be traced, Little Sister."

"But—"

"No buts," he scolded. "Now how about ATM cards, credit cards, stuff like that?"

"Are you throwing them out the window too?"

"No, I'm gonna shred those."

"Is that really necessary?"

"If I don't, then sure as the world you'll be tempted to use 'em." He stretched an open hand out toward me and waited. "You asked for my help. Well, I'm givin' it to you."

I reluctantly gave him my wallet.

He set it on the kitchen counter. "Now let me have another look at that eye." He examined me once more, then stood up. "You know what your daddy'd do if he was alive to see some piece of trash beat on you?"

"Dad would pretend he didn't see it."

He pointed at my neck and eye. "If your daddy saw that, he'd kill someone."

"That's why he'd pretend not to see it. So he wouldn't have to kill someone."

Shaking his head, Bud opened the fridge and removed something wrapped in white paper. "Put this on your face."

"What is it?"

He tore into the white paper and pulled out a hunk of brown flesh. "Dead cow."

I jerked back. "Don't you have an ice pack?"

"I been beat up more times than you. I know what works."

I took the steak and pressed it to my eye. Bud wiped his hands on his cutoffs. "Good girl. Now listen. Anybody tries somethin' like this again, you go straight for his privates and twist 'em off. It ain't proper fightin', but it ain't proper to be beatin' on a girl neither so I figure anything goes."

I laughed under the steak.

Bud took a seat at the table and reached for my free hand. For a moment I thought it was a tender gesture of reassurance, but then he spoke. "And if you do hit a fella, don't go makin' a fist round your thumb. It's the surest way to get yourself in a world of hurt. You hit the fella hard, you're gonna break that thumb." I made a fist, careful not to do it around my thumb, and he smiled. "Good girl. Just like that."

He dropped my hand and leaned back in his chair. "Now tell me about this here rat orgy you got yourself messed in with gangs and crooked cops and such." He grinned. "Or better yet, tell me about how you plan on gettin' out of it."

I lifted the bottom of the steak so it was nowhere near my mouth. "I don't know." I thought for a moment. "I think this guy Leland Warner may be the one behind everything."

Bud's voice filled the room. "You're in a mess with Leland Warner?"

"You know him?"

Bud paused, and when he next spoke, he'd recovered his easy-going tone. "I knew a guy, way back, who had a run-in with him." He paused again. I waited for more details, but he seemed to deliberately move on. "And I've seen him at that Dust Bowl Days Festival they put on over in Lamont."

I lowered the steak. "Is he a Dust Bowl survivor?"

"Keep that on your eye." Bud pushed my hand back into place. "Nah. He always had money. Warner likes to pretend he's an Okie, but he started out on top and he'll finish there."

"Why would anyone want to pretend to be an Okie? It's a derogatory word. Nobody would want to pretend to be that."

"I never minded bein' called Okie. It's the swear words that always come before it bothered me." He lifted his eyebrow in an accusing way and leaned across the table. "And I ain't never been ashamed of what I am a day in my life."

I put down the steak. "I'm not ashamed of who I am."

"I said keep that on your eye." Bud reached over and lifted my hand with the steak. "But honestly, Little Sister, if you're messed in with Leland Warner, you'd better run. He's got a nasty reputation, and, frankly, a sweet little girl like you's no match for a rich fella like that."

I shook my head, careful not to get steak juice on myself. "That's not an option."

"You're only sayin' that 'cause you've only ever lived here and it'd be scary enough on a normal day to leave. And today is probably the scariest day of your life so you're diggin' in with what you know. It's a mistake."

"I'm not leaving." My words were firm and left no opening for compromise. "I haven't done anything wrong and I'm not going to be run off. Now, are you going to help me or not?"

Bud sighed. "What do you need?"

"A car the police can't trace."

He reluctantly grinned. "I may know a fella who specializes in cars like that, but then what?"

I opened my mouth, but realized I didn't have an answer. "I need some time to figure things out. Everything's happened so fast."

"You go lie down and take a rest. I'll make some calls about that car." Bud reached over and took the steak out of my hand. "Old Pepper's in the bedroom. He'll keep you company."

"Maybe just fifteen minutes." I cleaned off my face, then started to leave. At the doorway leading to the rest of the house, I stopped and turned around. "Bud?"

He looked up from the table where he was rewrapping the steak. "Yeah?"

"Thanks."

His face lit up with the famous Bud Hawkins smile that had charmed an army of women and separated countless fools from their money. "Forget it. We're family."

I found Pepper, an old beagle/terrier mutt, asleep on Bud's bed. His black-and-white head lifted, sniffed in my direction, then he went back to sleep. I straightened out the quilt and checked my watch. It said two forty-five. Belly and Skinny were already looking for me.

When I woke up, the first thing I noticed was the amazing

smell. The air was salty and meaty and made saliva pour into my mouth. I heard sizzling and the scraping of metal on metal.

I rolled over onto my back and groaned. I was stiff and sore all over. Pepper was long gone, probably lured away by the promise of food falling on the kitchen floor, so I stretched out my arms and legs as far as I could. My neck felt worse, but the eye was better.

I looked at my watch and bolted upright. It said three forty-five.

In the kitchen Bud divided scrambled eggs onto two plates while Pepper waited expectantly at his feet. "Why didn't you wake me?" I said.

"Figured you needed to be sleepin'." He placed a well-done steak on one of the plates, then set it down on the table next to my wallet. "Now I figure you need to be eatin'."

I was seconds away from saliva actually flowing out the sides of my mouth, but I didn't sit down. "But what if the police discover we're related? They could be here any minute."

"Nah." Bud sat down with his own plate and twisted the top off a bottle of beer. "It'll be tomorrow at least before they put us together." He used his foot to kick the empty chair from the table. "Come on."

I reluctantly sat down. I opened my wallet to find all of my ATM and credit cards missing. At least he'd spared my driver's license.

"And take some of these." Bud pushed a bottle of Tylenol across the table.

I swallowed three with help from a glass of milk.

"Now eat up," he said.

I cut into the meat and took several bites. I think it was the best thing I ever tasted in my life. I was sopping up the leftover juices with eggs when the realization hit me. "Bud! This wasn't the steak I had on my eye?"

"Sure it is."

"That's gross."

He laughed and took a swig of his beer. "So how about you start from the startin'-off point of your mess?"

I quickly told him everything that had happened. "Obviously I can't go to the police. Someone at the crime scene last night must have tampered with the evidence and believes I recorded it. Until I know who's involved and how deep it goes, I won't know who to trust."

"And you think Warner's pullin' the strings?"

"He's the only one in this mess with enough money and influence to bribe cops."

Bud nodded. "Warner might be coverin' up for his son-in-law. Maybe Sinclair met up with Boyle, killed him, and stole the money he was carryin'."

"Why would Warner protect Sinclair from the police, but not the Eastside Crew?"

"Don't know. You're missin' out on most of the puzzle pieces. Like, what's this Sonoran Fancy the gang fella mentioned?"

I shrugged. "Whatever it is, Jason's men stole it and then Val hauled it on the truck and sold it. And it sounded like they'd done it before."

"They got lots of funny names for different kinds of weed. Sonoran Fancy sure sounds like one of 'em, and the Mexican cartels got lots of marijuana growin' up in the mountains around here." Bud shook his head. "But you rob one of those outfits, you don't come back a second or third time."

"Congratulations. You actually found a way this could be worse." I rolled my eyes. "A drug cartel, that's just what I need."

"Don't worry. Could be anythin' really. Electronics, tobacco, alcohol."

The last item on Bud's list gave me an idea. "Up until two weeks ago Sinclair worked at the Dewey Ridge Winery. He was in a perfect position to help Jason and his gang steal wine. And the murdered man was his assistant."

"Could be why he's not workin' there no more if folks were suspicious." Bud got up and took his plate to the sink. "So what's your next move?"

"I need some proof the police are involved. Then I'll go to the authorities."

"How you gettin' proof?"

"I don't know. I'd give anything to have Jason and Sinclair's conversation on tape." I paused. Was it really that simple? "What if I talk to Sinclair again, but this time record our conversation?"

"How you gonna do that?"

"At work sometimes we do hidden-camera exposés." I got up and joined Bud at the kitchen sink. "A couple months ago the engineers rigged up a tiny camera in a brooch for a sweeps piece. I'll wear it and he won't know he's being recorded."

"Folks don't like speakin' about their illegal-type shenanigans—especially when murder's in the stew."

"Sinclair talked to me earlier because he thought I was a blackmailer. All I have to do is tell him I want to sell the tape and then record what he says."

"How you gettin' your hands on this brooch? How you wrestlin' Sinclair down? Rich folks like that aren't in the phone book." He reached down and patted Pepper. "You're much better off runnin'."

"I'm not running." I looked around. "Where's your phone?"

Bud tensed. "Who you callin'?"

"My friend Marcie, at the station. She can bring me the brooch."

"Friends have a way of disownin' you when the law shows up."

"She already helped me once. It's worth a try, anyway."

Bud shrugged his shoulders. "Phone's in the livin' room, but you better let me make the call. Don't want somebody recognizin' your voice and raisin' the alarm."

We went to the living room, where I dialed the number and then handed Bud the phone. I heard Callum's voice answer in the usual way, and Bud asked for Marcie Walker. While we waited, I couldn't help looking at the framed photos on the walls. One set in particular caught my eye because they surrounded a strange ax mounted nearby.

"What's that thing?" I asked.

"Comes from when I was smoke jumpin' up in Alaska."

I looked closer at the black-and-white photos of young men

in old Forest Service uniforms. "You jumped out of planes and fought forest fires?"

"For a spell. I've done lots of stuff, for a spell."

Marcie's voice came through the phone line and Bud passed me the handset.

"Marcie Walker," she repeated.

I hesitated, then decided to take the plunge. "It's Lilly. I need your help."

"You need a lot more than my help," she yelled, but quickly dropped her voice to a whisper. "According to the police, you're going to need a good lawyer."

"They've been there?"

"They're here now. Callum had to cancel the five. They're saying it's going to tank us for sweeps."

"Never mind sweeps. What did the police say?"

"You held back the tape from last night to shield the killer. They want to arrest you as an accessory to murder . . . or maybe as a blackmailer. They can't seem to decide which." She gasped. "And Callum says Trent fired you."

"That must have gone over big. Are the other shooters having a party?"

"No. Everybody is upset. Rod was even rude to a policeman."

"Rod?"

"Ah-huh, and Callum just sent David in to watch the police search your locker in case they try and plant evidence."

I couldn't believe it. "Rod's being rude and David's watching my back?"

"Ah-huh, and Callum says Trent's a creep for firing you and we need to be circling the wagons—or something like that."

"I owe Callum an apology. Trent sent those men to my house, and now he's the one who told the police I'm holding back the tape."

"I don't know about any of that, but I think you need to turn yourself in."

"I want to, but I have to get proof first." I paused. "That's why I need you to bring me the little brooch camera we rigged up for the massage-parlor exposé. I can use it to prove I'm innocent."

"Lilly, I . . ."

"Please. I don't have anyone else to ask."

Marcie didn't make a sound. The newsroom hummed in the background.

"Okay," she finally said. "But this is a huge favor. If I ever need a kidney, you're first in line."

I let go of the breath I was holding and laughed. "Thank you. You can have both of them."

"Where are you?"

"I'm at my—" I started, but Bud grabbed the phone out of my hand and covered the mouthpiece.

"The first rule of bein' on the run is don't tell folks where you're holed up. Meet her someplace."

I quickly took the phone back, but kept the mouthpiece covered. "Where?"

"As far away from here as possible," he said. "Someplace on the south side of town."

I thought for a moment, then put the phone back to my ear. "Can you meet at the corn maze? It's deserted this time of year and it's easy to find."

"Okay. I'll meet you at the entrance, but I'm going to need some time. I have to find the brooch without looking suspicious. How about an hour?"

"Sounds good." I suddenly remembered the Sonoran Fancy. "Wait. There's one more thing. Can you find out if the Dewey Ridge Winery was robbed in the last few months? The murdered man worked there."

"I'll ask Callum to check. I'm doing a package on the murder so he won't think it's odd."

"Thank you." I paused. "Marcie, you're really coming through for me."

She hesitated, then said warmly, "That's what friends are for."

I hung up and turned to Bud, who was putting on a dirty, gray sweatshirt and flip-flops. "We're set," I said.

"I heard." He reached for an old can of peanuts sitting on top of his battered TV and removed a pair of keys. "You better freshen up while I get the car."

"It isn't here?"

"No. I park my baby around the corner at a neighbor's garage. Easier to get away if trouble comes knockin'."

I wanted to ask what kind of trouble he meant, but instead said, "Do you have a phone book?"

His eyes narrowed. "Why?"

"I need to make contact with Sinclair to set up the meeting."

His face relaxed. "Just so you don't tell nobody where you are."

"Okay." I rubbed my head and accidentally touched my sore eye. "I don't suppose we could stop at a drugstore? I need to get some makeup to cover up these bruises."

"There's some in the medicine cabinet."

I did a double take. "You have makeup?"

He laughed. "Think you're the only one who ever got a shiner?"

TEN

Tom Sinclair had no listing in the phone book or with information. I called every possible number for the Drillers, even the concession stand, but got a series of recordings telling me to call back in the spring.

Bud returned and found me staring at the open phone book.

"Don't say I told you so," I said.

"Not my style."

"No, I guess it's not." I returned his smile and felt a little of my tension ease. "And I haven't given up yet."

"What're you thinkin'?"

"I've met a lot of people covering stories over the years. If I can think of someone who has a connection to Warner or his business, it might give me a lead I can follow to Sinclair."

"Anybody who'd know Warner would know not to mouth off about it. Fellas like that stomp down hard to get things their way."

"You're right." Bud had given me an idea and I eagerly reached for the phone. "They do. Especially when TV reporters try to do stories about them."

I quickly dialed information. Within seconds the operator had a listing for Leanore Drucker. I called and spoke with her husband. He said she was volunteering that day at the Kern County Museum.

"Thanks," I told him, and hung up.

Bud must have sensed something was coming because he raised his eyebrows.

"What do you think about making a stop?" I asked.

He shook his head. "Dumb."

"But it's on our way to the maze. If there are cops around, we can keep going."

He turned and started for the kitchen. "First rule of bein' on the run is don't go paradin' round town."

"If you don't want to come, I can go by myself."

He stopped with his back to me, paused, then turned around. "We can stop, but it's dumb."

I covered my head with a John Deere baseball cap and swapped my KJAY polo for one of Bud's old Lynyrd Skynyrd T-shirts. I retrieved my jacket and camera equipment from the van and stored them in the backseat of Bud's 1971 Plymouth Fury.

"There are whole families living in apartments the size of your car." I settled into the passenger side of the bench seat and stretched out my legs.

"She's somethin'." His hand dropped to the seat between us and massaged the maroon paisley fabric. "Got her off my partner when he bought me out of Squirrel's Tattoo. Belonged to his grandma. Sat in her garage for thirty years beggin' to be let out."

I looked out the windshield across the expanse of gleaming white metal. The front hood seemed to stretch forever. "How much gas does this thing take?"

Bud put on a pair of scratched black sunglasses. "It's worth it."

Five minutes later Bud sailed his land yacht around the circular drive in front of the Kern County Museum and idled under the Beale Clock Tower. I'd been there the previous Friday to shoot the annual Clock Tower Wreath lighting ceremony. Some towns light giant Christmas trees the day after Thanksgiving. We light a giant wreath. I love that.

Bud scanned the front of the museum. "Looks okay, but the first sign of trouble you're back in this car."

"Sounds good." I jumped out and zipped my coat up. The winter cold felt stronger now that the sun was setting.

An older woman in a festive snowman pullover manned the

counter at the gift shop. She agreed to fetch Leanore out of the basement archives while I waited outside under the clock tower.

Originally constructed downtown, the Beale Clock Tower was rebuilt outside the Kern County Museum after a devastating earthquake in the early fifties. The earthquake is why Bakersfield looks like a snapshot from during the Eisenhower administration. Almost the entire town was rebuilt from scratch after most of the Victorian and art deco buildings were destroyed.

I waited for Leanore under one of the tower's Moorish arches while Bud smoked a cigarette in the car. After a few minutes an older woman in black slacks and a green blazer emerged form the main building. I stepped out from under the arch and waved. She saw me and hurried toward the tower.

"Lilly?" Her shoulder-length auburn hair formed a soft frame for her round face. "How are things at KJAY?"

I shifted my weight uneasily. "Same as usual."

Leanore's lips parted in the center as she smiled like a stereotypical sweet little old lady. "That bad?"

I laughed and lost most of my apprehension. "Worse, actually."

"Oh, dear. Maybe it is better I'm not there anymore." She waved a hand in the air. "No, no, that's not true. I really miss it."

I took a quick look at Bud in the car. He pulled back one of the sweatshirt's sleeves and pointed to a tattoo of a watch.

I turned back to Leanore. "I don't have a lot of time and I need to ask you a few questions."

She eyed Bud suspiciously, but said, "Go ahead."

"I need some background on Leland Warner and his family. Callum said you're the only one at KJAY who ever did a story on him."

She smiled. "Then he lied to you. I barely started before it was canceled."

"What happened?"

"Do you remember that series of biography pieces I did? Nice stories about notable residents and their lives in Kern County?"

I nodded. "I remember."

"Someone kept calling and leaving messages suggesting I do one on Leland Warner." She frowned. "I was stupid enough to take the bait."

"You think someone was setting you up?"

"Not me, Warner. I was a tool to annoy him. He likes his privacy."

I couldn't help smiling. "I may have heard that before."

"Well, at the time, I hadn't. He was a prominent businessman who supported local charities. I thought he'd be a good subject. Boy, was I wrong."

"What happened?"

"Trent called me into his office and said to drop it."

"Do you think Warner was giving orders to Trent?"

"I assumed Warner threatened to sue and made it clear that if Trent washed his back, then Warner would pay someone to wash Trent's."

"But that's so wrong. It goes against every principle of journalism. Why didn't you fight him?"

She smiled. "That's one of the things I've always liked about you. Somebody pushes, you push right back." The smile faded. "But I'm not that brave. I'd already been cut back to part-time. That job meant a lot to me and I didn't want to lose it."

"I'm sorry." I paused, then asked, "During your research, did you find out anything about Warner's family?"

She shook her head. "Only that his wife died some time ago. A daughter lives here, and I think a son lives on the East Coast."

I straightened like a bloodhound picking up the scent. "Do you know anything about the daughter? I think she's married."

Leanore shrugged. "Not a lot. Her name is Mary."

"Do you have a way to contact her husband or know someone who might?" She shook her head. "Do you know anything else about them? Even gossip."

Her lips pursed as she thought about something. "There was some talk a long time back. I think . . . when the daughter was a teenager."

"I won't use it on the air."

"Apparently she's a little high-strung. There was talk of an . . . incident."

Before I could prompt her to continue, a siren erupted down the street. I dived for the bushes. The siren got louder as the police car got closer, then faded as it passed us.

Leanore cleared her throat. "They're gone now."

"Thanks." I stood up, breaking several branches. Bud was giving me a nasty stare from the car. "Can you tell me real fast about Mary's incident?"

Leanore didn't miss a beat. "There was talk she attacked another girl in school. Some kind of rivalry over a boy. Rumors ran the gamut from the girl ended up disfigured all the way to she died. It was probably exaggerated or even made up."

"I understand." I hesitated for a moment. "Are you going to ask about what just happened?"

She smiled. "It was apparent from your lack of camera, van, and reporter that this was an unusual visit."

I brushed some dirt off my jeans. "It would take too long to explain, but . . . I'm sort of on the run from the police."

She pulled a twig from my hair. "That was apparent from your reaction to the siren."

I laughed. "Can you do me a favor and not mention to anyone that I came here? At least not for a few hours, anyway."

"I think that can be arranged."

Bud effortlessly steered the Fury down the deserted road. An unfinished subdivision, the construction workers already gone home, lined one side of the street with an orange grove on the other. The sunlight had faded, but it wasn't dark enough for the brand-new streetlights to turn on. The world was in a bluish middle ground between day and night.

"It's been a long time since I was down here," Bud said.

"Look at that." I pointed at a house set back a little distance from the road and surrounded by the orchard. It's old-fashioned construction, dirt driveway, and nearby chicken coop sat in stark contrast to the newness of the subdivision across the street. They even had an old-time racist lawn jockey. "It's odd, seeing the old ways right alongside the new."

"I'm as nostalgic as the next old fart, but some of them old ways stunk."

We continued several more blocks, then Bud slowed the car. "I think this might could be it."

Outside my window the line of orange trees ended and a wall of corn began. "That's the back side. In another block there's a big gravel road that leads to the parking lot."

Bud did a truncated three-point turn and backed the massive car down the small dirt road dividing the maze from the orchard.

"But we're meeting Marcie at the entrance," I said.

"First rule of bein' on the run. Always have a getaway car close, but not too close."

"What does that mean?"

"If you're walkin' into a trap, you don't want your getaway car fallin' into the net."

Bud brought the car to an unhurried stop three-fourths of the way down the dirt road. The engine idled to a slow purr and gently vibrated the white frame.

"It's not a trap," I said.

"I don't mean to be tellin' you your business." Bud turned the key and shut off the car. "But I've been around the cotton patch a time or two, so to speak. Sometimes people let you down. It's good to have an escape route. First sign of trouble, come runnin' back here and we'll take off."

I shook my head. "Marcie wouldn't do that."

Bud didn't say anything.

I reached for the door handle. "Okay. I guess there's nothing wrong with an escape route."

I walked along the line of corn until I found the back entrance. Bales of straw filled in a four-foot gap between the line of corn stalks. I pushed with both hands and the whole thing fell forward.

I took a last look at Bud in the car as I zipped up my blue jacket. A red dot glowed from the shadow of the interior as Bud sucked on a cigarette. I didn't want to admit it, but his warnings about Marcie had spooked me. If I was going to end up in police custody, I wanted it to be on my terms, with some proof to back up my story, and not because I'd been grabbed like a runner on *Cops*.

I raised my leg and took a giant step over a bale of straw. It was much darker inside the maze, and the corn had grown way past its prime. It fell over in places and created narrow tunnels. Worse yet, the straw that covered the floor had got wet, making it brown and slimy. It created the perfect dumping ground for old beer bottles, cigarette butts, and I don't want to know what else.

I made one wrong turn, but quickly corrected and found the right path. I emerged five minutes later onto a large, empty gravel parking lot bordered by more orange trees. A gravel road disappeared around the corner of the maze, and I knew at the end of it was the unseen street with the new subdivision. I knew this not because I could see through the wall of overgrown corn, but because I'd been coming to the corn maze for my entire life. I came first as a child with my family, then on school field trips, and finally as a shooter doing feel-good stories. It never changed. Every fall a farmer donated his land and a charity sold tickets, candied apples, and donkey rides. The layout was seared into my brain.

If I ran, as Bud wanted, I could find another town to live in. It would probably be a great place with everything that Bakersfield has and more. Maybe they'd even have a corn maze. The thing is, it wouldn't be my maze. It wouldn't be the one I'd outgrown at eight. It wouldn't belong to me. Nothing would.

I stood in the entryway as the light got dimmer and the wind got colder. Over the tops of the corn a streetlight flicked on. I blew on my hands before shoving them in my giant pockets.

I checked my watch. It read five twenty. Marcie had had over an hour to slip out of the station and meet me.

I jerked to attention at the sound of screeching tires and then the crunching of a car going fast on gravel. A KJAY news van turned the corner at a dangerous speed. Its headlights blinded me as the van charged. Bits of gravel flew like shrapnel as it came to a sudden stop.

Over the rumble of the engine a door opened and a single foot hit the ground. "Hurry, get in." It wasn't Marcie's voice.

"Rod?"

"We don't have much time."

I couldn't see him or anything else over the headlights. "Where's Marcie? Did she tell you I was here?"

"No, she told the police in exchange for an exclusive." Hurried footsteps crunched through the gravel and suddenly Rod was there. "The detectives are right behind me."

"I thought she might not come," I said quietly, "but I never thought she'd turn me in."

"I'm sorry. I know it's ugly, but we have to get out of here." He started back to the van, but stopped when he saw I hadn't moved. "Hurry."

"I don't suppose you brought the hidden camera?"

He patted his suit pocket. "It's right here." He looked nervously over his shoulder. "Now come on. We need to go."

I shook my head. "Thanks for coming to warn me, but I have a car on the other side of the maze. Give me the brooch and then you get out of here."

We both heard the soft crunch of tires on gravel at the same time.

"Too late," Rod whispered.

Neither of us moved for a few seconds as we listened to the slow, hesitant sound. Then, almost simultaneously, an engine roared and a piercing siren cut through the quiet.

I sprinted into the maze. I heard footsteps behind me and hoped they were Rod's. I didn't turn around to find out.

About halfway through I came to a crossroads and had to stop. The darkness and my own fear were playing tricks and I was unsure of the way.

Rod almost ran me down. "I'm sorry—"

I clamped my hand over his mouth. "Keep your voice down," I whispered. "They're probably in the maze with us."

He nodded and I dropped my hand.

"You know the way out, right?" he whispered.

"Yes."

"And you have a car waiting?"

"Yes."

"Excellent." He cheered for a moment, but then a crease formed on his forehead. "Why are we stopped?"

"I don't know the way."

He did a double take. "But you said—"

I covered his mouth again. Footsteps were coming closer. I looked down the darkened path and Rod followed my gaze.

"Tell me again why we didn't wait for backup?" I recognized Lucero's voice.

"Because that pretty boy was running down here to warn her," Handsome replied.

"Are you sure you're not a little ticked your girlfriend turned out to be playing you?"

Light from a flashlight cut through the gaps in the corn. Rod and I instinctively plunged into a crouch to avoid being seen.

"She's not my girlfriend and I didn't let her play me," Handsome shot back.

"This must be tough on you, Handsome. Women usually run in your direction, not away. Maybe your honey's playing hard to get."

"You won't be calling her my honey after I put her in the county lockup for a few nights. She'll be fresh meat in there."

I rocked backward and Rod reached out to steady me.

On the other side of the corn wall Lucero stopped and abandoned his teasing tone. "All kidding aside, I don't like that kind of talk."

"I don't care."

"Do you care that we're lost?" Lucero started to turn back.

"We should retrace our steps to the entrance and see if the black-and-whites are here. Then we can set up a perimeter."

"You do that. I'm going through."

"Fine." Lucero's footsteps faded away.

Handsome's flashlight cut through the corn separating our two paths. Shards of jagged light illuminated small pieces of Rod and myself and then disappeared. We each held our breath and waited till we were sure he'd moved on.

"What now?" Rod whispered.

I motioned for him to follow me and made a left at the crossroads. If I was right, we would be out of the maze in less than a minute. If I was wrong, we would find ourselves at a dead end. I didn't tell Rod and he followed without asking questions.

The final turn came and my muscles tensed in anticipation. A surge of adrenaline rushed through me as I spotted the fallen bales of hay at the back entrance. I jumped over them and ran for the Fury. I didn't care so much about making noise as getting to the waiting car before Lucero had time to set up his perimeter.

I pulled open the passenger door with Rod close behind me and got a nasty surprise.

The keys were in the ignition and Bud's flip-flops sat on the driver's seat, but otherwise the front seat was empty.

Rod tapped me from behind. "Shouldn't we get in and, you know, flee?"

I got in and slid to the driver's side.

Rod followed and shut the passenger door. "Is something wrong?"

"My uncle was here. I don't understand."

"Your uncle?" His head swung around and he looked out the back window. "Where would he go at a time like this?"

Suddenly every irresponsible thing Bud had ever done flashed before my eyes, and those were only the ones I knew about. "It doesn't matter." I turned the key in the ignition and the engine roared to life.

"Are you sure we should leave him?" Rod asked. "He could be in trouble."

I pulled out and down on the gear shift lever coming out of the steering column. "We're in trouble."

"Good point." Rod looked behind us and his whole body jerked. "Drive."

Handsome forced his way through the wall of corn behind us. I mashed the gas pedal and mowed down several stalks before spinning out into the street.

"He's coming," Rod warned.

I hit the gas again. We got almost a block before I had to slam on the brakes. A dark, shapeless blob came at us down the middle of the road.

I flicked on the headlights and Bud took the place of the blob. His bare white legs reflected the light as he ran toward us with something in his arms.

"He's still coming," Rod cried.

I turned in time to see Handsome clear the dirt road and start down the center of the street.

"I don't believe this." I stuck my head out the open window. "Bud, the police are here, hurry."

He threw open the backseat door and tossed something in. "Yeehaw," he yelped, and leaped in headfirst.

Handsome reached us at the same time.

ELEVEN

I floored it. Handsome dove for the back of the car and missed by inches.

"It's still open." Rod threw his torso over the backseat and reached for Bud's swinging door.

"Nothin' makes a man feel alive like runnin' from the law," Bud cried.

I tried to make a left at the first intersection, but misjudged the brakes. We came to a screeching halt. Rod fell backward and slammed his backside into the dashboard.

"Sorry." I mashed the gas again.

"I'm fine. Don't slow down." Rod threw himself back over the seat.

I accelerated without knowing where the road went. "Rod, get that door closed. I can't steer."

"I'm trying, but there's something hanging out."

Bud's lazy voice floated over the engine. "Simmer on down, son. You pull it in and I'll shut the door."

"Bud," I threatened. "My camera better not be hanging out the car."

Rod made a grunt and pulled on something. "I think it's the tripod."

"Don't worry, Little Sister, I'm sittin' on your camera."

"What?" I turned my head for a look, but the steering wheel followed. I overcorrected and Bud's open back door slammed shut. Rod fell into the front seat, bringing the tripod with him.

"Slow on down," Bud ordered. "Can't get away if we're mammocked up in a ditch."

I dropped our speed to sixty. The frame stopped shaking and the engine noise faded.

"This is the weirdest ten minutes of my life." Rod pulled the tripod closer as though he were trying to see it better in the dark. "I think we just committed a crime."

"Of course we did," I said. "We're running from the police. And what are you doing with my tripod?"

"That's not what I meant, and this isn't your tripod." Rod turned the object toward me, catching the light from the dashboard. "I think we may have stolen someone's lawn ornament."

"Bud," I shouted. "For the love of God, did you steal a lawn jockey?"

"The main thing—" Rod started, but had to pause when his voice cracked. "The main thing is not to panic."

"Sorry," Bud said. "Had to have it for my yard."

"You what?"

"Wait a minute," Rod cried, and pushed the jockey closer into the light. "Is this thing African-American?"

Bud cackled. "Mrs. Foote's boy is gonna have fits."

"Bud, this isn't a joke," I said. "We almost got caught because of you."

"The main thing is not to panic," Rod repeated, and tossed the jockey into the backseat as if it were radioactive.

"You been livin' a coddled life if you think that was close. When you're escapin' out the back of a cop car, that's almost gettin' caught."

"Of all the—"

"Maybe we should focus on our more immediate problems." Rod pulled the handkerchief from his coat pocket and ran the silky fabric over his forehead.

"Like what?" I said, transferring my anger.

"Like not going to jail."

"You're in luck youngins." Bud put his arms over the front seat and leaned forward. "Not goin' to jail's my specialty. Turn south up here."

I slowed the car at the intersection and made the turn.

Bud put a hand on Rod's shoulder. "I got a bag in the glove box, if you think you'll be chuckin' your crumpets."

It was too dark to see Rod's face, but his slouched outline didn't inspire confidence. He made another swipe at his forehead with the handkerchief. "I'm okay."

If you'd asked me an hour earlier, I'd have said nothing would ever go wrong in Rod Strong's charmed, color-coordinated life. How had he ended up in my uncle Bud's 1971 Fury with an offensive statue and homicide detectives in pursuit?

"I'm sorry I got you into this," I said.

"It's better than you being fresh meat in the county lockup." Rod shifted and put the handkerchief in his pocket. "And for the record, I'm nowhere near chucking my crumpets."

"If you say so, sonny." Bud pointed to the next intersection. "Turn left up there."

I made the turn and we emerged onto a neglected rural highway made of cracked and blistered asphalt. Grape and cotton fields ran into the growing darkness with occasional houses set back from the road.

"At least tell me where we're going," I said.

"Lamont's further on down the road a piece."

I hit the brakes. "But there's a sheriff's substation there. We're driving right into their hands."

"Exactly," Bud countered. "Last thing they'll expect."

"Because it's insane."

"More like touched in the head." I couldn't see Bud's face, but his voice sounded amused.

I turned around so I could look directly at him. "Please tell me you have some kind of plan. That you aren't just making this up as we go along."

Bud produced his trademark grin. "Most of those Lamont cops are gonna be chargin' outta the north and west, makin' like hell for the corn maze. That's why we're comin' into town from down south."

I turned to Rod. "What do you think?"

He looked at Bud, then back to me. "Of the three of us he seems to have the most experience with this kind of thing."

"I hope you know what you're doing, Bud." I turned around and put the car back in drive. "Otherwise we're all going to jail."

We drove for another ten minutes, then Bud said, "Slow on down. We're comin' up to Lamont."

The road doubled in size. Streetlights illuminated sidewalks lined with mom-and-pop stores. Some were already decorated for Christmas with FELIZ NAVIDAD scrolled on storefront windows.

"This street is so well lit," Rod said, echoing my own thoughts. "That police officer who chased us is going to send out a description of this car, and it's going to be very easy to spot us here."

"No problemo." Bud pointed to a do-it-yourself car wash half a block ahead. "Turn on in. The stalls got roofs. A chopper won't see us in there."

Rod's eyes widened. "You think they'll send a police helicopter after us?"

"Might could."

The car wash had a series of stalls with hoses for soap and water. Everything was self-serve, and customers fed money into machines to buy time with the equipment. The place was empty, and on Bud's orders I maneuvered the Fury into the last stall. A Dumpster blocked our view of the street, and a line of purple oleander covered a high fence running along the back.

When I killed the engine, Bud reached into the front seat and offered his hand to Rod. Dirt covered Bud's fingers and made his jagged nails look black. "Bud Hawkins. Lilly's uncle."

I expected Rod to balk at shaking the filthy hand of my thieving and disreputable uncle, but Rod took it without hesitation.

"Rod Strong. I work with Lilly at the TV station."

"You got a good grip there, boy." Bud slapped him on the back and got out of the car. Rod and I followed.

"Wait." Rod handed the flip-flops to Bud. "I think these are yours."

"I was wonderin' where those got to." Bud slipped them on and went to put some money in the pay machine at the entrance to the stall. He turned on the hose and missed spraying Rod by inches. "You okay, son?"

Rod, who'd jumped back from the water in terror, pointed to his coat sleeve. "Italian wool."

"You aren't really planning to wash the car?" I asked. "I can think of about a million more important things to do right now."

"You are just goin' to have to trust me, Little Sister. I always got an ace in the hole." Bud turned the hose on the car, and Rod retreated to the farthest corner of the stall. When Bud finished, I circled the Fury removing debris. Most of it was at the front end where cornstalks had become wedged in the concave grill and blocked most of the PLYMOUTH lettering.

As I threw the dead vegetation in the trash bin, a siren erupted.

Rod ran to the corner of the stall and peeked out. "Police."

"Where?" I said. "How many?"

"Coming down the road. Two of them. Sheriff's Department."

Bud kicked off his flip-flops. "If it all goes down the dumper, make a run for the back fence."

Rod looked with horror at his leather dress shoes, then peeked back out at the road. "They're going faster now."

The siren got louder and bounced off the cement walls of the stall. Around the edge of the Dumpster a car flashed by, followed by a second. The siren receded.

"Is that it?" I asked quietly.

Rod's head turned away from the street. "No, there's another one parked a couple blocks down."

I crossed to where Bud stood casually putting his flip-flops back on. "Why did I listen to you? We should have gotten out of here while we had the chance. Now we're trapped."

Bud lowered his bare knees to the wet ground between the car and stall wall. "Sure about that, Little Sister?"

"How much more trapped can we be?"

He ignored me and ran his hand over the rear door.

"What are you doing?" As I approached, I saw two ugly black scratches on the door. He rubbed the dark lines back and forth with more intensity than he'd shown for anything all day. The dark lines doubled in size, expanding under Bud's steady pressure.

"You're making the scratch worse," I said.

Bud stopped and stood up. "Am I?" He reached down and took hold of something. In a fluid motion he pulled off a chunk of white paint, revealing a dark maroon undercoat.

"What just happened?" Rod came up behind me and gazed over my shoulder at the car door.

"You thought I'd lost my touch." Bud cackled. "Well, this old fart still has a trick or two up his sleeve."

I knelt down. "But that's not possible."

Rod, careful not to let his clothes touch anything wet, leaned down and reached around my side. His clean, perfectly manicured hand examined the boundary between the dark and the light colors. "I've heard of this. It's plastic paint. They use it for commercials and movies."

I shot up and accidentally knocked Rod toward the wet car. He contorted his body in a curve and managed to freeze himself several inches from the Fury.

"Sorry." I offered him a hand.

He took it and straightened himself. "It also has obvious nefarious uses."

"Come again?" Bud looked from Rod to me.

"He means criminals use it to disguise their cars."

"That's puttin' it a tad bit strong. Even an honest, law-abidin' man can find himself a target of unwanted attention. Just look at you two."

"He has a point." Rod laughed. "In the last half hour I've assisted a fugitive and been chased by the police."

Bud tipped an imaginary hat at him. "See, it can happen to the nicest of folks."

Rod flashed his fake anchorman smile and I remembered I didn't like him.

"Let's get to work removing the white paint." I turned to Rod. "You should think about where you'd like to be dropped off when we're done."

The anchorman smile faded. "What are your plans?"

"You shouldn't be worrying about that. You should be trying to get as far away from me as possible."

"But you're in a lot of trouble." His white teeth caught the fluorescent light and reflected it back like a mirror. "I have an idea."

"I don't—"

"Let's hear it," Bud interrupted.

"Instead of going back to Bakersfield, why don't we head south to Los Angeles?"

I shook my head. "No way."

"My dad is a lawyer. He can give us good advice."

"Nice of you to offer, but I said no."

"Before we do anythin', this baby's gotta go from white to red." Bud grabbed hold of my arm and pulled me toward the rear of the car. "Rod, you take the front end. I'll get Lilly started back here and come check on you."

"We need to settle this first," I said.

"Later, Little Sister."

I allowed Bud to guide me to the rear of the car while Rod began work on the front hood. We both knelt at the rear bumper and went to work stripping it.

"I assume you wanted to talk privately," I said quietly. "It isn't fair to keep Rod involved. He's already risked too much."

"He ain't a pee-stained couch. We can't just drop him by the side of the road."

The rubbery paint yielded under my nail and I inched up a long swath of white. "Don't tell me you want to go to L.A.?"

"No way. Cops'll be checkin' out his friends and family by tomorrow at the latest." He stopped working and looked at his hands. His grin was gone and his lips were pulled back into a frown. "Your mama may not be the sweetest peach on the tree, but she's not stupid."

I gasped. "I'm not going to Fresno."

"I wouldn't do that to you." His grin came back. "I wouldn't do that to my worst enemy."

"Then what are you trying to say?"

He looked back down at his hands. "There's a reason your mama didn't want me round. I'm not sayin' she was right, but she wasn't exactly wrong. I tend to let folks down."

"It's okay about the lawn jockey. Just don't do it again."

"It's only that . . ." He pursed his lips as if he were taking a drag on a cigarette. For the first time in my life I thought he looked like an old man. I reached out and placed a hand over his. He looked up and tried to smile. "It's only that, I will do it again. Bound to happen."

I let go and returned to working on the bumper. "If you want out, say so. It wasn't fair of me to involve you in the first place."

"That's not what I'm sayin'. I'm not tryin' to lay out of it, but I'm not reliable. I'm not even reliable about bein' unreliable. No way to predict how I'll screw up or when it'll happen."

I nodded, but stayed focused on the paint. "Ah-huh."

"You need to understand that so it don't kick you in the teeth every time."

"Don't worry," I said, still unwilling to look at him. "I get it."

"And that's why I think Rod's a good man to have around."

"He's useless." I realized I was yelling and quickly lowered my voice. "You said yourself he was ready to puke back there."

"Pukin' and near-about pukin' ain't the same thing."

"That's not exactly a glowing recommendation."

"Then how about he's fightin' for you better than anybody else right now."

"Look at his competition. Marcie's the closest thing I've got to a friend and she sold me out to the cops. You're my family and you got bored and committed larceny. The guy I like just chased me through the streets trying to arrest me. All Rod has to do is breathe and he's better than the rest of you."

Bud's spine straightened. "You got eyes for a cop?"

I went back to peeling the paint. "If this hadn't happened, maybe the cop was going to ask me out, but that was before I was wanted for murder."

"No wonder he stuck with us so long." Bud chuckled. "He was worse than a bugger you can't thump off."

His amusement only fueled my frustration. "My point is, Rod doesn't exactly have to try very hard to look good."

"First rule of winnin' a fight. You need everybody you can get on your side."

I shook my head. "I want Rod out of this."

"Why? You give me a story about it not bein' fair to him, then you say he's useless, but you don't say what's really on your mind."

I glanced under the car and made sure Rod's feet were still on the other side. "I don't trust him."

"Now why—"

"I know, I know. You love him. Everybody loves him. To know him is to love him, but trust me, inside he's looking for an angle."

"My gut don't read him like that."

"Then why do you think he's so eager to get me to L.A.?"

"Same reason you don't want to leave Bako; it's his home base and he knows the lay of the land."

"Or maybe he saw what Marcie did and is trying the same thing on a bigger scale." Bud looked confused so I explained. "She told the police about the corn maze in exchange for an exclusive. If Rod got me to L.A., he could do the same thing with a TV station down there."

Bud squinted.

"You don't understand the TV business," I continued. "Everyone wants to get to a big market like L.A. It's all they think about."

"Then supposin' you're right about the boy. Supposin' he's

tryin' to snatch a crick in your neck. You cut him loose now, you never find out what he's up to."

"I don't want to know what he's up to. I just want him gone."

"Then if you won't keep him around to help, and you won't keep him around to find out what he's up to, keep him around so he won't talk to the cops." Bud gestured to the car. "We don't want him tattlin' about this here switcheroo with the color."

"You said we were getting a new car later tonight. After that it won't matter."

"Then at least keep him around till then."

I opened my mouth, but couldn't think of a good argument.

Bud went back to work on the bumper. "And in the meantime you'll get a better idea what he's made of. I think you're wrong about him, but if you're right, it'll show through."

I sulked for a moment, then walked to the front of the car. Rod looked up from working on the hood and smiled.

I didn't return his smile. "It's okay if you want to stay with us, but for the record I think you're . . ."

I lost my thought.

"What's wrong?" He followed my gaze to the maroon front of the car.

"You're practically done. We've barely got the back bumper uncovered and you've finished the entire hood."

"I'm good at picking up random skills, even if I don't like them. It's why I've been able to last this long as a reporter."

Before I could ask him what he meant, Bud joined us. "We need to be fixin' up some kind of plan."

"L.A. is out of the question," I told Rod.

He opened his mouth in what looked like the start of a knee-jerk denial, but stopped himself. "Why don't you tell me what this whole thing is about?"

I gave him a quick recap of my day while Bud worked on the car. I included my plan for recording Sinclair with the hidden camera before I went to the police.

"The stolen cargo didn't come from Dewey Ridge," Rod said when I'd finished, "because they haven't been robbed."

"How do you know?"

"Marcie had Callum check, and you know how thorough he is."

I did know. Callum was never wrong.

"I'm thinkin' pot." Bud rubbed away the last of the fake paint. "Sonoran Fancy's a terrific name for wacky tobacky."

"That, I will have to take your word for," Rod said. "But a subject I do know about is the Eastside Crew. I've done stories on the surge in gang violence, and this guy Jason has a very scary reputation. His two older brothers were killed in a gang war up in Fresno, and he went on a brutal revenge spree. When the Fresno PD stepped up enforcement, Jason targeted officers and their families."

"I heard he may have murdered a cop's wife," I said.

"What?" Bud looked horrified. "I been around and there are some lines nobody crosses. I don't care how mean and greedy they are."

"He didn't look mean or greedy." I touched my bruised neck. "He was a lot scarier than that."

Rod looked uneasily at my neck, but didn't remark on it. "That's how he holds on to power. After barely getting out of Fresno alive, he took over the Eastside Crew through fear and intimidation. A lot of their senior members resent him, but they're all too afraid to do anything about it. If he hesitates or shows weakness, they'll pounce."

"That's why I'm not going anywhere near him. Sinclair is harmless and will be easy to get talking." I gestured to Rod's suit pocket. "You do have the camera, right?"

"Yes." Rod took it out, but instead of giving it to me he glanced at Bud. "But I'm not sure about this."

I reached out and took the camera from him. "What aren't you sure about?"

"What if Sinclair discovers you're recording him? I know he doesn't appear dangerous, but you never know."

"He won't figure it out. I'm going to be sly."

Rod frowned. "No offense . . . the thing is . . . you're not exactly . . . I mean, not that it's a bad thing, but . . . what I mean to say is . . ."

"Spit it out," I ordered.

"Maybe your feelings are a little more apparent than you realize."

"Feelings? I'm not going on *Oprah*."

"No, I mean . . . Sometimes you may think you're being subtle, but your thoughts and opinions are very clear." He shot Bud a worried glance. "It's not a bad thing. You're just not . . . sly."

Bud shifted his weight. "I'm not in a real good place to say, what with our not seeing so much of each other since your younger days, but my gut tells me you're not a natural for a grift."

"Trust me," I said firmly. "I can handle Sinclair."

Rod didn't look convinced. "You'd be much better off coming with me to Los Angeles and talking to a lawyer."

"Getting people on-camera is what I know, so this is how I'm going to solve my problem." Despite Bud's wishes, I still wanted to get rid of Rod. "You know about lawyers. You should solve your problem by going to L.A. and getting legal advice."

He slowly shook his head. "No, you need me."

"I'm grateful for everything you've done," I said with absolutely no gratitude. "But I'm not exactly helpless."

He shook his head. "That's not what I meant. I may have overheard something significant this morning at the station. I tried to discuss it with you earlier, but you left to interview the murder victim's family."

A vague memory of Rod wanting to talk to me resurfaced. "Was it about the chief position?"

"Partly." He leaned forward in anticipation. "What if this morning someone substituted your tape with a black one? What if I knew how to get your tape back?"

TWELVE

Bud slowed the newly maroon Fury in front of the apartment building. The classic Southern California design, complete with lava rocks and palm trees, was common in downtown Bakersfield. I had only a vague memory of once dropping off equipment and couldn't say for certain we were in the right place. Fortunately a KJAY news van sat at the curb.

"This has to be it," I said.

Bud effortlessly maneuvered the Fury into an open space behind the van.

I turned to look at Rod in the backseat. "I still don't understand why you have to go in by yourself. Don't I have the right to confront him?"

"We been over this a hundred times." Bud cut the engine. "Marchin' up there on a tear ain't gonna get you this tape you're after."

If my refusal to accept his plan frustrated Rod, he didn't show it. "I know how upset you are, and rightly so, but I don't want him to feel threatened."

"I'm not going to threaten him."

Bud laughed. Rod was more discreet and looked away to hide his grin.

"Right now I'd say you're madder than a half-f'd fox in a forest fire," Bud said between chuckles. "Don't bother lyin' and sayin' how you're gonna be reasonable."

"I'm not lying," I lied. "I just want to talk to him."

"If by talk you mean put a hurt on him, then I believe you."

"And I may be wrong about what I overheard," Rod said. "He might have been bragging about something else or even making it up."

I abandoned my failing argument and tried another. "It could be dangerous to go up there alone. Maybe he's working for Warner or the crooked cops?"

Rod shook his head. "No. I think he saw your tape sitting in the basket of raw video and decided to act on the spur of the moment. Later, he went out to your van and turned your camera to black so you wouldn't get suspicious." Rod paused and his eyes avoided me. "I'm sorry to say this, but I believe it's one of many things he's done to keep you from becoming chief photog."

I thought of all the bad luck and equipment problems I'd had over the last six months. "When I get my hands on that—"

"That's exactly why it's better if I go by myself." Rod opened his door. "He may have destroyed the tape, but if he didn't, getting it back needs to be our top priority."

"You don't know which apartment it is. I can show you."

"No," Bud ordered. "You and I are sittin' right here."

"Don't worry. I'll find it." Rod exited the car. He passed under the white Christmas lights hanging from the branches of a palm tree and stopped at a row of secured mail cubbies. He zeroed in on one in particular and appeared to note the name and apartment number. But instead of going up to the second floor, where I remembered the apartment to be, he hesitated, then disappeared inside the first-floor hallway.

"Rod's going the wrong way." I opened the car door. "I better help him find the right apartment." I took the stairs two at a time and didn't look back. An exterior walkway ran around the building and led me to the rear side. I easily found the correct apartment. An inflatable hula dancer sat out front.

I raised my hand to knock, but stopped. I tried the knob. It was unlocked. I opened the door and went in.

The room smelled like funky Chinese food. One of the Wonder

Twins, shirtless and with a plastic cap covering his hair, stood in front of the only piece of furniture, a lime green sofa. He was picking up old fast-food cartons from the worn brown carpet. "Dude, I'm totally telling you we have to be careful. If we do it, like, all the time, it could totally damage our hair."

I closed the door behind me and his head jerked up. He froze with his hand about to toss a KFC bucket in a black trash bag. A look of absolute terror appeared on his face.

Unaware of my presence, the other one yelled from the bathroom, "Dude, I don't want black roots. My grandma always had black roots, and I'm totally not wanting to be my grandma."

I addressed the one by the couch. "Are you Teddy or Freddy?"

"Ted-Ted-dy," he stammered.

"Dude? Did you hear me?" I saw movement from the bathroom, and in the next instant Freddy appeared. "I don't want—"

He stopped in the bathroom doorway midsentence. In one gloved hand he held a small plastic bottle and in the other a strand of wet hair.

"Dude?" For a moment I thought he was going to freeze like Teddy, but instead he made a pathetic attempt at smiling. "Hey, Lilly? How about that? Dude, you droppin' in for a party?"

"I came to see you, Freddy."

He tried to laugh, but it sounded forced and nervous. "Callum said you'd been canned 'cause of that tape being black." Another nervous laugh. "He said the cops are totally looking for you too. You're, like, a wanted woman. Not that you're not always wanted, in a good way, but not like as a dangerous-criminal type, normally."

"Did you take the label off my tape and put it on a black one?"

Teddy dropped the KFC bucket and threw himself behind the couch.

I ignored him and advanced on Freddy. "How far back does this go? How long have you been sabotaging me?"

He backed up to the wall between the open bathroom door and a hallway. "Hey, hey. I resent the implication. Just because some bogeyman played hanky-panky, don't mean it was me."

"You're lying."

His pretense of innocence fell as his panicked eyes darted around the room. They settled on the open bathroom doorway.

I shook my head. "You won't make it."

He dropped the peroxide bottle and, instead of going for the bathroom, made a run for the hallway. "Help. Somebody help me."

I moved to cut him off. Before my fist could make contact with his jaw, someone grabbed me by the wrist.

"You don't listen so good, Little Sister." Bud pried open my fingers. "I said don't wrap your fingers round the thumb."

Freddy, cut off from the hallway, turned and stumbled for the bathroom. He tripped on the threshold and landed badly. He cried out and grabbed his knee.

"What's going on?" Rod stood at the open front door. "What are you both doing here? You're supposed to be in the car."

Bud let go of my hand. "Close that door, Rod."

"Rod, dude, is that you?" Freddy yelled while trying to squeeze himself behind the toilet. "Call the police. She's a dangerous fugitive and she's totally going to kill me."

"I should kill you."

Rod rushed to my side. "I know you're mad, but the important thing is not to panic or over—"

"I'm totally innocent," Freddy shouted. "Rod, tell her I'm innocent."

"You moron," I said. "Rod's the one who told me you did it. He heard you bragging to Teddy."

"Then he's lying." Freddy paused, then had a moment of fake inspiration. "Dude! What about David? I mean, it's totally none of my beeswax, but everybody knows you and David are like super cats-and-dogs on some kind of crazy fighting drug to make you, like, more fightier. If anybody did it, it's David. Go kill him."

Bud stepped between me and the bathroom. "This talk is all right, and everythin', but I think we're losin' sight of why we're here."

"Good point." I leaned around Bud. "You better not have destroyed my tape."

"I totally don't know what you're talking about." Freddy gave up trying to squeeze behind the toilet and settled for pulling himself into a ball under the pedestal sink. "Somebody stop her. She's totally dangerous and wanted by the cops."

"Now, now," Bud said to him. "Let's calm on down. Lilly's no dangerous criminal. Her temper's gotten the better of her, is all." He smiled. "Her mama was the same way. She could peel an orange with her tongue."

Nothing makes me angrier than having my temper compared to my mother's. "Freddy, if you don't give me that tape I'm going to peel you like an orange."

"All right. That's enough." Bud pointed to the other side of the living room. "You go over there and give me and this fella some breathin' room."

"But—"

"No buts, Lillian." Bud's face looked different. His lips were thinner and pressed into a tight line. All the easy good humor had vanished. "All you had to do was sit tight in the car, but you went ahead and made a right mess. Now you're gonna let me try and fix it."

Somewhere underneath my anger I knew I had acted badly, even stupidly. I shot another dirty look toward the bathroom, but reluctantly crossed the room.

"We really should get out of here," Rod said. "The police are probably on their way."

Bud approached the bathroom doorway. "I think the neighbors are used to hearin' all manner of strange things comin' from this here bachelor pad. I doubt we got to worry about one of 'em callin' the police."

I saw Freddy's hands swat at Bud's bare legs. "No way, man. I hear sirens. You should run."

"Now, son. Judgin' off the stink o' weed in this place, the last thing you want is the cops showin' up."

Freddy's swatting hands froze.

Rod sniffed. "Is that what that smell is?"

"That's medicinal, dude." Freddy's hostility faded. "My grandma was just visiting and she's got, like, cataracts."

Bud grinned. "You thinkin' of glaucoma, son."

"Whatever."

Rod put one hand on the door frame and leaned into the bathroom. "We'll be happy to let you get back to your medicinal pursuits just as soon as you . . ." He did a double take. "How do you live like this? I've seen cleaner gas station bathrooms."

"Dude, we weren't, like, expecting company." Freddy's hostility returned. "You don't get to bust into a man's crib and then get all judgy 'cause he didn't, like, tidy up."

Bud laughed. "As the great Eileen Barton sang, if you knew we was comin', you'd have baked a cake."

"Dude, get your head out of your butt. Everybody knows that's a Rosemary Clooney song."

"How is this helping?" I called from across the room.

Bud ignored me. "Now, all due respect to Rosie, 'If I Knew You Were Comin' I'd've Baked a Cake' was sung by Miss Eileen Barton."

"Dude, my grandma used to totally play that song and I'm sure it was Clooney."

Bud smiled. "Listenin' to music must ease the pain of her glaucoma."

"She's been dead for like . . . oh, right, yeah, grandma's glaucoma."

"Son, I think you and I got a similar way of lookin' at the world." Bud looked at Rod. "Why don't you give me and this here fella a few minutes alone?"

Rod nodded and joined me on the other side of the room. Bud returned his attention to the bathroom.

I didn't believe Freddy's claims of innocence, but something he'd said struck me. "What if David put him up to it?" I asked Rod.

He shook his head. "No. That's not—"

"But it makes perfect sense."

"No, it doesn't."

I pointed toward the bathroom. "Freddy's a harmless little dweeb. No way he'd take the initiative to do something like this on his own."

"Freddy played a serious of pranks on me when I started working at KJAY. He's actually very clever and nasty when he wants to be. He was also vocal about not wanting you to be chief."

"No, he wasn't."

"Behind your back, he was very vocal," Rod explained. "He believed you'd get him fired while David would be too soft to actually go through with it."

"Am I hearing things? David soft? And you don't seriously think Freddy is nastier than David?"

"David's too self-righteous to do something immoral. And he only wants the promotion because he's obsessed with being the best. Becoming chief through sabotage would be pointless for him."

"What are you talking about?" My voice rose. "David's a jerk, end of story. He has no depth. He doesn't have complicated psychoanalytical BS compulsions. His compulsion is to be a jerk."

Rod took his handkerchief from the suit pocket and ran it across his forehead. "I may not like David, but I can see he's more than just a generic blob called jerk. And if you tried harder to see him, what he really is, you'd understand why he's the last person who'd resort to sabotage."

"So you're saying I've completely misjudged Marcie, David, Teddy, and Freddy—pretty much everyone I work with."

"Not completely misjudged."

"Oh, not completely? That's a relief."

"Lillian," Bud called. "Maybe you can take a break from yellin' at our friend Rod?"

"I'm not yelling at him. We're having a heated discussion."

"Sounds to me like the heat's all comin' from you."

Rod smiled and even managed to diffuse the tension by laughing, but he sat down on the sofa like a tired man.

Bud turned back to the bathroom and squatted next to the toilet. "Now what say we stop goin' round in circles here?"

"I told you," I heard Freddy reply. "I'm not giving Lilly the tape."

My opinion of Bud rose. He'd got Freddy to admit to stealing the tape.

"That's a might bit contrary of you," Bud said. "And not necessarily the smartest way to play this."

"Dude, on her like best day, she's mean. Today she's totally psycho-dangerous and wanted by the police. The only thing keeping her from wailing on me is that tape. Once I give it to her, she's totally going to beat me up."

"I'm not mean." I took several steps toward the bathroom. "Name one time I ever said anything mean to you or anybody else at the station."

Freddy snorted. "You don't have to say things to get your point across. You're always giving dirty looks and acting all stuck-up like you're so much better than everybody else."

"That's not true."

"It's totally true. Teddy even tries to be nice and include you in stuff with the other shooters, but you always roll your eyes and hurt his feelings."

I started to repeat my denial, but stopped. Sometimes Teddy did invite me to things. Usually in the form of an idiotic monologue about all-you-can-eat crab legs or the monthly pie special at Marie Callender's, but he did it. Had he been making an effort to include me? Had I really hurt his feelings?

"David may be a jerk-off," Freddy yelled, "but at least he's not mean."

"This kind of yellin' is not goin' to help either of you." Bud reached for the door and closed himself in with Freddy.

The room was quiet for the first time since I'd entered the apartment. I'd thought it would feel good to confront Freddy. Maybe I should have stayed in the car.

I looked at Rod sitting on the couch and smothered the urge to ask him if I was mean. "Sorry I was yelling at you."

He smiled. Not a big, fake anchor smile. Not a grin. It was simple and warm. "Apology accepted. And for the record, you're not mean."

I felt my insides melt. An image of the dewy-faced writer who mooned at Rod popped into my head.

Rod ran a hand along the lime green sofa, then looked at his palm. "Why is the couch sticky?"

"I can think of a lot of reasons. And you don't want to know any of them."

Rod looked at me, then at his hand. He jerked himself off the couch. "I wish we'd gone to L.A."

"Or at least that I'd stayed in the car?"

He laughed and wiped his palm on his pants. "Or at least that."

"Sorry."

Rod put his hand against the wall and leaned on it. "It's okay. You've had a difficult day." He straightened and looked at his palm. "Why is the wall sticky?"

"I think, once again, that falls into the category of things you don't want to know."

We both laughed as Rod once again wiped his hand on his pants. Suddenly his laughter stopped. He reached down and picked up something from the floor, then glanced at the bathroom door. "We have to get Freddy out of the bathroom, right away."

"How right away?"

"By any means necessary. Whatever it takes."

"I like the sound of that." I took quick strides and threw open the bathroom door.

"Stay away from me," Freddy cried.

Bud rose from where he'd been sitting on the side of the bathtub. "Hold on there, Little Sister."

I grabbed both of Freddy's legs and dragged him out into the center of the living room.

"Not so fast." Bud put both arms around my waist and actually lifted me off the ground.

"It's okay." Rod rushed to shut the bathroom door, then stood in front of it. "Bud, put Lilly down. She's not going to hurt him."

Bud set me down and Freddy stood up.

"Freddy, you're in danger." Rod looked down at something in his hand and shook his head. "I promise that within the next minute you'll feel real terror."

Freddy started for the hallway. "Dude, I'm calling the cops."

Rod held up the small bottle of hair bleach Freddy had dropped earlier. "Is this what's in your hair?"

Freddy stopped. He reached up and touched one of the wet strands. "Dude?"

"Because it left a very ugly stain on your carpet." Rod gestured to an orange scar on the floor. "It must have nasty side effects." He looked at his watch. "How long have we been here? Five minutes? Ten minutes?"

Someone cried out.

Bud looked around the room. "Who the hell is that?"

"It's Teddy." I tried not to giggle. "He's behind the couch."

Bud stared at me the way my mother used to stare at him when he came shirtless to Sunday dinner. "Why didn't you say there was another fella behind the couch?"

"I forgot."

Rod smiled. "Hi, Teddy."

"Hi, Rod." Teddy rose from behind the sofa. He pulled off the shower cap and a mass of wet curls fell around his bare shoulders. "I'm totally sorry, Lilly. I swear I didn't help Freddy do anything bad." He looked at Rod. "I totally don't want my hair to fall out."

Rod nodded. "Do you know where the tape is?"

"Don't tell them," Freddy shouted. "It's our only leverage."

"We watched it, but nothing special happens." Teddy paused to take a nervous breath. "Freddy hid it with his stash. That's why he won't tell you where it is."

"Dude," Freddy exclaimed.

"Can I rinse my hair out now," Teddy begged, "please?"

"Of course." Rod opened the door to the bathroom and stepped aside. Teddy ran in and Rod shut the door behind him.

Rod looked at Freddy. "Where is your stash?"

Freddy didn't answer.

"Fine." Rod leaned against the door. "We'll all stand here and watch as your hair turns orange and falls out."

Freddy jumped from one leg to the other. "Dude. This is, like, against the Geneva Convention or something."

Rod glanced up. The tension in his face contradicted the casual stance of his body. "Where is your stash?"

Freddy made a squealing noise and pointed to the sofa. "Inside the first cushion."

Rod opened the bathroom door. Freddy ran in and pushed Teddy out from under the bathtub faucet.

THIRTEEN

I leaned into Rod and tried to view the small screen. "Are you done yet?"

"No. Almost, I think." He remained focused on my camera's viewfinder where the video from the orchard played. "You're interviewing the homicide detective."

"That's toward the end." I retreated to my half of the backseat.

We were parked outside a bar near the Dewey Ridge Winery waiting for Bud. In the hour since we'd left Teddy and Freddy's apartment I'd watched the tape twice, but wasn't any closer to understanding its importance.

After another minute Rod pushed stop and removed the earpiece. "There's nothing the least bit suspicious on this tape."

"We're missing something." I took my camera back and pushed rewind. "The viewfinder is so small. If we watched on a big screen, maybe we'd see something new."

"Maybe." Rod sounded skeptical. "It does make it hard to go to the police if we don't know what the tape proves."

I put the earpiece in. "I'm glad we got it back, but I'm still going ahead with my plan to record Sinclair. I need proof I can count on."

"If you can't find him, you can't record him."

"Hopefully Bud will learn something useful in the bar." I looked across the dark parking lot. "If he hasn't gotten drunk and forgotten about us."

"I'm sure he wouldn't do that."

I laughed. "You don't know Bud."

"I know he loves you."

"That's very sweet and very sentimental, but completely beside the point. Bud is who he is and that's not changing."

Rod looked straight at me. "People change all the time."

I laughed again. Not to be mean or to try to make a point, but because it's my natural reaction to funny things.

"I know that sounds corny," he continued, "but people aren't just one thing. You never know what they're going to do. Bud might—"

The music from inside the bar got louder, and we both turned to look at the front door. Six men, one of them Bud, poured into the dirt parking lot accompanied by rowdy laughter.

"Let me find my smokes and I'll be ready to go." Bud crossed the parking lot and opened the car door. "How you two doin'?" he asked quietly.

"We can't find anything suspicious or incriminating on the tape. It's just a bunch of police officers and techs doing their jobs." I paused while Bud lit a cigarette. "Have you been able to learn anything about Sinclair?"

He nodded. "Me and some of the fellas are goin' to check out the winery. See if we can come up with a phone number or address or somethin'."

Rod looked impressed. "How'd you pull that off?"

"I said he fired me from my maintenance job at the ballpark and I'm lookin' for a way to get some of my own back." Bud took a quick drag on his cigarette. "Some of the fellas work at the winery, and Sinclair's about as popular as a lard bucket full o'armpits. They all hate him."

That part of Bud's story I believed, but it was just about the only part. "I don't like you going off by yourself. And what does 'checking out the winery' mean, anyway?"

"Wait a minute or two until we're gone and then drive back towards Arvin." Bud crushed the remainder of his cigarette into the dirt. "There's a coffee-shop-type joint called the Top Hat Café.

They got a bar attached. You two wait in there and I'll come find you. Try to blend in." Before I could stop him, he slammed the door. "I'm good to go, boys."

Bud jumped into an old Dodge Ram with a camper shell, which immediately peeled out of the lot followed by an SUV.

"How long do you think we should wait?" Rod asked.

"This is good." I set my camera on the floor and jumped into the front.

"What are you doing?"

I started the engine and put on my seat belt. "I'm following him."

"What?" Rod threw a leg over and tried to join me. "But he said to wait at the restaurant."

"I told you, Bud isn't going to change." I jerked my head to avoid getting hit by Rod's expensive leather shoe as he pulled his other leg over. "He's up to something and we're following him." I drove out of the dirt parking lot. On the dark road ahead two sets of red taillights sped away.

"Wait a minute," Rod said. "We shouldn't panic."

"That's the important thing." I gave the Fury some gas and followed.

Rod nodded. "It is and I think we're . . . are you laughing?"

"Of course not." Good thing there wasn't enough light for Rod to see my face. "I promise, at the first sign of trouble we'll go find the restaurant and wait."

"At the first sign of trouble it'll be too late," he said, but fastened his seat belt.

We followed the red dots. I guessed in the darkness surrounding the road were grape fields, but couldn't see anything outside my headlights. Suddenly the red dots vanished. I sped up and stopped at a wide road cutting through thick trees. "They must have turned here." I followed.

"What's that?" Rod pointed to a lit section of road ahead. The SUV from the bar blocked a large metal gate. I slowed as we passed. Several security guards argued with the men in the SUV while a truck with the Dewey Ridge logo waited to exit.

"That's the winery," Rod said. "But why are they blocking the gate?"

I feared the SUV and the men inside were there to cause a diversion, but didn't tell Rod. "I don't know, but the pickup Bud took wasn't with them."

We followed the road as it curved, then I brought the car to an abrupt stop. A metal chain with a large, shiny PRIVATE PROPERTY sign lay on the ground at the entrance to a small dirt road.

"Looks like someone cut the chain," I said. "Three guesses who would do something like that."

I ignored Rod's protests and followed the dirt road. The trees were thick, and unusual for this area. Someone had gone to a lot of trouble to plant and maintain them. I remembered what Mrs. Boyle had said about Dewey Ridge not wanting anyone to know the wine was made in Kern County and guessed the trees were there for privacy.

The parked pickup truck appeared on the road ahead and I hit the brakes. I cut the engine, but left my headlights on. We got out. The dirt road ended nearby at a tall chain-link fence with vines blocking our view inside. The pickup was unlocked, but the interior held no clues as to where the occupants had gone.

Rod walked to the rear to investigate the camper shell. I was freezing in my thin T-shirt, so instead of joining him I started back to the Fury to get my jacket. That's when I saw a break in the ivy. I crouched down and looked closer. Someone had cut an opening in the fence large enough for a man to pass.

"This is weird," Rod said, looking in the truck's flatbed.

"Is there a bolt cutter in there?"

"As a matter of fact there is, but it's the wine that's odd."

"What?" I stood back up. "How much wine?"

"Two cases of Dewey Ridge chardonnay."

I quickly walked to the rear of the truck. Along with some random tools and the bolt cutter, the cases were haphazardly laying in the flatbed. "I'm going to kill Bud."

"Why? What's—"

I shushed him and pointed to the hole in the fence. A case of Dewey Ridge wine slid through the opening. The hands pushing the box turned into arms and finally a man. He stumbled as he stood and wiped his hands on already filthy jeans. The stranger appeared old enough to be my father, but that could have been the result of a hard life or hard drinking. I guessed the latter since even now he looked buzzed. His eyes fell on us and he did a double take.

"Where's Bud? I'm his niece."

The stranger hooked his thumb backward toward the fence.

"Are you stealing wine?" I asked.

"Hey." His outrage was magnified by whatever he'd been drinking. "It's all sitting in that SOB's office. Mr. Fancy Pants' private stash waiting for him to come back and get it. Weeks since he left. And it's just sitting there."

In my excitement I forgot that I disapproved of trespassing and robbery. "Is Bud in Tom Sinclair's office?"

His head bobbed in an exaggerated nod. "The SOB's gone, but his wine is just sitting—"

"I understand. Can you take me there?"

"Whoa, whoa," Rod exclaimed. "Hold on."

"Can you take me there?" I said again, and the man nodded. I ran to the Fury and put on my jacket.

"I said hold on." Rod followed. "This is a bad idea."

"Who knows what I'll be able to find in Sinclair's office." I pressed eject on my camera and returned the tape to its protective case. "And Val Boyle worked there too."

"You said Sinclair transferred to the Drillers weeks ago. There's probably nothing left to find." Rod watched as I slipped the tape in my pocket. "And taking our only evidence with you is an even worse idea."

"No offense, but I'm not letting this tape out of my sight."

Rod's voice rose. "You promised that at the first sign of trouble we'd go wait for Bud at the restaurant."

"There hasn't been any trouble yet."

Rod giggled, the high-pitched laugh I hated, but this time I heard it differently. What I'd always interpreted as mocking now sounded panicked. I stopped and looked at Rod, really looked at him. I didn't see a shallow Ken doll. I saw the man who'd come to the corn maze to warn me, I saw the man who'd told me I wasn't mean, and I saw a man who was now frightened.

"You're charging in without thinking this through." His face was pinched and worried. "Just like at Teddy and Freddy's apartment."

I had a moment of clarity and knew he was probably right. But knowing your instincts are dubious and being able to ignore your instincts are two totally different things. "I'm sorry. I have to go in there, but you don't. It's not fair to drag you down into my mess." I'd said similar things in my attempts to get rid of Rod, but now I really meant it. "Walk back to the main road. You'll find a pay phone eventually. Call your family or lawyer or whomever and have them come get you. You've helped me more than anybody else today. I don't want anything bad to happen to you."

"Please reconsider," he begged. "Think of the consequences if you get caught."

I started walking toward the opening in the fence where Bud's friend waited. "Don't worry. If I get caught, I'll say a lot of BS and try to smile a lot. You know, talk my way out of it or something."

Rod grabbed my arm. "Lilly, you couldn't talk your way out of a paper bag."

"Maybe I'll rise to the occasion." I tried to gently pull free. "What happened to people can change and you never know what they're going to do?"

He held on to me. "But I don't want that to change. That's why I like you."

Our eyes met. I couldn't remember feeling that uncomfortable in a long time and had to look away. The minute I broke eye contact he let go of my arm.

I couldn't get to the fence fast enough. "I mean it. I want you to leave and be safe, okay?" I didn't give Rod a chance to answer.

I pushed Bud's new friend through the opening ahead of me and followed.

I've never been to Napa or the wineries on the coast, but I have seen pictures. They're usually gold-tinted with lots of rustic oak barrels and sun-dappled grape leaves. Dewey Ridge looked more like a high-tech industrial compound. Powerful lights illuminated the main building's cavernous interior. Through open hangar doors I saw giant metal tanks in rows connected by scaffolding. Closer to the ground, a maze of pipes and hoses connected everything.

Attached to the side of the main building, a long row of glass-walled offices topped with a series of dark gray triangle roofs stretched out like an arm. My guide led me around to the far end of this second building where a door was propped opened.

"Wait," I said, and jumped back. "There's a camera over the door."

He didn't look concerned. "They're wiring up the whole place 'cause of those robberies." He paused and swayed slightly before regaining his balance. "But don't worry. None of it works yet."

I followed him inside, but then stopped. "You had robberies here?"

He waved his hand. "Nah."

Rod said there hadn't been any thefts, but he or Callum might have made a mistake. "This is really important. Did someone steal a lot of wine from Dewey Ridge? Maybe even several truckloads?"

"No way."

"But you just said there'd been robberies."

"Not here. Who'd steal this crap?" He paused, then laughed. "Except me."

He continued laughing as he led me down a hallway with a dozen offices on each side. At the end of the corridor the rooms were larger and equipped with an outer office for an assistant. We stopped at one of the last. The hallway itself ended nearby at a door marked HARDHAT ONLY.

"This is it." He pointed to the empty space on the door where a name plaque should be. "We had a party the day that SOB left. What a creep he was. Made the loaders wash his car. Got the crew boss canned because he complained."

I tuned out the man's rant and focused on the assistant's desk, which showed signs of recent use. I turned on what I hoped was Val Boyle's computer and, while it booted, checked the drawers. Aside from some generic office supplies I found nothing.

Behind me the door to the office opened and Bud wheeled out a dolly full of wine cases. "Little Sister, you sure don't follow orders so good."

"You're mad at me?" I gestured to the wine. "You're stealing and I'm the bad guy?"

Bud glanced at his friend, who'd seen an open bottle inside the office and gone for it. "Phil here offered to get me in if I helped move the vino. What was I supposed to do? Say no?"

"And you're not keeping any of it for yourself?"

"Maybe he offered to share." Bud managed to look bashful. "No harm in that. I nose around for you and make a little profit. Old-fashioned win-win."

I returned to checking the desk drawers. "And just how much nosing around have you done for me?"

"Been busy with the profit part. Might be a good thing you come to help. Don't know how long the boys can keep security busy out front. This ways, you can do the nosin' and I'll finish tendin' to the profit." Bud turned back into the office. "Phil, I got this here dolly from the big buildin' where we come in. I'm takin' the rest of the boxes out in one load through the back. Make sure the door stays propped open and don't turn no lights on. They'll know somethin's up."

Phil had sunk onto the floor of Sinclair's old office with his bottle. "Right-o."

"Phil doesn't look very reliable," I said.

"Fella's walkin' on a bit of a slant, but he's all right." Bud pulled back on the dolly and prepared to wheel it out. "But maybe keep one eye on him."

He left and I took a quick look inside Sinclair's office. The only light came from the hallway behind me, but I had no trouble seeing Phil on the floor drinking. Otherwise the room was empty except for a small desk and a computer in the corner. Even the walls had been stripped down to bare picture hooks.

I returned to Val's desk. Accessing the computer required a password. I tried some obvious ones, such as his mother's name, with no luck. I opened the drawers again, checked the phone's speed dial, and looked underneath the leather desk pad. I got up to investigate a printer by the window, but stopped.

On the floor next to the desk was a cardboard box. Someone had deposited Val's personal items inside. I searched it hoping to find an address book with Sinclair's contact info. No such luck. The meager contents consisted of shoe polish, a spare tie, several bus schedules, and two framed photos. I paused over the photos.

In one, Val wore his cap and gown while Diana kissed him. She looked much younger and stronger than the woman I'd met, even though the picture wasn't even two years old. The second photo I'd seen already on Diana's wall: younger versions of Val and Gideon clinging to each other with open and easy affection.

I returned the photos to the box. I'd found nothing. How much longer could I keep searching? I reentered Sinclair's office and peeked through the blinds. This side of the building faced the front gate and had a view of the SUV still blocking the truck's path. Three guards argued with Bud's new friends while several workers, probably all that were scheduled for this time in the evening, stood nearby watching the show.

Phil had resumed his monologue, but as he gulped chardonnay it had become both angrier and harder to understand. "Why don't you go check the door?" I told him as I turned on the computer in the corner. "Make sure it's still propped open for Bud."

He ignored me and continued ranting. The computer screen flickered to life and a Warner Land Holdings logo appeared. It was a different system from the one on Val's computer, which used Windows, but it too required a password.

I glanced at Phil. "Any ideas on how to get into this computer?"

"That's for the big shots, the grand pooh-bahs, the man." He paused for a swig of wine and discovered the bottle was empty. "Lowly little peons like me don't get access. Only the big shots like that SOB who—"

"Why don't you go make sure the door is still propped open."

"Right-o." He got himself up off the floor and stumbled out of the office.

I tried guessing Sinclair's password, as I had with Val's, with a similar outcome. On a whim I picked up the mouse pad and checked the underside. "Genghis Tom" was written on a Post-it note.

It worked and within seconds I was logged in under Sinclair's name, but my elation soon faded. I was inside Leland Warner's shipping system. The delivery and transport schedules for all of Warner's businesses were available with the click of a button. Impressive technology, but not what I needed.

I heard an angry shout outside and darted to the window. To my horror, the SUV and semi were both gone. The shouts came from Phil screaming obscenities at a guard.

I ran out of the office and down the hallway. A guard appeared at the back door. I immediately changed direction and sprinted for the door marked HARDHAT ONLY.

"Hey, you," I heard. "Stop right there."

I burst through the door. The bright lights disoriented me, but I recognized the metal tanks. I jumped over a set of pipes and around a staircase. A smash behind me echoed up into the catwalks. The guard had followed. I turned into the center aisle and ran toward the huge hangar doors. I could see the break in the fence ahead. As I left the building and felt my foot pound into the dirt, something flashed on my right. Seconds later I was on the ground.

FOURTEEN

Don't move." The guard who'd tackled me got up and brushed dirt off his khaki uniform pants.

Did he know about the hole in the fence ten feet away? Before I could make another run for it, the guard who'd been chasing me arrived. He yanked a Taser off his belt and tried to hold it steady while panting. "Don't worry, Greg, I've got her covered."

They cuffed my hands behind my back. Eventually I was taken to a small building next to the main gate. A dozen monitors hung from one of the walls, but an octopus of unconnected cables lay on the ground beneath them. Only two of the monitors had a working picture, and these showed different views of the front gate.

The guard who'd escorted me pointed to Phil passed out on the floor. "Sit down over there."

"This is all a big mistake," I told him.

A middle-aged man emerged from an office off the main room. All the guards wore Valsec uniforms and jackets, but this man's was neatly pressed and he wore a name tag identifying him as the chief of security. "You can tell the police it's a big mistake. Maybe they'll believe you."

I tried to smile and stay friendly. "I'm sure we can work this out without involving the authorities."

He gestured to the floor next to Phil. "I believe you were told to take a seat."

As they helped me down, I repeated my claims of innocence to no effect.

The guard who'd tackled me entered and went straight to his boss. "I'm sorry, Mr. Meyer, looks like whoever else was involved got away. I recovered the wine and did a quick search of the two vehicles, but no sign of additional suspects."

At least Rod escaped before things went bad. And Bud was still out there on the loose. Who knew what trick he might have up his sleeve to rescue me?

"Don't worry, Greg. We got the license plate off that SUV full of drunks. I'll give the number to the police and they can trace it."

"Excuse me," I interrupted. "Before you involve the authorities, there's something else you need to do first." Instead of continuing to deny involvement, I'd decided to try a new strategy. "Mr. Sinclair is a friend of mine. Call him and say Lilly Hawkins is here. He'll want to talk to me."

All three of them laughed.

The one named Greg seemed especially amused. "You're a personal friend of Mr. Tom Sinclair? A rich guy like that is friends with . . . you?"

I tried to wipe some of the dirt off my face with my shoulder. "I'm telling you with complete honesty that he wouldn't want the police called."

This unnerved Meyer, who stopped laughing. But after a moment he shook his head. "If it were just Phil Rumson over here, we might go ahead and handle it internally. But you and your pals in that SUV aren't employees. That makes it a police matter." Meyer turned and went back inside his office. "And I think it's about time I called them."

"Wait," I yelled. "You're making a mistake."

He ignored me. Rod was right; I couldn't talk my way out of a paper bag.

"Sir!" Greg pointed at the monitors. "We've got another one."

I turned and looked. Rod's smiling face filled one of the screens as he peered upward at the camera and waved.

Meyer rushed back out. "Is he alone?"

"Wait." I tried to stand, but Phil snored and rolled over onto my legs. "That man has nothing to do with the robbery."

"Does he look familiar?" Greg stared at the monitor. "Maybe he was in the SUV?"

Meyer leaned in and blocked my view. "No, but he does look familiar."

"No, he doesn't." I struggled with Phil's dead weight, but only became further entangled. "He's an innocent bystander."

"It's weird. I feel like I trust him," Meyer said. "You know what I mean? Like he's a war hero or something."

The other guard nodded. "Like, if I were in a fight, he'd be on my side."

I pictured Rod standing before the American flag in Trent's cheesy ads. I hadn't realized how effective they'd been.

Meyer pulled back from the monitor. "Regardless, I want him detained. You two get out there. Do whatever it takes to bring him in." The two men ran out the door. Meyer watched the monitor, then said to himself, "What's he doing now?"

On the screen Rod held something in his hand, which he raised to the camera. It was his station ID.

"K-J-A-Y," Meyer read slowly. "Rod Strong."

Suddenly Rod went down as the two guards tackled him.

I cried out. Phil roused, looked at me as if I were a pixie, and went back to sleep.

"Stop," Meyer yelled as he ran outside. "Stop, stop. He's the guy from TV."

A few minutes later I heard voices. Rod walked in with all three men.

"Of course you were only doing your job," Rod said.

"I hope we didn't ruin your suit." Meyer's tone had mellowed considerably.

"Nothing a good dry cleaner can't fix." Rod glanced around the room. His eyes landed on the twisted knot of limbs covering me. He immediately came to my aid. "There you are, Lilly. I explained how you're my shooter and we just happened to observe some thieves breaking into the winery."

"Oh, right." I stood with Rod's help. "Good thing you explained that."

Greg ran over and removed my cuffs. "We're so sorry. Why didn't you say you worked for Rod Strong?"

"I was—"

Rod cut me off. "Lilly was trying to be discreet. It's standard procedure."

"That's right. I—"

He cut me off again. "Lilly observed some men breaking through your fence so she followed hoping to apprehend them." Rod pulled me up and away from Phil. "You weren't hurt, were you?" He pretended to look at my wrists and whispered, "Say as little as possible."

Meyer chuckled. "I'm not buying it. I think you saw men breaking through the fence and decided to snoop around. You're here because of that young man who was murdered." He winked at me. "That's why you wanted us to call Mr. Sinclair, so you could ask him about his former assistant."

"Do you have his phone number?" In my excitement I forgot Rod's instruction to stay quiet. "Can you call him now? Please. He won't be mad."

Meyer shook his head. "I don't have the number, but even if I did, I couldn't give it out to the press. Our company has a strict policy of not speaking with the media."

"That's very understandable." Rod took my arm and steered me toward the door. "But we're on a deadline, and if you can't help us, we need to be on our way."

"Wait just a minute." Meyer stepped into our path. "You don't actually believe I'd let you go?"

Rod's anchor smile stayed firmly in place. "Is there a problem?"

"Not a problem." Meyer grinned. "But we don't get a lot of celebrity visitors. How about posing for a few photos?"

Rod dutifully posed for individual shots with each of the

guards. I took the opportunity to repeat my request that they contact Sinclair. Meyer said again that he didn't have the number. When Rod finished, we began to leave, but once again Meyer stopped us.

"If I got my wife on the phone, would you mind saying hi?" Meyer dragged Rod into his office. "She's a big fan of yours. This is going to make me a hero at home." Meyer closed the office door.

I was left to wait with the two guards.

"Your job is so cool," Greg said.

The other immediately backed him up. "Yeah, I'd trade places with you in a second."

"I don't know," I told him. "You get to tackle people."

They both laughed.

I pointed to Phil. "Is this the first time you've been robbed?"

Greg's posture straightened. "We're not supposed to talk to the media."

"Your boss isn't here and I won't tell anyone."

The other guard shrugged. "I don't see any harm in answering because the answer is yes, this is the first time."

"Then why the security upgrades? All these monitors and cameras can't be cheap."

"That's not because of us," Greg said. "We run a tight ship around here. The security upgrade is a companywide thing."

Sinclair helping Jason steal from Dewey Ridge made so much sense. Inside Man was a perfect roll for him—duplicitous, but not involved in the difficult or risky part of the crime. But given that Dewey Ridge was connected via computer to Warner's entire shipping network, wasn't Sinclair a potential Inside Man at all of Warner's businesses? "Was someone else in your company robbed?"

Greg glanced at the other guard. "We're not supposed to talk to the media."

"You already have. Don't worry, I won't tell anyone. It's completely off-the-record." I rubbed my arm and smiled. "And you tackled me really hard. I mean, come on."

Greg laughed. "I don't see what harm there is in telling you."

He glanced one more time at the other guard, then we all took a step closer to each other. "Three different almond distributors were robbed, but they were up north. The last one got hit two weeks ago. That's when the company decided to improve security."

"That's all?" I said. "Almonds?"

He nodded. "The thieves cut the fence in the middle of the night, found a loaded truck, and drove it straight out the front gate."

I indicated the wall of flat-screen monitors. "Isn't this is a lot to invest in security because some nuts went missing?"

The other guard laughed. "Have you bought a package of almonds lately? Those things are expensive."

I realized with a shock that he was right. Even the smallest package might cost several dollars at a convenience store.

"And you can get a lot of almonds in one of those tractor-trailers," he continued. "I heard the company lost over a million dollars."

"I heard one point five," Greg corrected.

Not drugs. Not cigarettes. Not alcohol. Was it possible? Had my life been ruined, had Val Boyle been murdered, over some nuts?

Whatever skepticism I still had faded when I heard Greg say, "I think these were a high-grade, fancy variety. They'd get top dollar."

I almost choked on my words. "You mean like Sonoran Fancy?"

He shrugged. "I guess."

I started to laugh, but outside a car horn honked.

Greg jumped to attention, and checked the two working monitors. They showed different angles of an older Honda waiting at the front gate.

"I've been here for three years without a single incident." The other guard checked his Taser, then put on his jacket. "Now in the space of two days we get an employee murdered, a robbery, newspeople sneaking in, and all kinds of strangers at the front gate."

"This is probably nothing," Greg told him, but also checked his

Taser. "HR packed up the murdered guy's personal things and left them in a box by his desk. Mr. Meyer mentioned someone from his family might stop by to pick them up."

"I hope it's that simple." The other guard stepped toward the monitor, trying to get a better look. "But it could be one of Phil's friends come back to spring him."

But it wasn't one of Phil's friends. I recognized Gideon's face as he leaned out the window to yell. Through the open door we all heard him. "Hello? Will somebody come out here already?" He honked the horn a few more times for good measure.

If Handsome and Lucero were keeping the family informed, then Gideon probably knew I was wanted for questioning.

I turned and went straight into Meyer's office.

Rod was on the phone. "That's a wonderful story idea. I'll pass it along to—"

"There's a strange man at the front gate." I took Meyer by the arm and herded him out of the office the same way he'd herded Rod in.

Meyer didn't question my panic. He ordered his two men to go investigate, then watched the action on the monitors.

"I'm sorry to be abrupt, Mrs. Meyer," Rod said into the phone, "but I really—"

I yanked the phone out of his hand and hung it up. "Val Boyle's cousin is here," I whispered. "He may know the police are after me. We have to run."

Rod giggled.

I put a reassuring hand on his arm. "It's going to be okay, but we have about five seconds to think of an excuse for Meyer."

"No matter what, it's going to look suspicious," Rod said. "But you should say as little as possible. People see right through you."

I whipped my hand away. "I may be bad at telling lies, but you're bad at coming up with them."

"Then you come up with the lie and I'll tell it."

"Fine. Say we got an emergency call about breaking news. Make it some huge thing and we have to race to the scene."

"Oh, that is smart." His smile faded. "But I don't have my cell phone. Bud took it."

"Meyer won't know." I pulled Rod out of the office.

Meyer heard us and turned around. "Everything okay? You two look a little shook up?"

"Got an emergency call about breaking news," Rod said. "Hazmat situation at an orphanage. They think it might be some kind of toxic gas." We both moved toward the door. "We're so sorry to run out of here, but it's a huge story."

I pulled Rod outside. "Bye. Thanks for everything. It's fastest if we go out the back where our car is." We hurried across the dirt lot. I glanced over my shoulder and saw the Honda entering the open gate behind us. "Hurry." I started running and Rod joined me. We sprinted around the side of the main building. On the back side of the property we found the hole in the fence and crawled through.

We jumped in the Fury and sped away. Out on the main road, I watched in the rearview mirror, but no one followed us. I relaxed a little.

"Do you know what happened to Bud?" I asked.

"No. I was walking out to the main road to find a pay phone when that SUV almost ran me over. I thought there might be trouble and doubled back, but I never saw Bud."

"We'll go to the restaurant and see if he turns up." I waited a moment, then took the plunge. "Thank you."

"What for?"

I kept my gaze on the road and didn't look at him. "Coming in and saving me instead of running away and saving yourself."

"Anyone would have done the same."

I wasn't so sure. Rod had put his reputation, his career, and himself in jeopardy. Most people would need a big payoff to attempt something so risky.

"Fortunately we're no worse for wear." He paused. "You do still have the tape?"

"In here." I pulled it out of my pocket. "Check and make sure it wasn't damaged when they tackled me."

He removed the tape from its protective case and held it up to the dashboard light. "Looks fine."

"Good. And we're actually better off. I discovered what Sonoran Fancy is."

"Really?" He slipped the tape inside his suit coat. "I'm betting drugs. Bud said pot, right?"

I almost asked for the tape back, but feared such a strong statement of mistrust would be hurtful. "Nuts."

"I'm sorry?"

"Sonoran Fancy is a kind of almond. If Val Boyle sold an entire semi full of the stuff, then he potentially had five hundred thousand dollars on him when he was killed."

"Really?"

"Really," I said. "And that's not all. The almonds belonged to none other than Leland Warner—and I don't think he's the kind of guy who appreciates getting robbed."

"Wow." Rod's voice sounded light and upbeat. "We got Sinclair's phone number and solved the mystery of the Sonoran Fancy."

My eyes glanced from the road to his smiling face. "What do you mean we got Sinclair's number?"

Rod pulled a slip of paper from his jacket pocket. "Meyer gave it to me. Off-the-record, of course."

FIFTEEN

The Top Hat Café turned out to be exactly where and what Bud had described. English and Spanish holiday greetings filled the windows. Inside, families with kids filled slightly worn green booths and maintained a constant hum of conversation and laughter.

The hostess greeted us with a friendly smile. "We stop serving dinner at ten, but I can still get you in."

Rod looked around. "We're looking for the bar."

She gestured to our right. "Through there."

We entered and had to pause to allow our eyes to adjust. Candles flickered on small tables, and soft, low light came from green lamps hung overhead. The walls were alternately covered in a silky, green fabric and beige tile bearing the image of a martini glass. I suspected that on closer inspection the fabric would be soiled and the tile chipped, but from a distance it looked swank.

A large group of office workers sat around a small table in the corner, but the bar itself was empty. Rod and I each took a seat on worn but comfortable red stools.

The bartender took a break from filling a jar with candy canes. He was Latino, with gray hair and a neatly trimmed mustache. "What can I get for a pair of sweethearts tonight?"

Rod glanced at me.

Drinking was the last thing I wanted to do, but Bud had said to blend in. "One tequila shooter. No chaser."

The bartender turned to Rod. "And for you?"

He hesitated, then said, "A cosmo, please."

"Only take a minute." The bartender ambled down the bar to make our drinks.

Rod gestured to the jukebox. "How about some music?"

I shrugged, but the bartender said, "Great idea."

Rod crossed the room and peered into the glass case where the songs were listed. "Hey, they've got Culture Club. I used to love them."

"Please, no," I begged. "I can't handle Boy George tonight."

"How about Joni Mitchell?"

I sighed. "Okay."

Rod put money in the machine and pressed some numbers.

The music started slow and dreamy, and Joni's older, deeper voice sang "At Last."

Rod returned to his stool. "You look relieved."

"I was expecting a song about being miserable. It's been too rough a day for that."

"Hey," the bartender called while yanking the cocktail shaker back and forth. "Why don't you dance with your boyfriend? A nice handsome boy and a nice romantic song like this—don't waste it."

Rod leaned toward me. "He'll get suspicious if we don't."

"Not a chance."

Rod took off his suit jacket and placed it on the stool next to him. He glanced down the bar, then whispered, "It might help us blend in."

"I don't think so."

The bartender brought us the drinks, winked, and retreated.

Rod lifted his martini glass. "Here's mud in your eye."

I touched the tip of my shooter to his glass. "Here's looking at you, kid." I swallowed half my liquor while Rod took a sip of his.

He set the glass back down and straightened his tie so it went smoothly into his vest. "Do you think it'll take Bud long to get here?"

"It depends on what happened to him. But he's the kind of guy who always has a backup plan. Maybe the SUV picked him up."

"He's quite a character." Rod laughed. "Half the time I have no idea what he's saying."

"When I was a kid, I thought he was making phrases up as he went along."

"There's an episode of *Star Trek, Next Generation,* not the original," Rod explained. "Captain Picard gets stranded on a planet with a member of an alien race and they can't understand each other's language. It turns out the alien's language is based on metaphor, and if you don't know the stories the metaphor is based on, you can't understand it." He smiled. "That's what being with Bud is like."

"I think that's the first time Bud's ever been compared to a character from *Star Trek.*"

Rod took another sip of his drink. "I have the DVD, if you ever want to watch."

I pulled back and stared. "Are you a Trekkie?"

"Absolutely. *Star Trek* is a gateway drug."

"Gateway to what?"

"Science fiction and then fantasy, and then one day you turn into a hard-core tweaker and graduate to manga."

I looked at the bar, then back at Rod. "I would not have thought that about you."

He picked up his cosmo and took a bigger drink. "What about you? What do you like?"

"Mysteries, I guess."

"I'm open to reading a mystery."

"You say it like you're agreeing to move in with me."

He held up a hand. "Hey, it's a big step. I've been on a steady diet of science fiction since I was a teenager."

The door opened and we both turned, hoping to see Bud. Instead an older man in a rumpled suit shuffled in and took a seat on the opposite end of the bar.

I raised my shooter to Rod and offered a toast. "To Uncle Bud."

He tapped my glass. "Uncle Bud."

I swallowed the rest of the liquor. I wasn't drunk or even tipsy, but I did feel a whole lot more relaxed.

"Is he literally your uncle?" Rod took a sip. "He seems too old. And why does he call you Little Sister?"

"I think it's a Southern expression, but I am the younger sister in my family."

"So that's your permanent label?"

"Something like that. And technically he's my half uncle. He and my father were born decades apart to different mothers." I couldn't suppress a knowing smile.

Rod noticed. "What are you smiling about?"

"Nothing."

"Come on. You're not telling me something."

I shook my head, but contradicted myself by giggling. "There's a kind of rumor. I don't know."

Rod scooted closer. "What?"

"My sister told me once, but she's not reliable."

"About Bud?"

I nodded.

"What is it? You have to tell me."

"It's possible . . . he might be my uncle and my grandfather."

Rod recoiled. "What?"

"Not by incest. Nothing gross. Just sleazy." I laughed. "My grandfather was an old man when he married his much younger second wife. He died of a heart attack before my dad was born."

"And?"

"My sister said she heard something once."

"What did she hear?"

I covered my eyes and giggled again. "That Bud got busy with his pretty, young widowed stepmother."

Rod's jaw dropped. "And got her pregnant?"

"I don't know."

"What does your grandma say?"

"She died when my dad was still a little boy."

Rod's eyes practically bulged out. "Wow."

"I can't believe I told you that. I've never told anybody that. I'm so embarrassed."

"Don't be embarrassed. It's great. The biggest secret we've got in my family is that Uncle Arthur blames his farts on the dog."

I laughed. "My dad would kill me if he knew I repeated that story. It's probably not even true."

"I won't tell him, I promise."

I laughed, but this time it was softer and a little more awkward. "He passed away."

Rod's smile faded. "I'm sorry."

"It was a long time ago. I took it bad, but it's fine now."

"How old were you?"

"Eighteen. He worked in the oil fields and there was an accident. Just one of those things."

"It must have been terrible."

"After it happened, I messed up . . . everything. I couldn't keep a job and I ran up credit-card debt. Those years were bad. My mom and I fought all the time. She kept trying to sue the oil company because they wouldn't pay dad's insurance. It was very stressful on her and I didn't help."

"Why wouldn't they pay?"

"I don't know. They said some stuff. . . . I guess I didn't want to know. I thought I was moving on, but all I did was screw up." I traced a circle around the rim of the empty shot glass. "Then my friend Jake got me on at KJAY."

"He was chief photog, right?"

"Eventually. He left before you got here. You would have liked him. Everybody likes him."

Rod nodded. "I've heard."

"We were old friends from high school. He vouched for me to Trent, got me on part-time. Everything got better after that."

As if reading my thoughts, Rod said, "I'm sure Trent will hire you back. We'll get everything straightened out and he'll have to hire you back."

"Thanks."

Rod took another drink.

The silence was verging on uncomfortable so I blurted out, "Now it's your turn to tell me a secret."

"I'm a Trekkie. There isn't much else."

"How about your name?"

"Rod Strong?"

"No, your real name."

Rod fished his wallet out of his jacket pocket. He opened it and showed me his driver's license. "See for yourself."

I read the name out loud. "Roderick Strong?"

"It's true no one ever called me Rod until I came to Bakersfield. Trent said it would be better on the air."

"What did they call you before?"

"Roddy."

"Roddy," I repeated.

"Feel free to call me that. I like it better." He returned the wallet to his pocket. "Why did you think my name was fake?"

"Anchors do that, change their names."

He shook his head. "I'm not an anchor."

"But you want to be."

He laughed, but shook his head again. "No, I don't."

"But . . ."

"But what?"

"Do you want to stay a reporter?"

Rod's face contorted in horror. "No. Ideally I'd like to be a producer, but I'd take almost anything that's not on camera."

"Then why are you reporting?"

"Trent advertised for a producer, but when I interviewed, he said I needed experience out in the field first."

My face scrunched up and caused my black eye to hurt. "What?"

"All my experience is from schools and universities. Don't get me wrong, getting a doctorate in communications is an enormous amount of work, and I'm an excellent journalist, but I always managed to avoid working in the real world. I was afraid if I didn't take Trent's offer, I'd end up a professional student." Rod shook his head. "It's been hard reporting. I don't have a natural talent for it."

I thought back to the way Rod acted on assignment: the nervous giggling, the endless talking with people before the interview—almost as if he was stalling. "Do you have stage fright?"

He took a large gulp of his drink. "Please don't tell anyone. It's so humiliating. I say I need time alone in the van to work on my hair, but I'm usually in there hyperventilating."

"But you were great just now with all the security guards."

"That's completely different. When the camera's on, I'm a basket case."

"I'm so sorry." I placed a hand on his shoulder. "You should have told me. I thought you were a jerk."

"I know."

I paused. "What do you mean, you know?"

"I told you, you're easy to read. Whatever you're thinking, it's pretty much written all over your face."

I looked down at the bar. How many times had I hurt his feelings without even knowing I was doing it?

Rod leaned closer. "I'm not complaining about that. I grew up in Hollywood. My mom's a producer and my dad's a lawyer. When you meet someone who's transparent—someone who's not saying one thing and thinking another—you hold on, even if they think you're a jerk."

"I'm not sure how I feel about that."

"Don't worry. And don't worry about my stage fright either. Trent promised me the six p.m. producer job when Susan goes on maternity leave. He's been letting me produce the morning show with Marcie for the last month to get ready."

I paused. "Trent told you that's why you were shadowing Marcie?"

"Ah-huh. A friend from school put in a good word for me at KTLA and I got offered a job on the assignment desk. Trent promised that if I stayed in Bakersfield, the next producer job was mine."

I didn't know who had killed Val Boyle. I didn't know why my life had been ruined in the space of a few hours. I didn't even know if Bud was my uncle or my grandfather, but I did know that Trent was never going to take Rod off the air, no matter what he'd promised. Rod was too much of a star for Trent to let him slip away. I was sure the next producer opening Trent had in mind would be Marcie's morning anchor job.

"Rod," I started, then hesitated.

"What is it? I can tell it's bad."

"If you're going to get what you want, you're going to have to be more aggressive."

"Oh."

"You trust people too much. You're a smart guy and you know what you want. You need to stand up for that."

He glanced at the jukebox. "Are you talking about work or other things too?"

"I'm talking about everything."

He smiled. "Want to dance?"

"What? No. That's not what I meant."

He offered his hand. "Come on, it'll be fun."

I shook my head.

"You're going to hurt my feelings." His smile wasn't wide and toothy like on TV. It curled up modestly. "Here I am following your advice, being more aggressive, putting myself out on a limb."

I felt my cheeks getting warm and looked at the bar. "What do you want to dance with me for? Half the girls in the newsroom are in love with you. They'd probably climb over my dead body to dance with you."

Rod's smile faltered and he took another sip of his drink.

"What?" I said. "You know it's true."

His shoulders hunched forward and his arms drew in like a turtle shrinking into its shell. "I don't pay any attention to that. It's not real."

"Not real? They melt like sherbet every time you walk by."

He laughed. "You sound like Bud. Maybe it's genetic."

"Seriously, Rod. They're all crazy about you."

"That's only because they don't know me. If they knew me, it would be different. So I don't pay attention."

"Who exactly are they're confusing you with?"

He hesitated. "You know . . . that guy. The one who's confident and cool. I'm not what they want."

"But you're confident and cool."

He cast a skeptical glance at me.

"Except for the giggling-when-you're-nervous thing . . . and having panic attacks in the van before a shoot . . . and probably lay off the *Star Trek* references."

"Exactly." Rod drained the remainder of the pink liquid from his glass.

"Hey, the football game's starting." The old man sitting down the bar from us pointed at a TV mounted above him. "Turn it on. The Patriots are playing the Falcons."

The bartender reached up and turned the channel to KKRN, our main competitors. On the TV a bright logo animation accompanied by intense yet uplifting music led into a wide shot of their anchor desk.

"What's this?" the old man complained. "That's news. I wanted the football game."

I gripped Rod's arm. "The police may have released our pictures."

The bartender spoke patiently to the old man. "They must have shown the West Coast game. You want to watch the news or should I turn it off?"

"Turn it off," Rod called down the bar. "I'll play more music from the jukebox."

The old man raised a hand toward the television. "No, I need my sports scores."

The bartender smiled and handed the man a candy cane from

the jar. "How about you watch, but only until you get your scores. That's a good compromise."

I started to step off the stool. "We should go."

Rod stopped me. "I haven't paid. Running out now will only draw more attention to us."

The television-picture cross faded to a two-shot of the KKRN ten-o'clock anchors. "Good evening, Kern County, thanks for being with us." The male anchor's voice quickly changed gears to somber and serious. "Tonight we have breaking developments in last night's shocking murder. Sources in the Kern County Sheriff's Department are indicating members of our rival station, KJAY, are wanted for questioning in last night's gruesome homicide."

I closed my eyes and tightened my hold on Rod.

"We'll bring you the developments as they unfold."

I exhaled and opened my eyes. Rod looked even more relieved than I felt.

"And in other news"—the female anchor took over from her partner—"we've obtained exclusive video of additional shocking behavior from the KJAY news staff."

Our heads shot back to the TV. "You're looking at amateur video taken this morning at Drillers stadium by the mother of the girl you see here." The anchor's voice continued over handheld video of the little sick girl throwing out the first pitch. "The girl is blind and was the Drillers' special guest of honor this morning."

I cringed when the grainy image swung around to reveal me squatting next to the camera and tripod. I wore the blue jacket that even now sat next to me on the bar stool. At least I had my back to the camera and my face wasn't visible.

"That's you, isn't it?" Rod asked quietly. "What happened this morning?"

"The fun came to a sudden and disturbing stop," the anchor continued, "during an interview with our rival station KJAY."

"No, no, no," I chanted under my breath.

The anchor's voice was slow and deliberate. "We warn you the following images are difficult to watch."

The entire bar stared as my hand reached for the baseball. I heard my own voice coming out of the television, and I knew it sounded normal to everyone else, but to me it reverberated in the deep distortion of slow motion.

"Caaaaaaaaaaaaatch." My arm pulled back and the ball went sailing. I think Rod may have said something, probably a swear, but all I could hear was the monstrous pounding of my heart.

The ball made contact and the little sick girl fell over.

Sounds of shock and outrage came not just from the bartender and the old man, but also the crowd in the corner. Several of them stood and pointed at the TV.

"Did you see that?" one of them shouted.

The old man slammed his fist down on the bar. "That's evil. Pure evil."

Even the bartender, who had seemed so nice and mellow, looked ready to join a lynching mob. "How about the way she taunted that little angel. Telling the poor kid to catch it."

"What were you thinking?" Rod whispered. "The kid's blind."

The image on the television was now sideways and on the ground because the mother had dropped the camera, but the audio track still ran. The little sick girl's sobbing filled the bar.

Rod eyed me with a mixture of shock and suspicion.

I grabbed his arm. "It was all a misunderstanding. I thought she could catch it."

Behind us the party in the corner was getting more and more worked up.

"They should lock that witch up so she can't attack anymore cripples," shouted a man.

"The kid wasn't even hurt," I explained to Rod. "The mom was fine with it."

"I only wish we could've seen her face," said the bartender. "'Cause if she ever comes in here, I'm going to do more than spit in her drink."

"I believe you," Rod whispered. "But if they show your face and these people recognize you, I'm going to be the only one who does."

Rod put an arm around me and turned to the bartender. "We sure wish we could get our hands on her."

"You're all a bunch of talk," a woman threatened from the corner table. "If you were real men, you'd go down to that TV station and do something about it."

"She's right."

"Let's go down there."

The bartender grabbed his head as if in agony. "If only we knew her name or what she looked like."

The entire room turned to the television. Someone had picked up the camera from the grass and, judging from the height and angle of the picture, didn't realize it was on.

The old man stood up and waved an angry fist at the TV. "Show her face, show her face."

The crowd in the corner joined his chant.

As if answering an angry and drunk prayer, the camera swung upward and stopped on a low and crooked close-up of my face.

SIXTEEN

"We have yet to identify this particular KJAY employee or discover if the mother of the victim will file charges for assault." The anchor's voice radiated with the kind of disgust reserved for war criminals and child murderers.

"Everybody take a good look." A man in the back stood and pointed at my frozen image on the monitor. "That's the face of evil."

"*El diablo, el diablo,*" a woman chanted.

The bartender turned away from the TV, and I knew it was all over. He was going to see me, seconds after looking at my image, and he'd have to make the connection. Frantically I tried to find somewhere to hide, but short of ducking under the barstool there was nothing.

Rod looked at me. Helpless panic spread all over his face. I don't know what terrified him more, our situation or what he was about to do. In any case, he took me completely by surprise.

I felt arms tighten around my waist and his body move toward me. I tried to ask what he was doing, but he swooped down and covered my mouth with his. His tender and intimate kiss sent a shock of sensation through me. My arms instinctively reached for his body. My hands moved slowly along his back exploring the surprisingly hard muscles under the expensive fabric.

An awkward quiet descended on the room and I knew everyone was watching us.

"Hey, bartender? Is that on the menu?" a man asked.

"I'll have some of what she's having," a woman added.

Laughter erupted from every person in the room. In the background the anchor's voice changed from somber outrage to giddy fun: "And in other news . . ."

"You mind gettin' your tongue out of my niece's mouth?"

Rod pulled away, but I kept my face buried in his chest. I saw Bud's bare legs standing nearby.

"Cut the lovebirds some slack," the bartender said. "You're embarrassing them."

Rod put his arm around me and further blocked my face from view. "Glad you made it, Bud. We were worried about you. But I guess you know how to take care of yourself."

"Sure as the world, son. Sure as the world."

"Maybe we should get out of here," I mumbled into Rod's chest.

He turned to the bartender. "How much do I owe you?"

"Fifteen."

Rod paid while still managing to hold on to me. "Keep the change."

The three of us exited the bar in silence. Rod kept his arm around me, but once inside the main dining room, I pulled away and turned to Bud. "They showed my picture on TV. Not about the murder, but it was bad. Rod was trying to hide my face."

Bud nodded. "Then we'd better get a move on."

Rod gestured to a sign marked RESTROOMS above a hallway next to the kitchen. "You two go ahead. I'll be right out."

Bud and I walked to the car and got in. Before he could quiz me about Rod, I said, "We got Sinclair's phone number and found out what Sonoran Fancy is." Bud didn't react. "It's a kind of almond, and the stolen ones belonged to Leland Warner."

"Sounds like you two been busy." Bud reached into his pocket for his lighter. "I called my fella again. We're pickin' up the new car later at Zingo's—around eleven." He lit a cigarette and blew out a cloud of smoke.

I resisted the urge to yank the cigarette out of his mouth. "Bud, this smoking thing is really bad."

He laughed.

"I'm serious."

"So am I." He flicked some ash out the window. "It's a real serious habit of mine."

I made disapproving sounds, but let it go. "Is Zingo's the truck stop across from the Crystal Palace?"

Bud nodded.

"That's not exactly a secluded spot."

"First rule of bein' on the run, hide in plain sight." He took a long drag on the cigarette and unleashed the noxious fumes. "Besides, I got a hankerin' for a chicken-fried steak, and Zingo's makes the best."

"I can't sit in this car while you smoke." I reached for the door.

"Where you goin'?"

I paused. "Back inside."

"Maybe not such a bright idea considerin' your picture was just on TV."

"I'm not going in the bar. I'll come out when Roddy . . ."

Bud raised his eyebrows.

" . . . when Rod's ready to go and you're done with that cancer stick."

Bud chuckled. "If you want more time alone with the fella, why don't you just say so?"

"If I did, I would, but I don't." I got out and slammed the door.

Truthfully, I did want time alone with Rod, but not for the reason Bud thought. The opposite, actually. I had to make sure Rod didn't get the wrong idea about the kiss, and the sooner we had that conversation the better.

I walked back in. The hostess greeted me with the same friendly smile. "You want a cup of coffee at the counter or something?"

"I won't be here long enough." I gestured to the hallway where the restrooms were. "I'm just waiting for my friend."

"Might be longer than you think. He's on the phone now."

I froze. "What?"

She pointed to an alcove on the opposite side of the kitchen.

"He's over there. Asked me where the pay phones were right after you left."

I felt all the energy drain from my body. "Thanks." I moved my legs, but it felt like running in sand. I knew what I'd find as though it had already happened. I took the last few steps and he came into view.

Rod, his face pinched and tense, spoke into the pay phone. "I told you she isn't going for it. I have the tape and I'm prepared to negotiate, but you'll have to come and get her yourself." He listened, then nodded. "We're at the Top Hat Café in Arvin. Her uncle is driving an old maroon Plymouth Fury."

My legs moved backward, as if on autopilot, until I could no longer see him. Then I turned and walked out. I don't remember getting to the car.

"Drive." I slammed the door shut and pushed down on the old-fashioned lock.

Bud sat up. "But Rod's still—"

"Drive now."

Bud started the car. "Freeway or back roads?"

"I don't know. Just get out of here."

Bud made a right at the road.

After we'd gone a few blocks Bud took the cigarette out of his mouth and checked his mirrors. "Okay. We're flown. You gonna spill it?"

"He's been playing me . . . us. He's been playing us."

Bud's voice was skeptical instead of outraged. "Rod?"

"Yes, Rod. He was on the phone with whoever he's working for."

He glanced from the road to me. "You heard him?"

"Yes. I heard the actual words coming out of his lying, scumbag mouth. He was cutting a deal to deliver me and the tape, which he now has because I was stupid enough to trust him with it."

"Are you sure, 'cause he seemed—"

My hand flew out and landed on the seat between us. "I told you, that's what he does. He makes people like him and then he uses them."

Bud tossed his cigarette out the window. "You should get out of town."

"No. We should pick up the car at Zingo's, and then I should record Sinclair, and then we should go to the police and get his butt locked up, and when all of that is taken care of, I should go find Rod and beat the living . . ."

A new realization hit me. I lowered my head and cradled it in my hands. "I don't believe it."

Bud eyed me warily. "What now?"

I closed my eyes, counted to ten. "I have the camera, but Rod has the phone number."

"That fella Sinclair's?"

I nodded.

"That's it then, Little Sister. It's over. You got no tape. You got no way of gettin' other proof. Your picture was on TV for somethin' else bad." While keeping one hand on the steering wheel, Bud pulled another cigarette out of his pocket. "You have got to get out of town." He put it in his mouth and lit up.

He was right, of course. I was radioactive. Multiple bad guys, the police, and now a lynching mob of little-sick-kid groupies were all after me. But if I was going down, I wanted it to be in the middle of a fight and not running away with my tail between my legs.

I reached across the seat, ripped the cigarette out of Bud's mouth, and threw it out the window. "You shouldn't smoke . . . and I'm only saying this once. I'm not getting run out of my town by a jackass like Sinclair and a scumbag like Rod and a harpy like that kid's mother. This will absolutely not end that way."

Bud frowned. "What harpy mother? You're bowed up so bad you're not thinkin' straight."

"It's too hard to explain right now, but she's a bad person who exploits her kid. She and Sinclair are made for each . . ."

At first Bud didn't say anything. His eyes swung from the road as he stole a frightened glance at me, but he remained silent. Finally, in a weary voice he said, "Lilly?"

"We have to go back to Bakersfield. I know how to find Sinclair."

"Are you sure this is the place?" Bud looked up and down the street. "All these houses look the same to me."

"I'm sure." I pointed to the large, modern-looking complex on our right. "They live around the corner from Bimat Elementary, next to the lake. I remember because it's named after my principal when we lived in Oildale." I gestured to the stop sign ahead of us. "You can pull over here."

"Why?"

"In case there's trouble waiting for me, I don't want you dragged into it."

Bud ignored me and turned the corner. A small man-made lake appeared. It was the chief amenity of this neighborhood in trendy northwest Bakersfield. "No doin'. If you're goin' over the cliff on a wild hog, I might as well follow."

"Bud . . ."

"No doin', Little Sister. Besides, you're not exactly on level ground. Mad as you are, you're likely to go off and crap a bug with a button on its collar."

I pointed at a peach-colored house two down from the corner. A series of decorative lights led up its walkway, and a ladybug flag hung next to the garage. "That's it."

Bud pulled the car into the driveway. I got out and made a beeline for the front door.

I rang the bell. From somewhere in the house chimes played "There's No Place Like Home." When I didn't get an immediate response, I began pounding my fist into the door. My hand began to hurt, but I continued.

"I think after all that poundin' maybe they got an inklin' you're out here," Bud said behind me.

Before I could reply, the door opened.

At first I didn't recognize her. The woman standing before me was so far removed from the chipper, fashionable publicity hound I knew and despised that I thought we were at the wrong house.

But she recognized me. "I guess you're here about the video I sold to the other TV station."

I shook my head. "Actually I need to get in touch with Tom Sinclair, but since you brought it up . . ." Barely suppressed anger bubbled up around my words. "How about that video?"

Her hand clutched the top of her faded denim shirt as though she were trying to keep the cold night air out. "It's very simple. They paid me for it and my daughter needed the money."

"Your daughter needed the money?" The echo of my voice reverberated across the neighborhood.

"That's right."

"Lilly, you goin' to introduce me?" Bud's lips spread into a half-smile and his forehead rose. His expression was unremarkable, but the effect on his overall face was amazing. The skin seemed to stretch itself out, removing wrinkles and making him look twenty years younger.

I shook my head. "No, I'm not going to introduce you because I'm done being polite and pretending I'm not disgusted by the way this lady exploits her kid."

I expected some kind of reaction from the mother, but she didn't even blink. "You may have always been polite, but you've made your dislike very clear from the first time I met you."

"Mommy?" a little girl voice's called from inside the house. "I'm all done."

The mother glanced over her shoulder, then back at me. "Wait here." She shut the door, but it didn't close all the way.

The Tylenol I'd taken earlier had begun to wear off and I rubbed my aching head.

Bud laughed. "Pretty clear you two don't shine to each other."

"No decent person would shine to her."

He raised an eyebrow. "Didn't seem so bad to me."

"You haven't seen her in action with the kid. It's disgusting."

Bud sighed and the twenty years reappeared on his face. "You may be right, but that don't sell the sugar on market day. We came here so's you could get a lead on Sinclair, and you just pissed off the lady who could be fixed to help us. What if she decides to leave us standin' out here all night?"

I used my foot to push the crack in the door open wider.

"Hold on," Bud whispered.

I ignored him and peeked into the house. After a short entryway I saw a great room with an open kitchen. The little girl knelt on a dining-room chair while the mother stood next to her. But with the exception of the dining room table, the entire room was empty.

I pushed open the door and entered. "Where is all your furniture?"

The mother jumped at the sound of my voice.

I continued toward them. On the table, different-colored beans sat in piles, and it looked as if the little girl had been sorting them by touch.

"Who's that?" the girl asked, and reached for her mother, who picked her up.

"Our friend from the TV station stopped by." The mother's voice sounded friendly and relaxed, but her body language was the opposite.

The girl noticed. "What's wrong, Mommy?"

Bud followed me into the room. "Nothin's wrong. We just heard the cutest little patch of sweet pea was livin' here, and I reckon it's true 'cause all them beans must a jumped clean out of their pods just to get a glimpse of you."

A high-pitched giggle came from where the little girl had her face buried in her mother's denim shirt.

Bud stepped toward them. "What's so funny?"

The girl pulled her head away from her mother. "You are." She quickly hid her face again amid a geyser of laughter.

"What's so funny about me?"

She turned her head in Bud's direction. "You talk funny?"

"I reckon it's everybody else who's talkin' funny."

"Silly." She reached out and grabbed for something in the air.

"Sweetie," the mother said, "do you want to touch the man's face?"

"I bet he's got a silly face."

"You're darn right about that." Bud took hold of the girl's hand and placed it on his cheek. "Cute and smart."

She giggled and pulled back. "Mommy buys the beans so I can pick them out."

The mother kissed the girl on the forehead. "And you did a fantastic job, sweetie."

She tilted her head up toward her mother. "Did I get them all right?"

"Almost all of them." The mother picked up a black bean from a pile of green peas and put it in the little girl's hand. "Don't worry. Next time you'll get them all." The mother set her down. "Now why don't you run along and get in bed."

The girl disappeared down a hallway, running her hand along the wainscot for guidance.

I waited for the sound of a door closing, then turned on the mother. "What happened to all the stuff people gave you? What about that giant TV with the special audio channels?"

She ignored me and began placing the beans in Ziploc bags.

"You sold it," I said. "Go on. Admit it."

I watched as her posture changed. She seemed to draw herself up, plant her feet, and prepare for battle. "I did sell it. I sold all of it."

"All of it? Everything people have been donating for months?"

"So what if I did? I had every right."

"People all over Bakersfield gave those things to your daughter, not you, your daughter, so she could have a better life."

"We didn't need those things." She raised her hand and gestured to the ceiling. "We needed a roof over our heads."

"You dragged your daughter around town like a circus freak

and made everybody feel sorry for her. You gobbled up as much attention and sympathy as you could and then turned around and made a quick buck."

"How dare you?" For the first time she looked really angry. "Who are you to judge me? You think you know everything?"

I laughed. "I know you care more about yourself than your kid."

"When we got the diagnosis, I quit my job so I could work full-time on Chelsea's condition. It's rare, and forty percent of cases end in death. Did you know that?" She didn't wait for an answer. "I thought if I worked myself hard enough, I could find a way to fix it. More research, more reading, more clinical trials, more holistic therapies—if I just kept going long enough and hard enough, I'd find something." She clenched her fists as tears formed in her eyes. "We spent every penny we had on treatments and cures and crackpot theories just in case something might stop it. And nothing did."

She took a breath and tried to continue, but the words choked in her throat. "Then one day I came home to find my husband's wedding ring sitting on the kitchen counter. His note said he was sorry. He couldn't even face us to say good-bye."

She looked me directly in the eye. "So, yes, I asked for help and people gave it and I take as much as I can get because I'm trying to hold on. I'm not even trying to fix it anymore. I don't even have hope anymore. All I'm trying to do is hold on."

She broke down into sobs. Bud gently placed an arm around her shoulders. "There, there, little lady. You been carryin' a heavy load."

After a few moments the mother lifted her head. She was still crying, but her words didn't hold any anger. "I sold all those things because I need money, not a big-screen TV. I sold that video of you throwing the baseball because I'm behind on the mortgage and if I missed another payment, I could lose the house."

Bud guided her to one of the dining-room chairs. "I'm sure you did what you had to do to keep a roof over your little girl's head.

And I know Lilly, and she might have been madder than a cat in a room full a rockin' chairs, but she's not the kind who'd grudge you for doin' that."

She looked at me. "I'm trying to sell the house, but my husband's name is on the title and I don't know where he is. If I default on the mortgage before I divorce him, we'll lose everything." She wiped away more tears.

"And maybe you're right," she said quietly. "Maybe I do enjoy the attention. Maybe it went to my head, but I'm all alone. I need something."

Bud sat down in the chair next to her. "Of course. It's just not right for a pretty lady like you to be all alone."

For a moment I thought she was going to cry again, but instead she smiled.

"Lilly," Bud gently ordered, "why don't you wait for me outside."

I went out to the car and lay down in the backseat.

Barely thirty seconds went by before I heard the front door open and close and then Bud's footsteps on the pavement. He got in and settled into the driver's seat.

"Bud?" I asked without moving my cheek from the cool maroon vinyl.

"Yeah?"

"Am I stupid?"

"Nah." He started the car and backed us out of the driveway.

"Am I stupid about people?"

He put the transmission in drive and moved the car forward.

"Am I really, really, irreversibly stupid about people?"

"Understandin' folks maybe ain't—"

I sat up. "Because the odds that I could be wrong about Marcie, Teddy and Freddy, David, Rod, and now this, all in one day, and not be so cosmically stupid, so completely worthless at understanding people . . . it's not possible."

"I think you oughta get credit for Rod. You had him pegged from the get-go. I'm the one who convinced you he was okay."

"Am I stupid?"

"If I say somethin', promise you won't take it too hard?"

I shook my head. "No."

"No, you won't take it too hard?"

"No, I won't promise."

He chuckled. "I love you, Little Sister. You don't got no falseness in you."

I flinched remembering Rod's similar words in the bar. "What's the thing you want to say that I'm going to try not to take too hard?"

He stopped the car at a stop sign and turned around to face me. "To understand folks you gots to be interested in 'em. You gots to be doin' more than just puttin' in your time." He handed me a slip of paper.

"What's this?"

"Compliments of Annette. It's that jackass fella's cell-phone number."

SEVENTEEN

I felt the car pull into a driveway, stop, and idle. I recognized the hum of the freeway nearby and sat up. My body felt as if it were made of cement. We were in the parking lot of the Crystal Palace, which meant we couldn't have been driving for more than fifteen minutes, but I felt as if I'd slept for weeks.

"Rise and shine, Goldilocks," Bud crooned. "This is your stop."

I gazed down the street at Zingo's neon sign calling to the drivers on the freeway. The parking lot full of big rigs was well lit, but the blazing light coming from the restaurant's windows made it look dim and full of shadows by comparison.

"Why are we here?" I asked. "Aren't we meeting your friend at Zingo's?"

"I'm meetin' him." Bud half turned to the backseat. "What time you got?"

I used up what felt like my last drop of energy and looked at my watch. "It's quarter past eleven."

"That's about right. You can kick up your heels here while I take care of business." He glanced at the parking lot across the street. "I shouldn't be too long."

"You mean wait here without you? Why?"

"'Cause Rod's probably blabbin' all over town what this here car looks like. If there's trouble, I'd just as soon you was out of it."

"But—"

"Not to mention my friend ain't goin' to be exactly pleased if I show up with company. An audience ain't proper protocol for this kind of transaction."

I forced air in and out of my lungs, but my overwhelming fatigue made even that a chore. "Can't I wait in the car?"

"No."

"I'm hungry."

"I'll get takeout. What you havin'?"

I looked back across at Zingo's and then at Bud's determined face. I was in no condition to win an argument with this man. "Tuna melt with fries."

"It'll be waitin' for you like a dog at the mail slot."

"Thanks." I reached for the car door and stumbled slightly getting out. I had the presence of mind to reach back in and retrieve my blue coat.

Buck Owens built the Crystal Palace to be an upscale honky-tonk—the kind of place where you could bring your family for a steak dinner or get a drink and listen to music. Its Old West architecture and interior design is a great showcase for Buck's memorabilia, and the stage has hosted some of the biggest names in country music. Even Buck's death a few years back hadn't lessened its popularity.

I went into the main showroom mostly because the lighting was dim and I didn't want anyone to recognize me from KKRN's news. Things were jumping even with an empty stage and no live music. Waiters darted back and forth between full tables on the first floor. A Dwight Yoakam music video played on the jumbo screens above the stage, and several couples had taken to the dance floor.

I headed for the stairs. The second-floor bar functioned more like the balcony in a theater with great views of the stage. A large group of friends were celebrating someone's birthday, and I took a seat as far away as possible.

The bartender came right over. "What can I get for you?"

"Mountain Dew."

"Sorry. How about Sierra Mist?"

"No thanks. You got Jolt cola?"

He shook his head. "Coke okay?"

I looked up to tell him no thanks, but noticed for the first time a large convertible mounted on the wall above the bar. The cream-colored car had horns attached to the front bumper and an old-time cowboy-and-Indians seat covering. "Whatever you've got will be fine," I said.

He glanced up at the car and smiled. "Some view, huh?"

He brought me my order and returned to the group at the other end of the bar. I sipped my soda. The song changed to Buck Owens singing "Santa Looked a Lot like Daddy" and everyone clapped. I found myself regretting I hadn't come to see Buck play before his death. A living legend had performed every Friday and Saturday night a few miles from my house and I'd never gone. Maybe Bud was right. Maybe I was just putting in my time.

"Are you a freebird or just looking for your sweet home Alabama?"

A good-looking cowboy type had sidled up to the bar next to me. His tan skin matched the light brown of his eyes.

"Excuse me?"

He pointed at my shirt. "Skynyrd, babe, all the way."

I looked down and remembered I was wearing Bud's Lynyrd Skynyrd T-shirt. "It's not mine."

"Oh, that's too bad. They rock."

Before I could warn him he'd caught me on the absolute wrong day, he sat down. "I'm so into all that old-school Southern rock. The Allman Brothers too."

I nodded. "That's great, but—"

"Hey, I've got a couple of their CDs out in my car. I could introduce you to them. It's nice and comfy in there too. . . ."

Suddenly his voice changed. "Maybe I better head back to my friends." He began backing away as if I were the creature from *Alien.*

Had he recognized me? I tried to stay calm. "You don't have to go."

He stopped. "You've got a strong go-away vibe."

"What kind of vibe did I have when you came over?"

"I don't know. Lonely and kind of sad."

I barely had time to digest this before a disturbing thought occurred to me. What if that's how people always saw me? Was I the lonely and sad girl? "If I ask you a frank question, will you give me a frank answer?"

He glanced nervously at his friends. "I guess."

"Why would you hit on a girl like that? Lonely and sad doesn't sound very appealing."

"If they're pretty, it's great." I must have sent out another bad vibe because he frowned. "I mean . . . they're just . . . those girls . . . it's easier to call the shots with them. You've got the upper hand from the get-go. If they're good-looking too, that's like the holy grail."

I felt my face harden. "So lonely and sad translates to undemanding and grateful?"

He turned his fingers into guns and shot them at me. "Not in your case." He started to walk away, but said over his shoulder, "And I don't think it would take a guy long to figure that out." He returned to his friends.

Was that why I routinely got dumped after the first date? Were the few men who asked me out expecting a pushover? And why would I go out with a guy like that?

I slid off the stool, picked up my coat, and navigated my way down the stairs. In the women's room I ran cold water on my neck and hands, careful to avoid my face where the makeup covered my black eye. The bruises on my neck were darkening, but they weren't noticeable yet. From one of the coat's pockets I pulled a bottle of Tylenol and swallowed two with water from the tap. I placed both hands on the sink, letting most of my weight rest on the porcelain, and dropped my chin onto my chest.

The door opened and a nice-looking woman in her forties walked in. She reflexively paused at the sight of me, the way anyone would when confronted with something not quite right, but recovered and went into a stall as though nothing had happened.

I dried my hands and headed for the parking lot to check for Bud.

What I saw outside sent a ripple of shock through my body. An army of cops had invaded Zingo's.

I turned and walked back into the lobby trying to suppress a primal scream. Rod's voice echoed in my head counseling me not to panic. It was good advice even if the source was dubious. Bud knew how to handle himself. He may even have got away.

I went into the gift shop. I used the last of my money to buy a cheap cowboy hat. Back in the bathroom I took the ponytail out. My hair fell down in an avalanche of long black curls. I took the hat out of its bag and put it on. I'd purposely bought it a little too big, and if I tilted my head down and let my hair fall forward around my face, it did a pretty good job of hiding me. I crammed my blue coat into the gift shop bag and left.

Outside I made an immediate left in the opposite direction from Zingo's. I wanted to run, but knew it would draw attention. After a few blocks I began to relax and think about my next move. I needed transportation. Everything depended on it. I continued walking through Westchester, the residential neighborhood between downtown and the freeway.

I stopped at the end of Teddy and Freddy's block. The van was still parked outside. No sign of the police. Keeping my hat low, I walked briskly down the street and directly to the driver's-side door of the van. It was unlocked, as I suspected it would be, so I got in. With an eye on the apartment building I began searching for a hidden key. This was Teddy and Freddy's van, after all. They lost keys all the time. They'd have to stash an emergency one in the van somewhere.

I looked up from rifling through the glove compartment and found a teenage boy staring at me. He stood frozen at the bottom of the stairs holding a bag of garbage in his hand.

I tried to smile, but he wasn't buying it. The boy dropped his bag of garbage and bolted up the stairs toward Teddy and Freddy's apartment.

I ran my hands underneath the seats. Nothing. I pulled out the rubber inserts in the cup holders and flipped down both visors. Nothing. I opened the armrest, got a whiff of something rotten, and immediately closed it again.

One of the Wonder Twins appeared on the second-floor walkway and charged down the stairs.

"Dude, thief, stop." He jerked open the passenger-side door. "I'll call . . ." He stopped when I took off the cowboy hat.

"You shouldn't leave the van unlocked."

"Oh, dude?" Teddy's hair was cut short and had an orange tint, but I still recognized him as the nice Wonder Twin.

The teenage boy ran up behind him. "See, I told you. I'll go tell Mom to call the cops."

"No. That's okay," Teddy told him. "She's cool. She works with us." He reached into his Bermuda shorts and pulled out his keys. "We're, like, trading nights with her. Freddy and me." He leaned into the open door while twisting one of the keys around the metal circle. "Callum called earlier."

I eyed the teenager who was standing nearby and listening to every word we said. "Did you tell Callum I'd been here?"

He smiled. "No, dude. That must have totally slipped our minds." The key twisted free and he tossed it in the open door. It landed on the passenger seat next to me. "But Callum said Rod was, like, you know, totally narcing it up. So, dude, maybe you should check in with Callum and get more info on that, 'cause, like, it would totally suck to trust the wrong person." He pointed to the back of the van. "The cell phone's in the back."

He started to close the door.

"Wait," I called, and he stopped. "I'm sorry if I ever hurt your feelings."

He smiled. "It's all good." He closed the door and walked away with the teenager.

I picked up the key and put it in the ignition. The van started and so did the heater and a cassette tape of something loud and awful. I turned the heater and the music off and looked out the window.

Teddy stood with the boy at the base of the stairs. He must have said something funny because the teenager laughed before picking up his garbage and disappearing with it around the back. Teddy watched him go and then looked back at me.

I raised my hand in a small wave and Teddy smiled, nodded, and went up the stairs.

The flashing gas indicator brought me back to planet Earth. I drove through the tree-lined streets of Westchester toward a gas station on Oak I'd never used before. I wanted to stay away from places I'd be recognized.

I filled up, using the station gas card the Wonder Twins kept in the glove compartment. Paying with the station gas card was risky since the cops could trace it, but I'd spent all my money and had no other choice. Next I found the cell phone Teddy had mentioned.

Callum picked up on the first ring. "What?"

"Does this mean you're not on my side anymore?"

I was treated to a long string of obscenities, some of which were used in completely original combinations.

"I'm not even sure what that last thing is," I said when he'd finally run down. "Was that a body part?"

"Jokes? You're making jokes now? Do you know how much trouble you're in?" I heard him take a giant breath and let it out. "Lilly, when I get my hands on you . . . What have you and Rod done? Do you know how short-staffed we are? I had to put the Wonder Twins on-call tonight. Now there's some giant smack-down going on at Zingo's, and I can't get those two bozos to answer a page. At this point, I wouldn't be surprised if the Penny Saver is scooping us."

"What about the smackdown?" I rushed to ask. "Have they captured anyone?"

"According to the scanner, there's a white male in custody."

Had Bud's luck really run out? It didn't seem possible.

"But you should be more concerned with Rod," Callum continued.

"What about him?"

"He's also in custody, but not for long. I've got a source who says Rod gave them a description of your car and who you were with in exchange for his release."

Hearing confirmation of Rod's treachery brought on a fresh wave of hurt and anger. "How did they catch Rod?"

"Turned himself in, like the smart boy he is."

"When was this?"

"Two hours ago."

The timing fit perfectly. Rod's description of the Fury must have led to Bud's arrest, and now Rod was going free. But did he still have the tape?

I took a breath. "You said they're letting him go?"

"Fast, huh? Shows what an expensive L.A. lawyer can do for you."

I didn't have an expensive L.A. lawyer. At the moment I didn't have much of anything. "Did Trent tell you he fired me?"

"Yes, but he'll come around. We'll get this whole thing straightened out and he'll come around."

"What if we don't get this whole thing straightened out?"

Callum sighed. "Listen. I'm going to talk sense now, and although it's hard for you, please listen." He paused. "You have to turn yourself in. Tell me where you are and I'll come get you and arrange some kind of peaceful surrender. I'll even arrange a lawyer."

"I'll take you up on that offer in a few hours, but I have an errand to run first."

I hung up before he could protest.

I took my jacket out of the bag and retrieved the small piece of paper Bud had given me. I entered the numbers into the cell phone and waited.

After several rings the voice mail picked up. I hung up and redialed.

This time he picked up on the fourth ring. "Tom Sinclair here."

EIGHTEEN

"This is Lilly Hawkins."

A long pause, then the salesman's voice he'd used at the ballpark turned on. "Lilly. I'm overjoyed to hear from you. I've been worried sick. After our misunderstanding this afternoon I wasn't sure what happened to you."

"Did I misunderstand you leaving me to be murdered?"

"You must know I was going for help."

I managed not to swear. My mother would have been proud. "That's the lamest thing I've ever heard, and I've heard some really lame things."

"Lilly, I am—"

I cut him off. "I have the tape."

Silence.

"I have the tape," I repeated. "I want to meet."

He cleared his throat. "What tape is that?"

I started to throw the phone, but at the last second didn't let go. Instead I channeled my anger into my voice. "Don't play games with me. I have had it. Do you know what today's been like? This is your only chance. I'm about five seconds from calling the cops and getting myself out of this mess."

"You can't do that." The salesman's voice vanished. "Please, I'm sure we can come to terms. How much do you want for it?"

How much? I hadn't thought that far ahead.

"The old man can pay cash," he offered. "And I'm sure there'll be enough for you and your reporter friend."

I jerked to attention. "Reporter friend?"

"The one in all the ads. Todd Burly, or whatever his name is. He left me a message."

"His name is Rod Strong and he's not my friend." If Rod was actually trying to sell me out to both the cops and Sinclair, you had to give him credit for nerve. Maybe he would go for a hat trick and call the Eastside Crew too. "What did he want?"

"His message implied he had the tape or at least knew where it was."

"He's lying," I lied.

"Don't worry. I passed him on to Leland's people to check out."

I could handle Sinclair, but what if Warner and his henchmen got involved? "That's fine, but don't pass me on to Leland's people too. This deal is between you and me. Otherwise I'm going straight to the police."

"But he's the one with the money."

"After we've met and come to terms, you can go to him for the money, but only then."

"Yes. Of course." Sinclair paused. "How about we meet at the ballpark? I have all the keys and I can send the security guard away. It'll be deserted. We can meet in my office by the front entrance."

He was right, the ballpark would be deserted, but I didn't know if I liked that. A lot of bad things can happen in deserted places. On the other hand, the layout gave me perfect cover to hide and watch for an ambush. "It has to be alone. If you tell anybody or bring some of Warner's thugs, the tape is going straight to the police."

"I swear I won't. You have my word."

"How soon can you meet?"

"I have to make up an excuse for my wife. She'll think it's odd I'm going out so late." He paused. "Let's say one."

It was just past midnight and I was only ten minutes away. I'd have plenty of time to hide and watch his arrival from safety. If he didn't come alone, or if it looked like an ambush, I could take off.

"It'll be close, but I should be able to make it by one." I hung up.

The lights were off at the ballpark. An empty security car sat at the entrance. I watched the parking lot. Nothing changed. The boredom and accumulated fatigue made it hard to stay awake. I listened to the police scanner, but the traffic about Zingo's had died down.

I spent a lot of time working out a strategy for dealing with Sinclair. If I was half as transparent as Rod and Bud seemed to think, then coaxing Sinclair into speaking would be difficult. Finally I decided to keep it simple; I'd try not to lie, but when I had to, I'd make it short and direct.

A little before one Sinclair's Jaguar turned off Chester Avenue and into the parking lot. He drove to the main gate and parked in a handicapped spot. He got out, looked around, started for the gate, stopped, looked around again, and went inside. A few minutes later the security guard walked out the main entrance, got in his car, and drove away. I waited another ten minutes. Nothing changed. No cars arrived. No thugs skulked in the shadows.

I parked the van behind the outfield wall on the third-base side. I switched on the hidden camera and attached the sequined flower to my jacket. It looked out of place on the water-resistant fabric, but I didn't have a lot of choices. I shook out my hair and decided to keep it down. Maybe if I looked pretty, Sinclair would be distracted and not notice I was lying. This was not my proudest moment.

I got out and I climbed onto the roof of the van. The outfield fence was short, and with the boost from the car I had no trouble hoisting myself over. I dropped onto the dirt at the far end of the field and walked toward the cheap seats. I made my way in darkness to the front of the ballpark, pausing every few yards to watch and listen, but heard nothing. I reached the alley behind the main stands and was relieved to see dim lighting. Not so dark I couldn't find my way, but not so light I'd be an obvious target. Still, it was creepy. No wind rattled the concession-stand shutters, but in the stillness wispy strands of fog had begun to creep in.

I found a door labeled GENERAL MANAGER and turned the handle.

"There you are." Sinclair stood up from behind a massive desk at the far end of the room. He wore Dockers and a purple polo shirt. "I thought you weren't coming."

The office was not large and reminded me of a galley kitchen. It didn't help that sports memorabilia filled the room. Some of it was hung and displayed, but most hadn't been properly unpacked. Half-opened cardboard boxes littered the office floor and the two oversize leather chairs in front of the desk.

"Come in, come in. How do you like my office?"

I stepped fully into the room and shut the door.

An oil painting of an older man hung on the far wall. He wore the same kind of cowboy suit Sinclair had been wearing that morning. I remembered what Bob had told me and guessed the painting was of Jim Ensley, the original owner of the team. His image appeared to be looking down at the latest general manager with an amused smile. I doubted the real man would feel that way had he lived to meet Tom Sinclair.

"I'm still unpacking. But my new desk is a big improvement. An important man should have an important desk."

I nodded.

"I'm so relieved you came." Sinclair started to come toward me, but had to pause and squeeze his body between the edge of the desk and a wall. "I know the two of us will sort this mess out like friends without Leland setting his usual bad tone." As he emerged from the tight space, his shoulder brushed against the wall and knocked down a framed program. He bent over to pick it up.

"How much is Warner already involved?" I angled myself so the brooch would have a clear shot of his response. "Did he order those two police officers to beat me up this morning?"

Sinclair stood back up with the frame. "I don't know the particulars. He said he was going to send someone to take care of things." He paused. "I understand how terrified you must be of Leland, but I promise to protect you."

"Why would you need to protect me?" My voice rose. "You didn't tell anyone else about this meeting, did you?"

"Only my wife, but you can trust her."

"You mean Leland Warner's daughter?"

"She's my wife first." He turned and replaced the frame on its hook. "Anyway, given the danger that tape puts her in, she's naturally anxious about our meeting."

The tape was a danger to her? I flashed back to the crime scene. There'd been police officers, coroners, photographers, but no heiresses.

I straightened and centered my body so the brooch had a perfect view. "Did she kill Val Boyle?"

"Of course not. He was dead when we got there."

Had he really just admitted to being at the crime scene?

"I believe you." I tried to sound reassuring and friendly. "But I'm confused about the timeline."

He must have sensed my insincerity because he looked up and stared at me. I didn't know what to do. My hand instinctively pushed a strand of hair away from my face.

He smiled. "I love your hair down." His creepy eyes ran up and down my body. "You should wear it like that all the time. You're such a pretty girl."

I knew what I had to do. I needed to play up to him in some awful and flirty way. I needed to ignore the bile rising in the back of my throat. I needed to do it because it was the safest way to get what I wanted. I needed to do it because I would be better off in the long run.

I looked up at the ceiling and mumbled some swearwords under my breath.

His smile faded. "Excuse me?"

"Okay, here's how this is going to go." I spoke decisively and without any of the fake affability I'd tried before. "I've had a bad day. I got very little sleep last night. I was humiliated in front of my coworkers. My home was broken into, my privacy invaded. I was threatened and beaten up by dirty cops. Then I was beaten up again later, by a gang." I crossed the room to where a bat in a glass case sat on the floor. I removed the bat. "My reward for all that? My boss fired me and tried to have me arrested. My friend, who I thought would help, turned me in to the cops. Then someone I thought was a jerk turned out to be a great guy. Only wait . . . here it comes . . . I was right the first time, he's a jerk and also turned me in to the cops." I swung the bat and tested the weight. "Oh, hey, did I mention my uncle's been arrested?"

Sinclair eyed the bat uneasily. "That's terrible."

"Yes, it is terrible, and that's why I have absolutely no patience left."

He shook his head. "I don't follow."

I raised and lowered the bat into the open palm of my free hand. "If you don't tell me exactly what I want to know, I'm going to start smashing things in this room." I smiled. "And, Tom, your kneecaps are in this room."

"Lilly, you don't—"

I slammed the bat into a framed baseball card on the wall. The glass smashed. Sinclair cried out and squeezed behind his desk.

"I know you helped Jason steal the almonds. I want the whole story in your own words."

"How did you—"

I turned, raised the bat over my head, and brought it down on his computer.

"I'll tell you, I'll tell you," he screamed. "Please don't hurt me."

I pulled back. "Start talking. From the beginning."

"Mary has a prenup, and if I divorce her, Leland will blackball me. I'll be unemployable for the rest of my life."

I rolled my eyes. "You want out and decided to rob your father-in-law to pay for it."

He threw his palms flat on the desk and leaned forward. "You don't know what it's like. I'm practically a prisoner. Mary won't even let me go out at night because of what happened with Gladys."

I did not want to know about Gladys. Gladys was not going to get me out of trouble. Gladys was not going to get Sinclair arrested, unless she was underage, which I doubted.

Sinclair pulled back and clenched his fist. "You should have seen the uproar over that. Leland was brutal. I'd always thought he was a monster, but I had no idea how bad it could get. And him with an army of floozies over the years. And Gladys wasn't a floozy. She had a very respectable job as a waitress."

Not underage, then. I smashed the bat into another frame on the wall. "You were telling me about almonds."

Sinclair jumped. "I had information, but I couldn't act on it myself."

"You got the Eastside Crew to do it for you."

Sinclair nodded. "Yes. Jason agreed to take the job if I told him exactly where to find the loaded trucks and on which nights."

"How was Val involved?"

"My buyer insisted the almonds be delivered to the port in Long Beach so he could ship them to Japan. That meant the driver needed a commercial driver's license to get through security, and none of Jason's men could pass the background check."

"So you compromised on Val."

Sinclair nodded. "Several of his friends from school are in the gang and vouched for him. All he had to do was drive the loaded truck over the grapevine to Long Beach and return with the money. Jason even provided a clean truck the police wouldn't be looking for."

I paused. "Did Val know the cargo was stolen?"

"Of course. He's the one who got me in touch with the Eastside Crew in the first place, although he made a lot of noise about not wanting to get involved."

I felt an invisible weight settle on me and lowered the bat. Mrs. Boyle thought she knew her son. Would she recover from learning she hadn't? "I guess he was saving for college."

"Yes, and I promised him promotions down the road. He really wanted to impress his mom. . . . Are you okay?"

"No. I'm not okay." I raised the bat again. "Because this time Val didn't make it back from Long Beach. What happened?"

Sinclair's face puckered. "It was Val's own fault. The first robberies went great, but then Leland transferred me out of Dewey Ridge and Val got paranoid. I told him Leland needed my marketing expertise for the Drillers, but Val became more and more convinced we were under suspicion."

And Val had almost certainly been right. If Warner suspected his son-in-law, but had no proof, then moving him to a business with nothing to steal from made a lot of sense.

"Jason's men had already taken our third shipment from one of Leland's packing companies up north," Sinclair continued. "They were holding it until Val was ready to drive to Long Beach, but he kept stalling. Val was convinced we were under surveillance. Finally Jason threatened him. He wanted their money, one way or the other, so Val agreed to go."

"And that was last night?"

Sinclair nodded. "Yes, but Val had a paranoid freak-out on the way back. He called from a pay phone at the base of the grapevine. He'd made the delivery and had the money, but he was sure someone was following him. He was supposed to meet Jason's people in Bakersfield, but he was too frightened."

"Then how did he end up dead in an orchard in Weedpatch?"

"I tried to calm him down, but he insisted I come meet him. He wanted out of the whole thing and threatened to abandon the truck and the money and hitchhike home. I told him to go to Valley Farms and wait for me. I used to work there and knew it would be deserted."

Sinclair didn't appear to realize he was hanging himself. If he was the only one who knew about Val going to the orchard, then he was the only one who could have committed the murder. "Is it possible Val called Jason and told him what was happening?"

"Jason denies it, but I think he and his men murdered Val and took the money. Now he's trying to get paid twice." Sinclair opened his arms. "And I can't pay him."

It was a good theory, but it didn't explain why the tape was a danger to Mary Sinclair or why her father would bribe the police to tamper with the crime scene. Those things brought the crime back home to Sinclair.

I tightened my grip on the bat and now thought of it more as a defensive weapon. "What happened when you got to the orchard?"

"Val was dead." Sinclair didn't sound sorry or even upset. "That was pretty much it."

"Was the money there?"

"I didn't hang out to check." He shook his head. "I asked Mary this morning, but she doesn't know."

"You brought your wife to the meeting?"

"You know that," he said defensively. "She's on your tape."

Was it possible? Did my video place Leland Warner's daughter at the scene of a murder?

"And I had to bring her," Sinclair continued. "She overheard Val's call and had an attack. Calming her down took forever and then I was afraid to leave her alone. She kept threatening to call her father."

Every nerve in my body came to life. "Did she threaten to call her father tonight?"

"Yes, but this time I talked her out of it."

"She threatened to call her father and you left her alone?"

"But last night I took her with me and you know how that ended."

I didn't know, but I wasn't going to stick around to find out. I dropped the bat and tore out of the office. I ran through the alley and then into the stands. The farther I got from home plate, the less light I had. Soon, the near total darkness forced me to slow down. About halfway to the van I heard a noise and ducked between rows of seats. I cautiously peered back. Skinny and Belly were entering the stands behind home plate. I crawled as fast as I could through the peanut shells and spilled beer.

I reached the outfield wall and turned around. Skinny and Belly had split up. Each walked slowly through his half of the ballpark, methodically searching the seats. The fog was getting thicker and highlighted the beams of their flashlights. Skinny was closest to me, but even he hadn't reached third base. I hit the dirt and hoped the darkness provided cover as I sprinted to where I'd come over the back wall. I jumped up and pulled myself over the fence. I held on tight, stifling the urge to cry out as the wood cut into my abdomen. I lowered myself onto the roof of the news van and then slid to the ground.

I was breathing hard, but felt a surge of relief as I opened the driver's-side door.

That's when the world fell down on me.

I stumbled and reached for the car door. More than anything else I was confused. At first I didn't even understand I'd been hit. I felt a pair of hands pull me up and knew for the first time I wasn't alone.

He half pushed, half dragged me. I fell onto the dirt and tried to raise my head, but felt a stabbing pain and immediately lowered it.

Voices. He was calling for help.

I made one last attempt to raise myself. I lifted my head and pushed up with my legs. A wave of nausea burst from my empty stomach, and I doubled over with the dry heaves.

It was the last thing I remember.

NINETEEN

"You awake back there?"

I flirted with recognizing the voice, but the elusive identification disappeared when I tried to move my head. Pain shot down the back of my neck and into my shoulders. I must have cried out because the voice returned.

"You are waking up. Good, we're almost there."

I opened my eyes. I was lying across a backseat breathing in new-car smell. My hands were cuffed behind me.

The voice had come from the front seat, where I made out the back of a man's head. My first thought, that I was under arrest, filled me with horror. I would be stripped, searched, interrogated, and finally left to spend the night in a locked cell with criminals—and all that was if Skinny and Belly didn't kill me while in custody. But looking around, I realized there was no protective barrier between the front and back seats, no police scanner rattling in the background, and no signs of wear to the plush interior. This wasn't a police car, but something about it felt institutional.

We turned off smooth asphalt and onto something rough and uneven. Through the windows I saw only darkness and realized we were out of the city—probably on a dirt road in a rural part of the county. This frightened me more than being handcuffed.

After a few minutes we turned onto another dirt road and stopped. A man's voice called from outside the car, followed by a loud mechanical sound. I tried to raise my throbbing head so this person could see me, so that someone would know I was there. I forced myself up onto an elbow and almost passed out from the effort.

The mechanical sound stopped and the car began to move. With my last bit of strength I forced myself into a sitting position and looked out the back window. A large gate closed behind us as a man in a uniform walked toward a small booth.

I took a deep breath and yelled, "Help."

The uniformed man jumped at the sound of my voice, but quickly looked away and entered the booth.

"You should have saved your strength," the driver said. "Travis is the only one on guard tonight because he's very good at not seeing things."

The large gate finished sealing itself shut. I fell back onto the seat, out of breath and disappointed. We drove for several minutes before the driver slowed the car again and then came to a complete stop.

"We're getting out now." The voice sounded familiar, but once again I failed to identify it. "Don't cause me any trouble. It wouldn't be good for either of us."

He opened his door and I heard the soft scuff of shoes touching dirt. A few seconds later he'd opened my door. "I think it's best if you help yourself out of the car. No offense, but you put up quite a fight back there. I think I'd rather give you a wide berth."

At that point I couldn't have swatted a fly, but my pride swelled a little.

"Come on now. Your feet aren't tied."

I turned onto my back and managed to sit up. My head felt like a lead weight and I almost fell backward.

"That's good. Now step out of the car."

I swung my feet out the open door and sat, half in the car and half out. The air was cold and smelled of earth and manure.

"Where am I?" I tried to gently shake my hair out of my face.

"Someplace very few people ever see." A bright light shone behind the man, highlighting his outline, but keeping his face in darkness. In one hand he held my blue jacket, and I remembered the camera and Sinclair's confession with a dawning awareness of my failure. I was captured, bound, and the piece of evidence that could clear me was now in this man's hands.

"Come on. You don't want to keep him waiting."

I raised my head and looked around. The harsh light flooding the entire area came from the top of a large two-story, Craftsman-style house.

"Where are we?"

"Stand up, you can do it."

I turned my head and took a long look around. Fog was rapidly descending, but it hadn't dramatically affected visibility yet. In addition to the main house, two garages and a stable ringed the large clearing. Surrounding everything were trees. Not small orchard trees, but huge monsters full of branches and foliage that blocked everything. Behind us a dirt road cut a path through the woods and disappeared.

I leaned forward and pushed up with my legs. I stumbled slightly, but leaned against the open car door for balance. "Why am I here?"

"At this rate we're never getting inside." He opened a Valsec Security jacket and turned his body to the light. In a holster under his arm rested a small gun.

I tilted my head up and got my first good look at him. Unlike his voice, which had hovered on the edge of being identified, I recognized his face immediately. He'd radiated the same kindly innocence the night before—over the police tape at the entrance to the orchard. His eyes even had the same sly twinkle as when he'd offered the tip about sneaking into the crime scene. This man didn't look like a thug. He didn't look like someone I should be afraid of. He looked like someone you'd confuse for a friend of your dad's.

He smiled. "See, I wasn't kidding about the gun, so don't try anything."

He let the Valsec jacket fall closed over the same khaki uniform he'd been wearing the night before. "Name's Frank, by the way." His arm went around my waist and he helped me toward the house. "I got to hand it to you kid. I've seen big guys go down faster. That part where you were retching and still trying to stand was great."

"Thanks." We'd taken several steps and I was leaning heavily on him.

"You didn't have a chance, but you kept at it. That's nice to see."

"Glad you liked it." I turned and glanced at the car. It was the same one he'd been sitting in with the female guard the night before.

"I should have guessed you wouldn't go down without a fight. You're a persistent little thing. When you started throwing pebbles at my car last night I couldn't believe it."

"You could have ignored me."

We reached three small steps leading up to the porch. On the other side of the railing, plants overflowed from pots and tumbled down from hanging baskets. The lighting here was subtle and carefully designed to highlight the plants and the wood.

He shook his head. "Too risky. I needed to get rid of you."

"That's why you told me how to sneak in?" I raised my right leg to the first step. "And here I thought you really liked me."

I felt a boost as he helped me up. "It should have been a win-win. I get what I want; you go away; and you get what you want; a better story. Why you had to stick around and take those pictures of me and Mrs. Sinclair sitting in the car, I'll never know."

"Mrs. Sinclair?" Understanding broke through my clouded and overworked brain. "You don't mean your partner in the car? Sleeping beauty?"

"The very one."

I glared at him. "That's what this is all about? Those shots I pretended to roll off. I did it for the cop so he wouldn't get suspicious. There wasn't even enough light."

"And all you have to do is produce the tape and prove it."

We reached the top of the stairs and stood before a pair of double doors with beautiful stained-glass inserts.

"I can't do that," I said.

He sighed and reached for the doorbell. "That makes everything so much harder." Movement flashed from behind the glass and his hand paused in front of the bell.

Mary Sinclair threw open both doors at the same time. Her shoulder-length hair hung limp around her pale face. Her talonlike hands were in perpetual motion. They darted from the crisp collar of her oxford shirt to the seam of her khakis as she took several steps back.

The smell from the interior of the house came pouring out on warm air. It was a strange combination of foul and sweet. Like wet dog and potpourri.

My escort closed the doors behind us and casually tossed my coat on a nearby chair. "See, Mrs. Sinclair, no problems."

She didn't even look at me. "Where's Tom?"

"He's right behind us." Frank guided me down a step into a sunken living room with a leather sofa and several arts-and-crafts-style chairs. The room's light was soft and came from a fireplace and stained-glass lamps. "He had to lock up the ballpark."

"Where's my news van?" I'd already totaled one today and didn't relish telling Callum I'd stolen a second and then lost it.

"I left it there. Keys are in the ignition."

Mary's hands came together as if in prayer. "Oh, Frank, I wish I knew where Tom was."

"Don't worry. He'll be along any minute."

"But I've been calling his cell and all I get is voice mail."

"He's right behind us. I promise." With his back to Mary Sinclair, Frank helped me onto the leather sofa and moved a pillow out of my way.

"Is she always this batty?" I whispered. "She seemed pretty mellow last night."

Frank rolled his eyes and whispered back, "She'd had a Xanax by then. You should have seen her when I got there. If she hadn't been so damn hysterical, we would have gotten away before the police arrived."

I looked at the nervous wreck across the room. She stood at the window pulling back the drapes, looking out the window, then replacing the fabric, only to start again a few seconds later.

Frank ran a hand over the back of my head. "You've got a bump there, but it's nothing serious."

I leaned back onto the sofa cushion and adjusted my hands so I wasn't sitting on them. "Can you unlock these handcuffs?"

"No."

"Please. My wrists and shoulders are killing me."

"I take those off and you're out the door." He laughed. "Not that you'd get far, but I don't particularly want to chase you. Those cuffs are staying on."

He was right, of course. I saw my coat by the door and wondered if Frank had found the camera. Splitting head or not, it would be worth grabbing the coat and making a run for it. To do that I'd have to get the cuffs off.

"Not that I want you to be uncomfortable." Frank placed a pillow behind my head, then turned to the window. "Mrs. Sinclair, why don't you come and sit down? Can I get you something to drink?"

She didn't move. "If he was right behind you, why isn't he here yet?"

"Maybe he decided to stop at your house. He didn't know you'd be here."

"This isn't your place?" I asked.

"No, it's Daddy's," she said without looking away from the window. "I don't like this. The fog's coming in. What if he's had an accident?"

Frank lowered his voice so it sounded soothing and confident. "I'm sure Mr. Sinclair will be here very soon."

I felt a little guilty for what I was about to do, but I had to get the cuffs off. "He mentioned something about looking in on Gladys."

Mary Sinclair dropped the drape and fell back against the window. "What?"

Frank's bland features lit up with surprise.

"I don't know," I continued. "But I think he said something about meeting her when she got off her shift at the restaurant."

"That's impossible." Frank took quick steps to Mary. "She doesn't even live here anymore. We paid her to leave town."

"Maybe I got the name wrong, but I'm pretty sure he said Gladys."

"No," Mary cried.

"Mrs. Sinclair," Frank pleaded. "Think it through and you'll see how ridiculous this is."

Mary started sobbing.

Frank tried to guide her to a chair. "He can't be with her because she's long gone. I'd know if she came back."

She pulled away from his gentle grip and ran back to the window. "Where is he? What if he's left me?"

I pushed up with my legs, almost losing my balance, but managed to stand. This was my chance and I marshaled all my energy to take it. "You need to send Frank out to look for him."

"Nobody is going anywhere." Frank stepped down into the living room and casually pushed me off my feet. I fell backward onto the couch. "Mr. Sinclair is probably driving through the gate as we speak."

"What if he's not?" Mary turned from the window. "What if he's never coming back? You have to find him."

Frank glared at me. I tried not to look too happy, but it was hard. We both knew if he left, I'd have her unlocking the cuffs in minutes.

"Mrs. Sinclair." He spoke slowly and calmly. "Do you think that's what Mr. Warner would want me to do? Leave you alone at a time like this with a woman who's blackmailing you?"

Mary looked at me.

"I'm not blackmailing anyone," I said. "Your husband and I worked everything out."

Frank leaned over me and lowered his voice. "You want me to gag you? 'Cause I will."

"No." My voice was the only weapon I had left. "Don't do that."

"Are you going to behave?"

I nodded.

He stood back up and walked to the window. He put an arm around Mary Sinclair and guided her to a chair by the fire. "How about this? If Mr. Sinclair isn't here in fifteen minutes, and your father says it's okay, I'll go look for him."

Her face shot up. "Really? You will?"

"Of course I will."

She relaxed into the chair and wiped the tears from her face.

Frank sat down next to me. "Nice try."

"Is that the kind of thing you do for Leland Warner? Pay off his son-in-law's girlfriends?"

"Technically I'm a senior adviser at Valsec Security. But it just so happens Valsec is owned by Mr. Warner and only services his properties." Frank winked at me. "And I play Mr. Fix It from time to time. It's not a nine-to-five job."

"Are you former law enforcement?"

"Bakersfield PD." He actually sounded proud. "It comes in handy. Sometimes I can offer freelance work to the right kind of officer."

"You mean like the cops you sent to my house this morning?"

"Exactly like that. It also comes in handy when I need information." He paused. "For instance, I know your uncle was taken into custody tonight."

I tried to sit up, but didn't get far. "Is he okay?"

"They haven't charged him with anything yet, probably because they think he's cooperating."

I stopped moving. Bud wouldn't betray me. Or would he? "What do you mean, they think he's cooperating?"

"He told them he dropped you off in a cornfield on the south side of town. They've got a big manhunt going down there—which I like since we're on the north side of town."

I remembered what Callum had said about Rod. "Do they have anybody else in custody?"

"If you're worried about your boyfriend, they released him two hours ago."

"He's not my boyfriend," I said louder than I intended.

"That's a good thing because he sold you out to us and the Sheriff's Department."

"If you know he's dishonest, why are you making a deal with him?"

"We haven't yet." Frank shrugged. "But I've got people making contact. Ideally, we'll work out a combined arrangement with you and your boyfriend. Then we can finally put this whole thing to rest."

I paused. "You called him my boyfriend again just to annoy me, didn't you?"

He laughed. "You jump to the bait way too easy."

I tried to look outraged, but only managed to dislodge the pillow behind my head. "How do I know you won't kill us both once you have the tape?"

"Who do you think we are?" Frank picked up the pillow and replaced it. "No reason for us to take a chance like that. And I think Mr. Warner will be very generous. He doesn't want any trouble."

"How long has it been, Frank?" Mary Sinclair sat on the edge of her chair looking at us with pulsing, almost manic eyes. She showed no evidence of understanding or caring about our conversation.

Frank looked at his watch. "Only a couple minutes. Don't worry. He's on his way."

She got up and used a phone on the side table.

Frank whispered, "Now she's starting to get me worried. I want to go chase him out of some girl's bed about as much as I want to chase you through the woods."

A high-pitched cry came from the other side of the room. We both looked at Mary as she slammed the phone down. "It's still his voice mail. I can't stand it."

Frank jumped to his feet. "It's all right, Mrs. Sinclair. Why don't you come sit by the fire again."

"Why is this happening? I don't understand. Ever since last night. It won't stop."

Her instability frightened me the same way Jason's rage had. They were both unreasonable and unpredictable. But was she dangerous? "What happened in the orchard last night?"

Frank shot me a threatening look, but kept his voice calm when he spoke to her. "Don't distress yourself. Talking about it will only upset you."

"It's that boy's fault," she said with venom. "Why did he call? Why couldn't he leave us alone?"

"It's going to be okay, Mrs. Sinclair. I promise. Just come and sit down." Frank took her arm and tried to guide her back to the fire, but she refused to move.

"I didn't want Tom to go," she said. "I begged him not to. I knew something terrible would happen and it did and it's still happening."

"Mrs. Sinclair, you shouldn't talk about these things."

"I should have called Daddy, but Tom wouldn't let me. When we got there . . ." Her whole body shook and she leaned on Frank for support. "When we found him it was so terrible. He was like a monster, lying there with no face."

She broke down crying and Frank was finally able to bring her back to the chair by the fire.

I relaxed a little. Her statement, although somewhat hysterical, supported Sinclair's story that Val was dead when they arrived. If I had to be held against my will, I preferred it not be by a murderer and his family.

Mary's tears ebbed and she patted Frank's arm. "I don't know what I'd do without you, Frank. You saved me last night."

"Why were you there?" I asked him.

He glanced from me to Mary. "I don't think we should—"

"I called Daddy on my cell phone." Mary took a tissue from her pocket and blew her nose. "Then Daddy called Frank, who came to the rescue. We were driving away when the police stopped us."

Warner's calling Frank to clean up the mess made sense. Of

course the arrival of the police must have limited what Frank could do. "Who called 911?" I asked Mary.

She shook her head. "It wasn't me. When I saw their lights, I wanted to scream, but Frank gave me his jacket and let me sit in the car."

I looked at Frank for confirmation. He reluctantly smiled. "I told them she was my partner and we were on rounds."

"They believed that?"

"Why wouldn't they?" He shrugged. "Arvin PD called Valsec when they got the 911 call. They expected us to be there. I told the police I needed to call headquarters and check in. What I really did was cancel the team on its way."

Mary's face contorted as if she'd tasted something bitter. "But they wouldn't let us leave. They made us sit in the car for hours and hours."

Frank chuckled softly. "It was five a.m. before we got out of there."

I kept my attention focused on Mary. "But where was your husband?"

Frank made a noise, got a scathing look from Mary, and then tried to act as if he'd been coughing.

"He drove you down there," I said. "You both discovered the body. Where did he and the car go?"

She looked down at her twisting hands. "The truth is . . . Tom is very sensitive and he had a kind of episode where he wasn't himself. Kind of like temporary insanity."

In my mind I saw Sinclair's Jaguar peeling away from Mrs. Boyle's house. "Are you trying to tell me that he ran away and left you there with a dead body?"

She didn't answer.

"Let me get this straight—your husband drags you to a murder scene and then drives away without you?"

Her hands flew to her neck. "He didn't know what he was doing."

"What do you see in this guy?"

"A question I've asked every day since she first brought him home from college." The voice was deep and powerful. It came from behind me, and though I'd never heard it before, I knew to whom it belonged.

TWENTY

From my position on the couch I couldn't see Leland Warner, but I heard him and saw his effect on the other two people in the room.

Frank jumped up. His muscles were rigid where they'd previously been slack, and his face was blank where it had been friendly.

"Daddy, how can you say such a thing?" Mary looked smaller and fatter, as though her flesh were pressed down and out. "You know Tom loves me."

"I don't know any such thing." I heard him take slow, deliberate steps and followed the sound of his voice as he came around the couch and faced Mary. "As a matter of fact I think something very different."

He wore a plaid shirt tucked into the kind of cheap, old-fashioned jeans they sell at discount stores. A thick leather belt at his waist encircled a painfully thin, stopped-over frame. What little weight he had was supported by a nicked and scarred cane.

Mary jumped out of her seat. "Daddy, don't say horrible things. I'm all on edge."

I got my first look at his face as he placed a hand on Mary's head. His look of disinterest conflicted with the concern in his voice. "I'm sorry, kitten. I know you've had a bad time." He glanced at me with the same bored expression, then slowly took the few steps to Mary's vacated seat. Mary followed and hovered attentively as he carefully lowered himself into the chair. She took his cane and leaned it against the large stone hearth. The light from the fire flickered in the polished silver of the handle.

Warner dismissed her with a simple "Thank you," and she returned to the front window to look for Sinclair.

"This young lady also looks like she's had a bad time." Warner had spoken without actually looking at me.

"I had to hit her over the head to subdue her." Frank shifted his weight from one leg to the other. "And Dick and Dale may have gotten a little carried away this morning."

I chuckled and Warner looked directly at me for the first time. "You think being beaten is funny?"

"Dick and Dale? Please tell me that's some kind of alias. Those can't be their real names."

Warner turned his attention back to the fire. "Frank, did you arrive in time to prevent Tom from making a bigger ass of himself than usual?"

Mary made a noise, but didn't say anything.

"Miss Hawkins was recording Mr. Sinclair with a small device hidden in her jacket." Frank looked at me. "I destroyed it."

"Of course you did," I said, and buried my last shred of hope with a sarcastic remark.

"Good work." Warner rubbed a long, thin finger along his forehead. "Hopefully we're near the end of this disaster."

The old man lowered his hand and looked at me again. I met his gaze and openly studied him. His face was a maze of crevices, valleys, and canyons. Wrinkle trenches combined with folds of drooping skin and pocks like craters. Wild and overgrown eyebrows dominated his face. With a shock I realized his look of disinterest was the result of drooping eyelids that made him appear to be watching the world with barely opened eyes.

"I understand you had an idea to blackmail us," he said.

"Whoever was the first idiot to say that and started this entire ridiculous nightmare going, please find me that person so I can wring their neck."

His thin lips flipped into a skeptical smile. "You weren't after money?"

With nothing to take to the police to prove my story, with my hands cuffed behind my back, with no hope of escape, and with nothing to leverage or bargain with, I had no options left but the truth. "The video Frank thinks I shot of your daughter doesn't exist. Even if you get your hands on the tape, those images won't be on it because there wasn't enough light. I only took those shots because I was planning to sneak inside and didn't want the police officer to get suspicious." Warner continued to stare at me. His eyes, peeking out from behind those deceptive folds of skin, made me feel antsy and exposed. "I'm telling the truth. There's nothing to blackmail you with."

"You could be lying and planning to sell the tape to one of my business rivals? My only daughter embroiled in a murder would distract me—something quite a few people could take advantage of."

"There's nothing on the tape that implicates your daughter or anyone else," I said as though the matter were closed. "It's just the police processing the crime scene."

His eyes stayed fixed on me. "You're either telling the truth or an excellent liar."

"I'm telling the truth."

"Probably not." He looked at Frank. "Get her file for me, will you please? It's on my desk."

Frank disappeared into the back of the house.

"I'm not lying," I repeated. "If you'd left me alone I wouldn't even know your daughter had been there."

Frank returned and handed Warner a blue folder.

"Thank you." Warner took a pair of reading glasses from his shirt pocket and began casually flipping through the pages. Frank walked backward to one of the other chairs, as if he were afraid to show Warner his back.

"Your whole life distilled into a few dozen pages," Warner said.

"What is that? Some kind of background check?" I leaned forward, but couldn't see.

"Basically, and it's told me that you're a bit of an outsider. You don't talk to your family and you don't have any friends. Why is that?"

I straightened. "I'm very close to my uncle." Of course that was a recent development, but I didn't feel the need to share it.

"Really? I'm glad." The corners of his drooping mouth turned up as he enjoyed the moment. "You see, I was afraid your father's suicide left you an emotionally crippled loner. It's good to hear I was wrong."

For a few moments nobody spoke. The only sound came from the logs in the fireplace.

I broke the silence by laughing. "That's the best you can do—a stupid lie about how my father died? Was that supposed to be shocking? Am I supposed to start crying?"

"I thought you knew he killed himself." He cringed in mock dismay. "I would never have mentioned it if I thought you didn't know."

"You can't change facts. The police—"

"You're right." Warner looked at the page in front of him and nodded. "The death certificate does indicate an accidental death. But the company's investigation is much more interesting. Lots of interviews with coworkers, family members." He held up several sheets of paper. "This report says deliberate operator error."

I rolled my eyes and relaxed back into the cushions. "The company made stuff up so they wouldn't have to pay out on his insurance. Really, if this is the best you've got, it's pathetic."

He returned the pages to the pile on his lap and continued to leaf through. "Could be the company was trying to cover themselves. That's what I'd do in their place." He paused and withdrew several more sheets from the pile. "Of course the interviews don't paint a pretty picture. Withdrawn, even from his own family. Chronically depressed . . . and of course it wasn't your father's first suicide attempt. That does seem significant."

I looked up.

"Oh, you didn't know about that?" he said in the kindliest voice imaginable.

"That's because it's not true."

He offered the papers to me. "Would you like to see?"

I leaned forward like a fish chasing the worm. "You're making—"

"Then again, maybe I shouldn't." He quickly withdrew the papers. "Maybe the kind thing would be to let it drop."

"There's nothing to show me because he never tried to kill himself, ever."

"That's the spirit. It's important you believe there's nothing on these pages because I'd feel terrible if I'd inadvertently planted a seed of doubt in your mind."

"You haven't made me doubt anything."

"Maybe you've always known."

I looked from his face to the folder in his lap. "You're never going to show me those papers, are you? No matter what I say or do?"

"It depends." The sagging corners of his mouth tilted up again. "I always like a bargaining chip in my back pocket."

I smiled. "Go to hell."

He nodded as though he were taking it under advisement. "Do you think suicides go to hell?"

I had a flash of sympathy for Sinclair and then, for the first time in my life, a strong desire to pound my fists into a frail, old man.

Warner appeared to sense this and nodded as though a store clerk had handed him the socks he'd asked for. He closed the file in his lap. "I think you're telling the truth about your video. You seem to be a straightforward sort of person and very easy to read. Of course I could be wrong." He turned to Frank. "Why don't you get her a whiskey?"

Frank's rubber soles squeaked on the wood floor as he walked behind me. Crystal tapped crystal with a melodic ping and then I heard liquid being poured.

Mary broke the silence. "Daddy, I'm so worried about Tom. Can Frank go look for him?"

Warner looked at Frank behind me. "Didn't you bring him with you?"

"He's driving his own car." Frank returned with a glass of brown liquid. "He had to lock up the ballpark."

Mary let the curtain fall at the window. "But, Daddy, he should be here by now and it's foggy."

Frank's cell phone rang on his hip. "He probably stopped at home." He placed the whiskey on the coffee table and answered the call.

I couldn't hear the voice on the other end of the line, but Frank looked happy.

Frank covered the phone with his hand and turned to Warner. "They picked up the reporter we were looking for."

I jerked forward. "Rod?"

Frank nodded, then looked back at Warner. "He wants to make a deal, but will only speak with you or Mr. Sinclair."

"Have them bring him here," Warner said. "We can sort this mess out once and for all."

Frank nodded, raised the phone back to his head, and said, "Bring him to the ranch, ASAP. . . . No, it's only Travis. Nobody will see you." Frank turned off the phone and sat back down.

"But, Daddy," Mary pleaded. "What about Tom?"

Warner sighed. "Have you tried calling his cell phone?"

"Yes. He doesn't answer. It's just the voice mail." Mary flew across the room and landed at Warner's feet. "Don't you see? That proves there's something wrong. Frank has to go look for him."

Warner looked at Frank, who shook his head and then gestured to me. Warner nodded and looked down at his daughter. "This isn't a good time for Frank to go out. When his people arrive, we can send them back out to look for Tom."

"But, Daddy—"

"No buts." He picked up his cane and raised himself out of the chair. "I'm going to take my pills and lie down. Come and get me when everyone has arrived."

Frank stood. “Of course, sir.”

Mary sulked as he left the room, but soon distracted herself by dialing Sinclair’s cell phone again.

Frank glanced longingly at the whiskey, then picked it up and brought it toward me.

“You go ahead and have it.”

Frank smiled and pulled back. “He doesn’t break out the good stuff for the hired help. I think he really likes you.”

“If that’s how he treats somebody he likes, I’d hate to see what he does to people he loves.”

Frank glanced at Mary, then downed a large gulp of the alcohol.

Twenty minutes later Mary was still dialing the phone, listening expectantly, then hanging up when the voice mail picked up. Headlights flashed in the front windows and she abruptly dropped the phone.

“Tom.” Mary ran to the double doors. Her shoulders tensed in anticipation and then sank. “It’s not him.”

Frank let out a long breath and abandoned his comfortable seat. “Don’t overexcite yourself, Mrs. Sinclair.”

I tried to sit up. “Is it Rod?”

Frank had reached the doors and was now unlocking the bolts. “And friends.”

Mary returned to where she’d dropped the phone and redialed.

Footsteps sounded on the same steps I’d climbed forty minutes earlier, then Belly walked through the entryway followed by Rod and Skinny.

Rod had shaved and done whatever it is he does to his hair, but he wore the same suit.

Frank offered his hand to Rod. “Thanks for making the trip.”

Rod, looking eerily like the smiling reporter from KJAY’s cheesy ads, shook Frank’s hand. “My pleasure. Having Leland Warner behind me will be a big boost for my career.”

“I’m sure it will,” Frank agreed. “We’re waiting on Mr. Sinclair. Then we’ll all put our heads together. I’m sure if you and Lilly cooperate, you’ll be generously rewarded.”

A flicker of something unpleasant crossed Rod's face but he recovered so quickly I doubted Frank noticed. "I'd rather not involve Lilly. I've got the tape. We can proceed without her."

"Too late." Frank gestured to me.

Belly advanced while wagging a finger at me. "Missy, missy, missy. You didn't meet us at two. Peggy Sue shouldn't stand her best boys up at the big dance. That ain't right."

"I got a feeling Peggy Sue's best boys would rather tug on each other's—"

"Maybe it's not a good idea to antagonize them." Rod shot forward and blocked Belly's path to me.

Skinny smiled from the doorway. "We made a bit of a mess at your place when we found you weren't home."

I smiled back. "Lovely. Just lovely."

Belly pointed at Rod. "Got your boyfriend's place too."

"You did what?" Rod asked at the same time as I said, "He's not my boyfriend."

"Dale, come here," Frank called from the still open double doors.

Belly turned around, but not before winking at me.

"We'll just be a minute," Frank told Rod. "Why don't you have a seat?"

Rod sat down on the edge of the sofa and watched the three men conferring in the open doorway. They spoke quietly and were far enough away that their voices reached us as indecipherable mumbles.

"You're lucky my hands are tied," I said.

Rod turned a worried face toward me. "Are you okay? They haven't hurt you, have they?"

"Like you care."

"How can you say that?"

I snorted. "Give the act a rest. I'm not buying it anymore."

He took a furtive look at the men in the doorway, then lowered his voice. "Why did you leave me in Arvin?"

"Don't act all innocent. I know what you're doing here."

He shook his head. "Listen, I did call Sinclair, but—"

"Don't get me wrong. You've got a great routine. First-class all the way. Butter me up with all your nice-guy manners and then throw in a little vulnerable geek and you're gold. You're in like Flint and I bought it hook, line and sinker, but I'm not buying it anymore."

"What are you talking about? Who's Flint?"

"James Coburn. You're mother's a producer. You should know about old movies."

"You're not making sense." Suddenly his eyes widened. "Did they hit you over the head?"

"Yes, but I'm making perfect sense."

He held up his hand. "How many fingers am I holding up?"

"Stop it. The only thing wrong with me is I was stupid enough to think you were a sweet guy and had to get the rug pulled out from under me."

His hand dropped. "What are you're talking about?"

"I heard you on the phone at the restaurant. Don't play innocent."

He tensed, drew back slightly, then leaned in close to whisper, "Lilly, I don't know what you think you heard, but I can explain."

"I'm sure you can, and I'm sure you'll come up with some devious way to make me believe you, which is why I'm not going to listen. You are a liar, end of story."

He sighed and pulled back to his seat on the edge of the couch. "When this is all over, I hope you'll give me a chance to explain."

I rolled my eyes so he turned his attention to the conference still going on at the door. "Have you figured who tampered with the crime scene and why?"

Given how little I trusted him, I should probably have kept my mouth shut, but the change in subject was a welcome diversion. "No one tampered with the crime scene. Dick and Dale appear to be the only cops on Warner's payroll."

"Then why does everyone want the tape?"

I indicated Mary in the corner still dialing the cell phone.

"That's Leland Warner's daughter. They think I shot video of her sitting in a car at the front of the orchard. It proves she was there last night." I shook my head. "I mean, if it hadn't been too dark and the shots had come out, it would have proven it."

I gave him a quick review of what I'd learned.

"Where's Sinclair?" he asked when I'd finished.

"I don't know." I gestured with my head to the group at the door. "I think Frank is going to send Dick and Dale out looking for him."

"Are you sure they're cops?"

I nodded. "Bakersfield PD."

Headlights flashed in the windows. Mary dropped the cell phone and rammed through the men at the door like a three-hundred-pound linebacker. She was outside before any of them could stop her.

Frank put his hand inside his coat and rested it on the gun. "Dick, you stay here." He gestured to us. "Keep an eye on them. Dale, you come with me."

Frank and Belly joined Mary outside. Skinny stayed in the doorway. I heard several car doors open and close. After a few seconds Skinny ran outside.

Rod sat up in alarm. "I don't understand. This isn't right."

"Right for what?"

Rod jumped up. "Stay here."

"Like hell." I scooted to the edge of the couch and pushed up. I lost my balance and almost fell over. Rod had already reached the front door. I followed and stumbled into his back.

He put an arm around me and propped me up. "You should go back to the couch."

What I saw in front of the house made me agree. Frank, Dick, and Dale were facing down my worst nightmare and several members of his gang. To the side, two more of Jason's men held Sinclair while Mary clung to his neck with both hands. Behind them two black SUVs blocked the driveway.

Rod bent his head and leaned down. "I don't know who they are, but I think everybody has guns."

My voice caught as I said, "It's the Eastside Crew."

Rod remained bent over in a kind of standing fetal position talking into his crotch. "The driveway's blocked."

"Rod, this is no time to lose it." I took a step backward. "We have to get out of here."

"What's going on?" Warner bellowed from behind me. I tried to duck out of view, but it was too late. Everyone turned toward Warner's voice. When Jason saw me, his scowl transformed into a sick smile.

Warner reached my side and stopped when he saw the scene in front of his house. The shock only fazed him for a moment. "Mary, come here at once." He took several decisive steps onto the porch. "Let go of Tom and come here."

Mary stayed where she was. "They won't let Tom go. Daddy, make them let him go."

"Dad, please." Sinclair was struggling to stand against Mary's weight. "I had no choice. They were waiting for me at home. I had to bring them here."

Jason stepped forward. "Old man, Tommy Boy owes me and says you're gonna make good for him."

"I don't know anything about your dealings with my son-in-law." Warner paused, then raised a bushy eyebrow. "Boy."

I think it would have been less insulting if he'd actually used the N-word.

The two men stared at each other. Jason's silence was terrifying. Even Mary knew enough to keep her mouth shut.

"Me and your . . . boy," Jason said, and gestured to Sinclair, "we had an agreement. I held up my end of the deal. Now he can cry about Val getting jacked, but I don't care. Tommy Boy is going to make good or else you'll make good for him."

"Please," Sinclair whimpered. "I swear I didn't take the money. Val was dead when we got there."

"Are you deaf? I don't care. The point is you're responsible." Jason turned to Warner. "And you're responsible for him."

"You're out of your mind if you think I'm going to be extorted like this." Warner waved his cane. "Mary, come inside immediately."

"No, Daddy. I won't leave Tom."

Jason gestured to his men, who then let go of Sinclair. Mary cried out and threw her arms even farther around his neck. Frank, Dick, and Dale all seemed to relax, but kept their hands hovering over their guns.

"See, I can't let it stand." Jason's hand darted toward Mary. He ripped her away from Sinclair by the hair and shoved a gun at her head. He faced Warner. "Now me and you are gonna work something out."

Frank, Dick, and Dale each drew their guns. Jason's men drew theirs.

The situation no longer felt merely dangerous. Violence had become a certainty.

Rod, who was no longer bent over, motioned toward the inside of the house. I nodded and slowly took a step backward away from the door.

"No, you don't, girl." Jason was looking right at me. "You and your shorty come out here." He turned the gun on us.

I had an insane desire to yell that Rod was not my shorty, but remained frozen.

"Do what he says," Warner told me, then cautiously stepped down the stairs and out of the way of stray bullets.

"I'll come out, but he's staying inside." I motioned to Rod with my head. "He doesn't have anything to do with this."

Jason, still holding a whimpering Mary, shook his head. "I said both of you."

I worked hard to keep my voice steady. "I said just me."

"It's okay. We'll cooperate." Rod moved down the steps. "But don't hurt anyone."

"How about I hurt you?" Jason threatened.

I followed Rod. "There's no reason to hurt either of us. What

Sinclair told you about me is a lie. I'm not blackmailing anyone. All I did was photograph his wife in a car last night. I don't know anything that could incriminate you."

"You and me got a whole lot of other issues, goes way beyond this." Jason dropped Mary, who fell into the dirt at his feet. He ignored her and stared at me. His focus was total, as if we were the only two people there. "Nice girls shouldn't play with Mace."

Jason handed his gun to one of his men and drew a switchblade from a pocket. He looked at Warner a few feet from me. "Consider this a preview of what's coming for your daughter if you don't make things right."

Jason hit the button and the long steel blade popped into view.

TWENTY-ONE

With my arms still cuffed behind me I was defenseless. I looked to Frank, Dick, and Dale for help, but they stood motionless.

"Think they'll stop me?" Jason laughed and came at me with the knife.

The sound of rushing water flooded my ears. I stumbled backward and Rod quickly stepped in front of me.

Jason came to a sudden stop. His hand with the knife remained raised.

"Wait a minute." Rod dabbed at his forehead with his blue silk handkerchief. "There's no reason this has to turn violent. I'm sure we can work something out."

"Out of my way," Jason ordered.

A high-pitched giggle bubbled up from inside Rod.

"You think that's funny?" Jason switched the knife to his left hand. His fist shot at Rod's stomach.

"No," I cried.

Rod crumpled into the dirt and moaned as his eyes rolled back into his head. At the same time a high-pitched sound came from his gut. With dawning understanding I recognized it as feedback.

Jason's man jumped back and pointed at Rod. "He's wired up. He's wired up."

Frank turned on Dick and Dale. "Did you search him?"

The glance Dick and Dale exchanged confirmed they hadn't.

"Of all the—"

Sirens cut Frank off.

Jason didn't react. Everyone else ran as the police lights flashed against the fog, but he didn't move. Without taking his eyes off Rod he raised the knife.

I used the only weapon I had. My body smashed into Jason like a battering ram. We both fell.

"This is the police," a voice called over a speaker. "Drop your weapons and put your hands in the air."

I don't know who fired the first shot, or the second, or the third. I didn't see any of it. Instead I kept my body flat, my eyes closed, and my head facedown in the dirt.

Until strong hands ripped me onto my back. I looked up to see Jason raise the knife.

Someone moved behind him. A flash of silver descended and Jason collapsed. I kicked his unconscious body away. "Thank you."

Warner inverted the cane he'd used to strike Jason and grasped the silver handle. He placed the tip of the cane in the dirt and leaned on it. "You're welcome."

The first ambulance took Dick and a gang member, both of whom had been shot. The second took the security guard who'd been badly beaten at the front gate, and Jason, who had a severe head injury. Mary had to be sedated, and even that put only a mild dent in her hysteria. We were only too happy to let Warner take her in the third ambulance, even though she had no injuries. Sinclair, Frank, and Dale all lawyered up and were taken to Sheriff's Department headquarters in handcuffs. Even Warner and Mary's ambulance had a police escort—and not the good kind.

The clearing in front of Warner's house had been transformed. Plastic markers indicating shell casings were everywhere. A line of Sheriff's Department vehicles ran down the dirt road as far as the eye could see. Every few moments a bright flash lit the scene as a TI took a photo. Two detective sergeants were there, and the sheriff himself had stopped in.

"Next ambulance is a couple minutes away." Handsome leapt up the porch steps. "The fog's slowing them down."

I looked up at Rod. He was sitting in a cedar chair next to where I sat on the floor of the porch. "You should be next. You could have some freaky internal injury the EMT couldn't find."

Rod smiled and adjusted the ice packs on his abdomen. "I doubt it."

"I'm sorry it went down that way." Handsome glanced at me without making eye contact. "Neither of you were supposed to get hurt."

"It's not your fault," I said.

He nodded. "It was a tough call deciding when to come in. We weren't expecting the Eastside Crew, and we didn't have good intelligence about the layout in here."

"I'm grateful you were here at all." I smiled at Handsome and then Rod. "Both of you."

"At least nobody got away and nobody died." Handsome glanced at the police cruisers, where Jason's men were waiting for the Gang Enforcement Unit. "And we've taken a lot of bad guys off the street. Even two dirty cops."

"What's going to happen to them?" I asked. "And Frank?"

"With your testimony we can get all three for assault and kidnapping. Once I build a case against Sinclair, we'll also charge them with accessory to murder."

I'd told Handsome and Lucero everything I knew, but we hadn't had a chance to discuss what it meant. "You're sure Sinclair killed Val Boyle?"

"Of course. It's plain as day." Handsome's voice carried a hint of annoyance. "The kid called him to back out. Sinclair went down to the orchard, lost his temper, and shot him. Then he panics, grabs the money, and drives off."

"Leaving his wife?"

"That's why they call it panicking, sweetheart." Handsome grinned. "He wasn't thinking straight."

I shook my head. "But Mary supported his story."

"She's batty. You can't go off what she says."

"But why would he stick around town?" I asked. "Why not run away? He'd have to know that Jason would be looking for him, not to mention the police."

"He probably figured Warner would bail him out."

Rod shifted his weight and an ice pack fell onto the porch floor. "Is there someone else you suspect?"

"Sinclair told me Val called from a pay phone at the base of the grapevine. What if he made a second call to someone else?" I looked at Handsome. "You said the 911 call came from gang territory. What if Val called Jason and told him that instead of coming to Bakersfield he was meeting Sinclair in the orchard? Maybe Jason decided to kill him and take the money."

Handsome chuckled. "You're overthinking things. The simplest answer is usually the right answer. Sinclair made the call himself to divert suspicion."

That simple solution tied up all the loose ends. "I only wish Sinclair would confess," I said. "I'd feel a lot better if he actually said the words."

"I've got men searching his house right now." Handsome waved a dismissive hand at me. "We'll find the money or the murder weapon, and that'll be as good as a confession."

"Hey," Lucero called to Handsome. He was standing next to a TI writing something in his notebook. "You want to quit spending time with your honey and do some work?"

I felt an intense desire to study my hand.

"Coming," Handsome called. "Always a smart-ass."

Handsome left to join Lucero. I picked up Rod's fallen ice pack.

"Thanks," he said, and took it from me.

"I'm the one who should thank you—wearing a wire for the police and then stepping between me and Jason—you probably saved my life."

He shook his head. "You saved my life. Jason was going to stab me until you knocked him down."

"I guess we're even."

Rod smiled, then paused. "I'd like to explain about my phone call at the coffee shop. I don't know how much you heard—"

"Let's not talk about it."

"I was calling my parents."

I didn't look at him. "We'd decided not to do that."

"You decided and I went along with it." He leaned forward. "But in the bar you said I needed to be more aggressive. When they showed your picture on TV, I decided to take action. I couldn't say anything in the restaurant because I thought we'd be overheard. I was going to tell you as soon as I got to the car."

"But I heard you on the phone. You said, 'She's not going for it. You'll have to come get us.' You even mentioned a deal."

"I was telling my dad that you were never going to come down to L.A. and he'd have to come up to Bakersfield. The deal was with the police to turn ourselves in."

"Oh." It made sense. I had no reason to be suspicious or wary, but something inside me wanted to get away from him.

"When I got off the phone and discovered you and Bud were gone, I didn't know what to do."

"Why did you turn yourself in? You didn't have to do that. You could have gone to L.A."

"Once I realized you were gone, I called my dad again. He arranged everything by phone through his contacts in the L.A. district attorney's office. Just to be safe, I left the tape at the restaurant where my dad could pick it up later." Rod pointed to Handsome. His face was flush with success as he laughed at something Lucero said. "Those two came for me. I told them everything and suggested setting Sinclair up. It was your exact plan except for the police being on the other end of the microphone."

I raised a skeptical eyebrow. "They believed you?"

"Not exactly, but it didn't hurt to let me call Sinclair. When Frank called back, making vague threats and promising money, that's when they got interested. I agreed to wear a wire, and Lucero put out a fake story about a manhunt on the south side of town to divert suspicion. They also picked Bud up from my description of the car and told everyone that's why I was being released."

"It was very brave of you to meet Dick and Dale wearing a wire. Thank you."

Rod blushed and cleared his throat. "I was wondering . . ."

"Yes?"

He hesitated. "Sorry. I'm a little embarrassed."

I felt a warning twinge, but asked anyway. "Why are you embarrassed?"

"Because I'm going to ask you out."

"Oh."

He raised both hands as if I were a frightened animal. "Hear me out."

"I don't do so well with long-term things."

"We can take it slow."

I shook my head. "And a short-term thing wouldn't be good since we work together."

"We'll start with dinner. No big deal. Just two people having a meal together."

I made another attempt at letting him down easily. "I don't think it's a good idea."

"I know it's awkward about work, but we'll figure something out."

"Things like that don't get worked out." I tried to change the subject. "Did you know the little sick kid's father ran off and left them high and dry? They may lose the house."

He ignored me. "Nobody at the station will mind if we're a couple. It isn't like one of us is the other's boss."

I jumped up. "You're taking an awful lot for granted here. What makes you think I even like you that way?"

Rod smiled and gazed down at the floor. He looked like a timid, geeky teenager. "Come on. You're crazy about me."

"I am not."

His shy eyes looked up. "Sure you are."

"Hey, guys," Handsome called. "Ambulances are here. Two at the same time."

I took decisive steps off the porch and walked to Handsome. "Hey, why don't you ride in the ambulance with me?" I put a hand on Handsome's arm. "I'm sure we've got stuff to talk about."

He looked back toward the porch. "What about your friend?"

"He's taking the other one." I didn't know if Rod had followed me, and I didn't turn around to see. "He could have internal injuries. This way they can focus more on him."

"Sounds good." Handsome looked at Lucero. "Do you mind waiting for Gang Enforcement while I ride with her to the hospital?"

Lucero didn't look happy, but nodded.

I let Handsome and the EMT help me inside the back of the first ambulance and sat down on a stretcher. I deliberately looked the other way in case Rod was standing outside the back doors.

Handsome followed me in and waved the EMT away. "I'm coming with. You can ride up front."

The EMT closed the door, and a few minutes later we started moving.

I lay down on the stretcher. "This has been the worst day, ever."

Handsome covered me with a blanket. "You should have told me this morning what was going on. I could have helped you."

He hadn't seemed eager to help me in the corn maze, but I kept that thought to myself. "I was frightened. I knew Dick and Dale were cops and they made some pretty awful threats."

"Still. It was dumb to try and handle things by yourself."

I decided to change the subject. "Has my uncle been released yet?"

"Should be. We never charged him with anything so it won't take long."

"Thanks."

"When I saw you at the victim's house," he said, continuing

his previous topic, "I knew something was wrong. You looked so helpless with that shiner. It was really stupid not to tell me then."

Had he really just called me helpless and stupid?

He sat down. "You shouldn't try to do things on your own like that."

"Rod wanted to go to the police from the beginning. I probably should have listened to him."

He looked away. "I guess your boyfriend's pretty smart."

"He's not my boyfriend."

Handsome grinned. "I was hoping you'd say that."

"Why?"

"It means I can ask you out for coffee."

"You mean a date?"

"Kind of." He adjusted the blanket. "Maybe a predate."

"That's really sweet." Although I didn't think asking a girl on a predate was all that sweet. "And if you'd asked me yesterday, I'd probably have fainted."

His smile froze. "If I'd asked you yesterday? You mean you're saying no?"

I looked at the man sitting next to me. He was strong, smart, and courageous. He was a catch and he wanted me. But he was also arrogant, condescending, and hadn't even been nice, let alone interested in dating me, until he'd seen me with a black eye. What had the guy at the Crystal Palace said? Sad and lonely translates into needy and grateful.

"Yes," I answered, then realized it could be misinterpreted. "I mean no. . . . I mean yes, I'm saying no."

He pulled back. "What?"

"No offense. I'm flattered and you're a great guy."

His green eyes fixed on me and didn't move. Finally he shook his head and looked out the back window.

"I guess this is going to be an awkward ride," I said.

His head jerked back. "Is that my fault?"

"You should have asked at the end of the trip."

"I wasn't expecting *you* to turn *me* down."

I pulled the blanket up. "Maybe we should talk about something else."

"Did you throw a baseball at that little sick kid?"

"How about we don't talk at all?"

I got home at 8:00 a.m. and found my landlord having hysterics in what remained of my apartment. Dick and Dale had really thrown themselves into their work. My mattress and couch had been sliced open and the stuffing torn out. Every jar and can in the cupboard had been emptied on the walls, furniture, ceilings—pretty much wherever they thought it would do the most harm.

"Do you know how long it's going to take me to get this place back together?" my landlord shouted. "Do you know how long before it's rentable? . . . Hello? Are you even listening to me?"

"Sorry." I looked down from examining a chunk of mattress stuffing stuck to the ceiling. "They caught the guys who did it and they're cops. I'm sure the city will make some kind of restitution."

"Are you kidding me? Do you know how long that could take, and it might not cover all this damage. There's even a hole in the wall by the front door."

"Ah, really? . . . Ah . . . that's awful."

He stared at me as though I were the creature from the black lagoon. "You're bad news. Pack up your stuff and get out."

"You can't do that. I know I'm month to month, but you can't kick me out today."

"This place isn't going to be livable for a long time. By then your month will be up." He started for the front door and called back to me, "And don't even think about trying to get your deposit back."

The phone rang around ten as I was returning, on foot, from scrounging for boxes. I let the answering machine, which had miraculously survived the trashing, pick it up.

"Lilly, this is your mother. Call me when you get home from

work. We need to talk about Clem's shower. I've picked out your gift."

I reached down to the floor where the phone lay and picked up the receiver. "Mom, I'm here."

"What are you doing home?" Her voice filled with hope. "Have you left that awful job?"

"I hope not." I rubbed my good eye. "It's not an awful job."

"Yes, it is. You need to get into a nice line of work. Something where you can meet men who are real prospects. Your sister was only—"

"Did dad kill himself?"

For the first time in my life I left my mother speechless.

"Did dad kill himself?" My voice was surprisingly steady and matter-of-fact.

"Of course not." She sounded both chipper and angry at the same time.

"Did he leave you a note or anything?"

"How can you ask me something like that?"

"Did he leave you a note?"

"Of course not."

"He was sad, though, wasn't he? I remember him being kind of depressed all the time."

The chipper tone disappeared, leaving just the anger. "Why are you doing this?"

"Did he ever try to kill himself before the accident?"

"Of course not."

"Would you tell me if he had?" She didn't answer. I started to hang up the phone, but stopped. "Go ahead and buy Clem whatever you've got picked out. I'll send you a check."

I hung up. My mother didn't call back for six months.

After packing for an hour I took a nap on the floor. I woke up at two in the afternoon dehydrated and sore. I took some of the pills they'd given me at the hospital, checked all my various lumps and bruises, and showered.

I took my jacket and stepped outside. I found Leland Warner standing on the walkway outside my bungalow.

"Hello." He was wearing a similar outfit to that of the previous night, but he'd protected himself from the cold with a brown canvas field coat. His weight was supported by the same cane he'd used to save my life.

"I'm on my way out." I closed and locked the door.

He smiled, but it was slightly more forced than the previous night. "Then I'm glad I caught you."

"Do you know what your goons did to my place? I have to move."

"I'd like to compensate you for your losses."

"Drop the polite BS. Why are you here?"

He abandoned the forced smile. "You're a straightforward person so I'll be blunt."

"Please."

"I'd like you to stop cooperating with the police."

I laughed. "I bet you would."

"It's not for me." He adjusted his weight on the cane. "I'm not anticipating any legal trouble."

"What are you talking about? You gave orders to beat me up. You had me kidnapped and brought to your house."

"My son-in-law has confessed to giving those orders, and the men who attacked you all confirm they were reporting to Tom."

I remembered Bud saying that Warner was born on top and would end that way. "I saw you, with my own two eyes, giving Frank orders, and I'm not changing my story."

"It'll be your word against everyone else's, but that's not why I'm here." He paused. "The police are moving to press formal murder charges against Tom. They may charge Mary as an accessory."

"If Sinclair killed Val Boyle, then she is an accessory."

"She swears to me that the young man was already dead when they arrived."

"And if that's true, then I'm sure you'll hire an amazing lawyer who will find a way to prove it."

"Please, my daughter is not well." His voice shook with emotion. "Even if she's eventually exonerated, the strain of this will drag her down. She might never recover."

"I'm not going to lie to the police."

He withdrew the blue folder from inside his coat. "Would you be willing to lie in exchange for the truth about your father?"

I almost laughed. "You really are awful."

"It's a fair trade."

"No deal." I started down the walkway.

"Don't assume it's bad news," he said as I passed. "Maybe I made up that business about the suicide. Wouldn't you like to know, one way or the other, for sure?"

I stopped and turned around. "Would you like to know about Mary and what happened in the orchard?" His expression didn't change, but I saw alarm behind those drooping eyelids. "Would you like to know, one way or the other, for sure, just how far Mary would have gone to hold on to Sinclair?"

"I don't know what you're talking about."

I stepped toward him. "Everyone thinks Mary is covering for Sinclair, but maybe it's the other way around. His running away from the orchard makes a lot more sense if his wife had just committed murder."

"That's ridiculous."

"Once Sinclair made enough money, he was sure to leave her. No Val, no money, no threat to her marriage. She had opportunity and motive. I think deep down you're terrified she's a killer. That's why you were so desperate to get the tape. You don't want her anywhere near the police."

He opened his mouth to protest, but I cut him off. "Didn't you push a lot harder than you had to? Hiring dirty cops to beat up journalists is pretty risky. Weren't you desperate?"

"I know my daughter. She's not a killer."

"I'm not saying you believe it, just that you're frightened it might be true." I smiled and pointed at the blue folder. "So you ask me if I want to know some truths about my father. Maybe they'll be good truths. Maybe they'll be bad truths." I paused. "What would you do? Would you like to learn some truths about Mary?"

He looked down at the folder in his hand and then up at me. He rolled it up and shoved it back inside his jacket. "Then what do you want? Please don't say money. It'll be a great disappointment to me."

I shook my head. "I'm not making any kind of trade. Absolutely, end of story, not going to happen."

He paused, then nodded. "All right then."

I waited, but he didn't say anything else.

Finally I broke the silence. "Aren't you going to say it?"

"What's that?"

"You saved my life. I owe you."

He shook his head. "No. I won't say that."

I softened. "The truth is, I already told the police I have doubts about Sinclair committing the murder. It's in my official statement."

"Thank you."

"And maybe I won't raise a big stink about you giving Frank orders."

"Thank you again."

"But I won't lie."

He smiled and began walking out to his waiting car. Over his shoulder he said, "You know, you're very like him."

"Who's that?"

"Your uncle Allen." He chuckled. "Last night you mentioned you were very close to him."

"Are you talking about Bud?" I yelled.

But he didn't answer.

TWENTY-TWO

I waited at the side entrance for someone to use his or her key card to enter the station. Mine had been deactivated. Former employees who are wanted in connection with a murder aren't usually welcome. After ten minutes one of the engineers went in and I grabbed the door behind him.

The newsroom was busy, but when I entered, an audible gasp could be heard. I walked up to Callum, sitting on the assignment desk.

"Lilly." He hung up one of the phones in his hands. "Where in the name of my great-aunt Irene are my news vans?"

"I can explain."

He waved the remaining phone at me. "I know, I know. You're a hero, you're lucky to be alive, you're the greatest thing since sliced bread, but where are the vans?"

"One is in my uncle's backyard, and I think the other is still parked behind the ballpark."

"You think? That's great."

I glanced around the newsroom. "Is Rod here?"

"No. Came in this morning. Said he was going back to L.A. for a couple days to recover." A desk assistant handed Callum the latest faxes. "Said he might not be back. Doesn't like reporting. . . . Are you okay?"

"Fine." I rubbed my forehead. "I have a headache. Is Trent in?"

"Going to get your job back?" Callum smiled with satisfaction. "He's in his office. Go get 'em, kid."

I walked into Trent's office without knocking and closed the door behind me.

Trent looked up from his computer ready to yell at someone, but seeing me, checked himself.

I took a seat. "How's your eye?"

He reached for the remote and lowered the volume on CNN. "I already called payroll and had you reinstated."

"You mean I don't have to threaten you with a lawsuit or tell the world what a spineless creep you were?"

He crossed his arms and spoke in a low and angry monotone. "Don't think you've got a blank check to do whatever you like around here."

"When I return to work next week, I expect to be treated just like everybody else, but today I've got a few requests."

His arms dropped suddenly. "I won't be blackmailed."

My smile deepened. "I think you value your career and are going to do whatever it takes to keep me quiet about my completely erroneous firing—not to mention the way you gave crooked cops the name and address of an employee and then sat back and let them go at her. You'll never get out of Bakersfield if a story like that makes the rounds."

"I don't have to take this."

"Yes, you do, but don't worry. I'm done making you squirm. I'm ready to move on to my actual demands."

He dropped his pretense of outrage. "What do you want?"

"Hire Leanore Drucker back for starters, and up her to two pieces a week. She wasn't getting enough airtime."

"Leanore?" Shock registered on his face. "That's what you want? For me to hire Leanore back?"

I shook my head. "That's not all. The little sick girl too."

"What about her?"

"We spend all our time doing stories about other people making donations. I think it's time we made one of our own."

"I can't write checks because I feel like it. We have a budget. Do you understand? A budget."

"I'm talking about a couple hundred dollars for charity. Make it part of the Season of Caring Campaign. It'll make us look good."

He mumbled something under his breath and moved some papers around the desk.

"I also want you to meet with a minister who thinks we might have some racial bias in our coverage."

"You what?"

"I'm going to give him your number so you two can set something up." I put up a hand to silence his protests. "And I'm serious about this. It's nonnegotiable."

He rolled his eyes. "Anything else?"

"Last thing. I'm going to be the next chief photog."

This time he didn't say anything.

"You said I was the best," I continued. "You said I was the leading candidate before my run of bad luck."

"You were, but—"

"Turns out Freddy manufactured the bad luck for me. He even switched my tape yesterday morning with a black one."

He pulled back in surprise. "Can you prove this?"

"Feel free to check with Rod and Teddy. They'll both back me up. Freddy probably will too, if you press him hard enough."

"Even if it's true, I can't just—"

"Have you offered it to David?"

"No, but—"

"Then it's not his yet." I stood up. "I'm taking a few days off. I'll start my new duties on Monday."

Trent looked around the room, appeared to decide something, then looked back at me. "If what you say about Freddy is true, then you should have the job. That's why I'm going along with this. Not because you have some kind of hold over me. Do we understand each other? From now on I'm treating you like any other employee, and if you don't perform, I'll fire you."

I nodded. "We understand each other."

"And you're going to have to make a real effort with the rest of the shooters."

"I will."

"Good." He reached for the remote, but realized I showed no sign of leaving. "Don't worry. I'll fire Freddy. It's way overdue."

"No. That's not what I want."

Trent looked at me as if I were crazy. "Why not?"

"I'm going to try and work it out with him."

"Then what is it you do want?"

I hesitated. Rod needed a producing job. It would be easy to push Trent—easy to keep Rod in town.

I walked to the door and opened it. "Why don't you get a check cut and I'll run it over to the little sick girl's mom." I closed the door behind me and returned to the newsroom.

Teddy and Freddy stood at the assignment desk with Callum. Freddy's hair was just as short and just as orange as Teddy's. He appeared to be arguing with Callum about something.

Callum saw me. "How'd it go? Are you back on the clock?"

Teddy's eyes widened and his mouth stretched into a goofy grin. "Trent gave you your job back?"

"Better than that. Guess who's going to be the next chief photog?"

Freddy sputtered some angry, disjointed words, then stormed out, leaving Teddy behind looking confused and uncertain.

I gestured to the door Freddy had just slammed and said to Teddy, "You better go after him."

"Totally," he said with obvious relief, and left.

Callum picked up a fax and began reading it. I approached the assignment desk, but he didn't acknowledge me. Finally, without looking up, he said, "You could be great at that job."

"I'll need you to tell me when I'm screwing up."

"You going to listen?"

"Probably not."

He smiled and put the fax down. "I got an auto-versus-tractor out by Highway 178."

"Trent gave me the rest of the week off."

He nodded. "Maybe David can do it before he shoots the

murder victim's memorial service." He reached for a phone. "And before you take off for the week, I want a complete, exclusive sit-down interview about everything that's happened. We'll run it in pieces every night this week and promote the hell out of it." He pointed the phone at me. "And I want those vans back."

"I'd like to keep one. I need to move out of my apartment."

Callum shook his head. "I didn't hear you request a company vehicle for personal use. You said you were taking one as a backup to the on-call shooter."

"Exactly, that's what I said." I reached out and stopped his dialing. "Did you say Val Boyle's funeral is this afternoon?"

"Not a funeral. Coroner's backed up with autopsies. This is a memorial service at the church." Callum looked at the clock on the wall. "Starts in an hour. David's about to leave."

I left him to make his call and followed Teddy and Freddy. They'd gone through the door leading to the equipment room, where the shooters have their lockers. Inside, David and Freddy argued while Teddy hung back eating a bag of smiley-face sun cookies. Freddy and David stopped talking as soon as they saw me.

"Hi," I said.

David scowled. "This moron just told me what he's been doing to your equipment. I swear I had nothing to do with it."

"I believe you, but the truth is we've never gotten along." I hesitated, but decided to continue. "I know I haven't always been easy to work with or even friendly."

"Ha," Freddy said. "That's putting it mildly."

I ignored him and kept looking at David. "But it hasn't all been me. If there's bad blood between us, then we share responsibility for it."

David looked away, then reluctantly nodded.

"You're a great shooter and the station is lucky to have you," I continued. "But I have more seniority and experience and I'm going to be the next chief."

"I totally told him already," Freddy said. "And for the record, I wouldn't want to work for you, even if you begged me."

I continued to speak to David. "You staying here is the best thing for KJAY, but if you can't deal with me as chief, then you need to get your résumé out there and move on to a bigger market."

He nodded again. "I understand." He picked up his gear and exited.

Freddy stomped his foot. "This is totally bogus."

I stayed calm. "Thank you for not calling the cops on me last night."

"That was totally Teddy. I wanted to."

"I'm glad you didn't." I looked at Teddy. "Thank you."

He took a tentative step forward. "It seemed like you were totally up in it, you know." He offered the white bakery bag.

I pulled a cookie out. "Thanks."

"Dude! Don't give her a cookie. She's totally going to get us fired."

I took a heavenly bite. The mixture of sugar, butter, and flour melted in my mouth. "Most people in your position would have called the police last night. I'd like to focus on how you helped me and not the other things. As far as I'm concerned, we're all starting with a blank slate."

Freddy eyed me suspiciously. "Totes for real?"

"Totes for real."

Freddy's crossed arms relaxed a tiny bit. "Well, you know, we're not like rats or anything. We don't go squealing to the cops."

I nodded. "Here's the bottom line. If you have a problem with me being chief, you need to find somewhere else to work. I'm not firing you or telling you to go, but I'm not putting up with any attitude either—and there will be consequences if you screw up."

Freddy relaxed even more. "Yeah, well, maybe we need somebody around here who, like, cracks the whip. Jake used to get on us a lot, but things ran smoother. This was a better place to work back then."

The door opened and Marcie entered. No one spoke for a minute.

"Callum would like me to interview you." She paused and,

when I didn't answer, took a step backward. "If you'd rather wait until someone else is available, I understand. I can—"

"No. I want to get it done so I can go home." I looked at Teddy and Freddy. "Why don't you give us a minute alone?"

They both scurried out.

"Have you heard from Sacramento?" I asked.

Despite an obvious effort to remain stoic, her face lit up with joy. "Yes. I got it. I start in two weeks."

I let my relief translate into a smile. "That's great. I'm sure we can tactfully avoid each other until then."

"Lilly, I know you're upset about what happened, but—"

"I can see now that we were never friends, just friendly." I paused. "That's probably my fault. I never made any effort to know you better."

She shook her head. "It's not like that. I think of you as a friend. I genuinely like you."

"Don't you see how much worse that is? You're my friend, but you sold me out anyway." I started to walk out. "On second thought, I will wait for someone else to do the interview."

After I finished, the Wonder Twins ran me over to Bud's house. No one answered my repeated knocks at the back door.

"Maybe he's, like, walking the dog." Teddy rubbed his shoe against the tin shed, trying to remove the dog poop he'd stepped in.

"I don't think that dog walks anymore." I stopped peering into the window and stepped down onto the brown grass. "But you're right. It looks like he took Pepper with him. That probably means he'll be gone for a while."

Freddy poked the web of shattered glass hanging from the van's rear door. "I want to know how you did so much righteous damage to this thing. Dude, Lilly, you are one badass chick."

"Totally," Teddy rushed to agree. His puppy-dog eyes reminded me of the women in the newsroom who gazed at Rod. "You're totally awesome."

"Not really."

Freddy jabbed at the glass again and it fell off. "Dude, you, like, took on the cops, and gangs, and like a huge conspiracy thing, and a murderer, and best of all you trashed two news vans."

"Trashing vans is a total fantasy of ours," Teddy explained.

I shook my head. "Don't ever say that in front of Callum."

We sent Teddy back to the station in the busted van. It still drove okay, and Teddy looked happy behind the wheel. Maybe that was another fantasy of his.

Freddy drove me over to the little sick girl's house and waited in the van as I rang the doorbell. No one answered at first, but since the mom's car was in the driveway, I kept trying.

Finally I heard footsteps and a tentative female voice. "Who is it?"

"It's Lilly Hawkins from KJAY."

The door opened a crack. I could barely see her through the thin slit.

"I understand if you don't want to see me." I could barely bring myself to look her in the eye. "I said terrible things last night. You have every right to be angry."

"Oh, no, don't worry about it." Her voice sounded upbeat and almost cheerful. "I understand you were going through a lot yesterday."

I felt a wave of relief and realized I'd been holding all my muscles rigid. "Is your daughter at home? I'd like to apologize to her as well."

She jerked her body and seemed to kick at something behind her. "No, she's spending the night at a friend's house."

"Oh, that's too bad." I raised the hand holding the check and offered it to her. "KJAY is making a donation to help your daughter. It's part of our season-of-caring promotion. I hope it helps."

"Thank you. That's so generous." She opened the crack farther and reached for the check. I saw for the first time she was wearing a pink flannel robe. At her feet a familiar face tried to squeeze between her legs and the door frame.

I swallowed a lump in my throat. "Hi, Pepper."

Her cheeks turned bright red as she tried to stammer a reply. "Um . . . that's . . . um . . ."

"Can I speak to my uncle?"

"Just a minute." She closed the door.

A few seconds later I heard loud steps, and the door swung full open. "Lilly." Bud grabbed me in a giant bear hug. He wore shorts and a man's dress shirt that clearly didn't belong to him. In his hand he held a spatula. "Come on in. I'm fixin' somethin' to eat."

"Are you crazy? What are you doing here?"

He let go of me. "We're both consentin' adults."

"Bud, it's the little sick girl's mother. You can't break her heart. The town will lynch you."

He looked into the house, then closed the door behind him. "The truth is, I haven't spent a night in jail in about twenty years, and it didn't feel so good."

"I'm sorry that happened." I looked away. "It wasn't fair to drag you into my mess."

"Nah. That's not what I mean, Little Sister. I was glad to help you out. Best thing I done in a long time." He put a hand on my shoulder. "But I had a lot of time to think, and what I'm tryin' to say is, when you find yourself at my age, sittin' in a cage with a bunch of smelly druggies, pimps, and crazies, well, you take a look at your life and it's not a good look. I'm too old to be runnin' round gettin' into trouble, and more important, it ain't much fun no more."

"What are you saying? You're settling down with a woman you've known a day?"

"Settlin' down for a bit," he said with a twinkle in his eye. "I'm gonna help Annette keep the mortgage up till she gets things sorted out. After that, we're agreed to play it by ear."

"What about her daughter?"

"Annette says she might could get worse." He frowned. "But right now she needs what Annette calls a positive male role model."

I raised an eyebrow. My mother would have been proud. "And that's going to be you?"

"Probably not, but we can hope for a miracle." He pulled up a sleeve. "Check these babies out."

"Are those nicotine patches?"

He nodded. "You know it."

"I don't think you're supposed to wear three at once."

"Me and nicotine been together a long time. This here is gonna be an ugly breakup."

I reached out and hugged him.

I had a sudden thought and pulled back. "Is your name Allen?"

He laughed. "How'd you come to hear that? Not even your mama knows about that."

"Leland Warner told me."

"Oh." His face melted into an inscrutable mask.

"Well? Aren't you going to say something?"

He shrugged. "I told you I had a run-in with the fella, back in the day."

"No," I reminded him. "You said you knew a guy who had a run-in with him, back in the day."

"Near about the same."

"No, it's not."

He put an arm around me. "Now, Little Sister, you are goin' to have to trust me when I tell you this is another story for another day and you best better put it out of your mind." He hooked his thumb back toward the house. "Now, why don't you come on in and get somethin' to eat. Annette's all embarrassed, but she'll get over that soon enough."

I shook my head. "I can't. I want to stop in at Val Boyle's memorial service. I'm worried about his mother."

"How about tomorrow, then?"

I shook my head again. "I have to move. My place is trashed and the landlord wants me out."

"Where you goin'?"

I laughed. "I have no idea."

"How about my place?"

"Really?"

"Sure. I'm gonna be bunkin' over here. You'd be doin' me a favor."

I remembered the lawn and hesitated. "Can I clean up the front of the house?"

"I told you, I'm turnin' over a new leaf. I'll haul all that crud to the dump myself."

"You really don't mind if I move in?"

He answered by hugging me tighter. "Only don't go in the third bedroom. There's some stuff in there you don't want to see . . . or the shed out back."

The ballpark was our final stop. It looked cold and beautiful in the twilight. Freddy sat in his van, the engine idling, while I got out and checked the abandoned one. Frank had said the keys were in the ignition and he hadn't lied.

Freddy stuck his head out the driver's-side window. "I'm kind of disappointed. I was hoping you'd, like, you know, totaled this one too."

"One a day is my limit."

By the time I'd gotten back to my apartment and found some dressier clothes that had survived Belly and Skinny's rampage, day had turned to night. I expected the service to be over, but hoped Diana Boyle might still be there.

I found Reverend Phillips's church five blocks from Diana's house. It had a full parking lot, but the church itself was empty. Light and voices poured out an adjacent building so I walked in. The room surprised me. I expected a quiet and solemn collection of mourners. Instead, over a hundred people talked in normal voices while helping themselves to a huge potluck meal. Most wore black, but the room felt alive and full of energy.

Reverend Phillips spotted me in the doorway and frowned. He

put down his plate and came toward me. "No press here. I told all your friends earlier, this is private."

"I'm not here to take pictures. I came to pay my respects to Mrs. Boyle."

He looked at my black slacks and matching jacket. "Do I have your word?"

"Yes."

He nodded. "Your news director left a message for me this afternoon. Thank you."

"If we're making mistakes, we want to fix them." I paused. "And I keep my word."

"That's why I'm letting you stay." He walked back to where he'd set down his plate and resumed his conversation.

Now alone, I recognized surreptitious looks coming from some of the mourners. I wasn't the only white person in the room, but I was definitely in the minority, and I didn't have any friends or acquaintances to talk with. I located Diana sitting between Rachel and a woman I'd never met. I guessed she was Diana's sister and Gideon's mother. I wanted to pay my respects and leave, but the crowd around them was too large.

I took a plate and helped myself to some food. As I ate by myself, I observed the constantly shifting and changing group of people around the three women. I had feared the revelation of Val's criminal activities would destroy his mother's fragile state of mind. Examining her now, I decided it hadn't. She looked slightly more animated than the day before, and as people expressed their sympathy and support, she appeared to draw strength from them.

I'd started on some lasagna when I noticed Rachel get up and go to the coffee urn.

I approached her cautiously. "Hi. I'm Lilly Hawkins, the shooter who came to Mrs. Boyle's house yesterday."

She glanced up from filling a styrofoam cup with steaming black liquid. "Thanks for coming. It'll mean a lot to Diana." She paused. "About yesterday . . ." She set the cup down. "I hope you don't think badly of us for stopping the interview."

"I would have done the same thing in your place."

She frowned. "I know it looks like we were bought off by those lawyers, but . . ."

"I'm sure Val would have wanted you all to be taken care of."

"You're very nice to say that, but I can see how it looks. Especially now that the police are saying Val's boss may be the one who killed him."

I was surprised by how much I liked her. The clawing attention-grabber from the day before had been replaced by a friendly and intelligent young woman. I guessed the change was due to the absence of my camera. It wouldn't be the first time a desire to get on TV had made someone temporarily insane.

"Don't worry," I told her. "Whatever documents you signed won't prevent you from telling the truth in a criminal investigation, and I do believe Val would have wanted his mother taken care of."

"Thank you." Rachel glanced at Mrs. Boyle. "I better get back. You should come and say hi to Diana. Gideon's around here somewhere too."

Rachel picked up two cups of coffee and started to leave.

I eyed Diana as she took a man's outstretched hand in both of hers. "Rachel?" She paused and I continued, "How is Diana, really? Is she going to be okay?"

Rachel looked around to make sure no one could hear, then leaned in close. "Between you and me, I was very worried. Yesterday afternoon, when Reverend Philips brought Val's personal things from the police, she had a . . . I guess the word is *breakdown*." Rachel glanced at Diana. "Her father's watch was missing—the one she'd given Val when he graduated. It was the last straw."

I didn't know what to say so I fell back on an old standard. "I'm sorry."

Rachel smiled. "Don't worry. She's stronger today. Maybe she needed to get it out of her system."

I nodded and concern turned to curiosity. "That's weird about the watch."

Rachel dismissed the idea with a casual flick of her head. "Not really. Turns out Val left it in his desk at work. Gideon found it when he picked up Val's things from the winery last night."

Could I have missed a watch hidden among Val's things? I'd looked through the entire box carefully, and there hadn't been much in it. "Did Gideon bring Val's things home in an old cardboard box?"

Rachel nodded. "The winery people packed it up that way."

"From his desk at Dewey Ridge?"

She nodded again. "Diana made a big deal this morning about giving the watch back to Gideon, as the man of the family now. It was very emotional."

Why would Gideon lie about finding the watch? I could think of only one possible answer—he couldn't say where he'd really got it.

TWENTY-THREE

I asked Rachel several follow-up questions, culminating with where Gideon lived. She hesitated, confusion and curiosity both apparent on her face, but told me anyway. I asked her not to repeat our conversation, but her excited eyes reminded me of the attention-hungry girl from the day before. I drove quickly to the address she'd given me in the hopes I could get in, find some proof, and get out before she was tempted to tell someone.

The house was dark and empty. I knocked on the front door just in case, but I already knew no one was home. I got my hiking boots out of the back of the van and switched them with the suede pumps I'd worn to the memorial service. After slipping on my blue coat, I checked my camera and loaded it with a fresh battery and tape. I found an open bathroom window and climbed in with my camera.

Even in the dim light I could see the shabbiness of the place. It wasn't modest but clean, like Diana's house. This home was small and the residents were careless with what they did have. I found Gideon's bedroom and turned on a light. A giant poster of a woman in a bikini hung above the bed. A flat-screen TV, still in the box, sat on a desk next to a new video-game system.

I turned on the camera and set it on the desk so it would have a wide view of the room as I searched. I began by thoroughly checking his dresser. Next I turned to the bed and lifted up the mattress. Wads of hundred-dollar bills sat next to a stack of dirty magazines. There had to be tens of thousands of dollars in the careless bundles—not nearly the missing amount, but still suspicious.

Removing the money and taking it to the police wouldn't prove much. It would only be my word where I found it. I took a cellphone picture and sent it to Lucero along with a brief text message explaining where I was.

I continued searching. A solid mass of laundry covered the floor of the closet. I tapped it with my foot and felt something solid. I pushed back the clothes and found a new black suitcase. I opened it. A large gun rested snugly on top of more money than I'd seen in my entire life.

Somewhere in the house a door burst open. Pounding footsteps charged down the hall. I barely had time to stand before Gideon was in the room. He saw me. He saw the open suitcase.

"I can explain." He wore a brand-new black suit and took huge gulps of air as he tried to catch his breath. "It's not like it looks. I can explain. Please let me explain."

"Okay." I picked up my camera. It was still recording, but I didn't care. I just wanted something heavy I could use as a weapon. "I'm listening."

Gideon finished catching his breath. He looked at the open suitcase. "He called me for help. He was scared. He was going to that orchard and he wanted me to come get him. I only went there to help. I thought it would be like the old days. I thought, I have to go, my brother needs me."

His face contorted, but then he suppressed whatever emotions threatened to escape. "That's why I took my mom's gun. He was scared, but wouldn't tell me why. It would've been stupid to go without protection."

I nodded.

Gideon shut the door and began pacing around the room. "When I got there and saw all that money . . . all that money and he wanted to leave it for his rich boss to take. Can you believe that? Leave all that money." His pace quickened. "He wouldn't listen to me. He said I was stupid. He said I'd end up in jail like my father."

Gideon stopped pacing and looked at me. "That's not going to happen. I'm going to have what I want and I'm going to be strong and I'm going to take care of Aunt Diana and my mom and everyone else."

He pointed to the watch on his wrist. "I'm the one who cares about family. Not Val." He took a step toward me. His voice became louder and more emotional. "Val wasn't staying. He was going to some fancy school and ditching us first chance he got. You should have heard the way he talked—even to his mom—like we were embarrassments or something. But I'm staying. I'm the one who's going to be here. I'm the one who knows what's important."

He waited for me to respond. I had no idea what to say. In the ensuing silence we both heard a siren.

"You called them?" He made a noise like a scream and lunged. Without thinking I swung the still-recording camera at him. He took a blow to the head and staggered back. He swayed as though disoriented and reached for the wall.

I dropped the camera and ran. The front door stood open at the end of the hallway. I was steps from making it when my legs went out from under me. He pulled me down and clutched the lower half of my body. I kicked myself free. Instead of running out the door, I turned. My fist connected with his face. Crippling pain shot up my arm.

That's when I felt hands pulling me from behind and saw the uniformed officers.

I didn't put up a fight as they cuffed me, but Gideon freaked out. He began sobbing and wouldn't get off the floor.

Lucero arrived and ordered me taken to the kitchen. I refused medical assistance and waited. I don't know how long. It felt like hours. Sheriff's Department and Bakersfield PD came and went. I saw Handsome, but he didn't respond to my calls, and the officer who was babysitting me said to be quiet. A team of Sheriff's Department TIs arrived and was directed to the rear of the house. After a while one came in and took my prints.

Gideon's mother returned and a nasty scene ensued. I didn't see anything, but her voice carried. Later I heard sobbing and guessed it was her. For the first time in the evening I was glad to be sequestered in the kitchen and away from the emotional carnage.

Finally Lucero, looking cranky and tired, walked in. He pointed to me. "Get those off her."

The Bakersfield PD officer leaned in and unlocked the cuffs.

"Thanks, you can go." Once we were alone, Lucero joined me at the small table. "You okay?"

I looked at my hand. The knuckles were red and swollen. "I think I may have broken my thumb when I hit him."

"Why didn't you tell the EMT?"

"I wasn't thinking."

"That's you in a nutshell." He gave me a paternal smile and reached for my hand. He gently touched the thumb.

"Ow." I winced and pulled away.

"Next time you punch a guy, don't wrap your fingers around the thumb."

Before I could reply, Handsome walked in. He spoke to Lucero as though I weren't in the room. "He's going to have to go in the ambulance. He's got a bad concussion."

"I swung my camera at him."

Handsome didn't look at me, but Lucero turned. "We know. You recorded it, along with his confession. Not that I'm complaining about the confession, but next time you trespass, don't bring a camera along to provide proof of your crime."

"Am I in trouble?"

"You were," Lucero said, "but I doubt his mom will press charges. When she found out what he'd done, she tried to kill him herself."

I relaxed and for the first time became aware of just how much my hand hurt. "Will the confession hold up in court?"

"Doesn't matter. The money and gun are going to hang him." Lucero shook his head. "Not a real bright kid. He should have at least gotten rid of the gun. I guess his cousin was the smart one in the family."

How many times had Gideon heard that? How much of what happened was because of simple greed and how much because of anger?

"He was smart enough to make the 911 call from gang territory," I said. "If I hadn't been at the winery last night and searched Val's things, no one ever would have found out about the watch. He might have gotten away with it."

"Maybe," Lucero replied. "But most likely he'd have spent the money and got caught that way. You don't want something bad enough to kill for it and then leave it in your closet."

I shook my head. "The murder wasn't just about the money. It's more complicated than that."

Handsome grunted and looked at me for the first time. "It's never complicated. You know how many of these cases I've seen? It's always the same. If a woman gets killed, it's almost always her husband or boyfriend. If a young black man gets killed, it's almost always another young black man. People don't change. Even the way they die is predictable."

"You're wrong." I returned his stare. "Gideon really loved Val. Maybe if he hadn't, there wouldn't have been enough anger in him to pull the trigger. It wasn't simply the money. People aren't just one thing. You don't always know what they're going to do."

Handsome rolled his eyes and walked out.

Lucero watched him go and then turned to me. "You know, I really hate that guy."

After getting a splint for my thumb, Lucero made me come to the Sheriff's Department headquarters on Norris Road to make my official statement. While I waited, someone from Gang Enforcement stopped by to give me an update on Jason. He'd already been disowned by the Eastside Crew as their new leadership tried to consolidate power, and it was doubtful I'd face any retaliation. Jason himself was looking at a long prison sentence and wasn't likely to be a threat.

It was early morning by the time Lucero returned me to

Gideon's house and my news van. I drove back to my apartment, laid newspapers down on the floor, and slept next to the remains of my bed. Later that day I finished packing everything salvageable and loaded it in the news van. I was going to be short on clothes until my new credit cards arrived, but at least some of my books had survived.

I made the short drive to Oildale and found Bud had kept his word. The front yard wasn't well landscaped, but the lawn garbage had all been removed. A small rental truck sat at the curb so I expected to find Bud inside the house moving his things.

I was wrong.

Rod sat on the living-room floor stocking a bookcase from an open carton. The collar and tails of a rumpled white dress shirt peaked out from the top and bottom of his striped sweater. His hair was a little less perfect, but it made him look even more like an ad from a fashion magazine. About half a dozen open boxes peppered the room.

I took several more steps into the house. "Rod?"

He saw me and relief showed all over his face.

"What are you doing here? I thought you went to L.A.?"

"I came back." He put down the books and stood. "Callum called and told me what happened last night. Are you all right?"

"Sure. I'm fine." I held up my hand with the splint. "It's only my thumb this time."

He appeared on the cusp of saying something, but instead his entire demeanor shifted from intense to cheerful. "Guess what? I followed your advice." He reached for the books he'd set down. "I told Trent he was either taking me off the air or I'd quit."

I tensed. "What did he say?"

"Starting Monday I'll be writing for the six." He smiled and resumed stocking the bookcase.

"That's fantastic. The six? That's our most important show."

"And when Susan goes on maternity leave, I'm going to produce. You were right. I needed to be more aggressive."

"This is so great." My excitement turned to confusion as I

watched him place another book on the shelf. "Wait a minute. What are you doing here?" I glanced around the room. In addition to the many half-opened boxes I saw a chenille throw, some decorative pillows, and what I can only describe as an elf chessboard. "Why are there elves in my uncle's house?"

He scanned the room and stopped at the chessboard. "Actually only the bishops are elves. The pawns are Hobbits and Gandalf is the king."

"But what's it doing here?"

"Warner's henchmen trashed my place too. I'm staying here until it's fixed."

"What?" My voice almost cracked. "Bud invited you?"

"Ah-huh." He reached down and pulled another stack of books from the open carton. "He called the station looking for me. Did you know he's at the little sick girl's house?"

"But he told me *I* could stay here."

Rod's head jerked up. "He did?"

"Yes, and I don't have anywhere else to go."

Rod stood. He started to say something, but stopped. He looked uncertain.

"I'm sorry, Rod, but you're going to have to find another place."

"It's just . . ." He paused and thought for a moment. "I'm sorry, but I don't think I will." He knelt down and resumed stocking the bookcase.

"What do you mean, you don't think you will?"

"This is the new Roddy. I'm more assertive."

"But you have to go," I ordered.

"No, I don't. Bud offered it to me just as much as you." He smiled. "And I call dibs."

"Dibs? We're not in kindergarten."

"You're only saying that because you didn't call it first."

I tried to calm down. "I'm sorry Bud promised us each this house, but you're going to have to leave. I don't have money for another place and Bud is my uncle. Family is better than dibs."

"Nothing is better than dibs and I called it first, so you can't kick me out."

"He's right, lady." The voice came from a strange man standing at the open living-room window. "I heard him."

I looked at Rod, who didn't seem the least alarmed, then back at the man. "Who are you?"

The man adjusted a drill and placed it against the outside of the house. "I'm Ted. I'm installing your new cable modem." He turned on the drill, and seconds later the metal tip broke through the living-room wall.

I turned on Rod. "You're having cable installed?"

"I play some online RPGs so I need a high-speed Internet connection."

"But . . . that's . . . but," I stammered, then recovered. "This is crazy. One of us has to go and it's not going to be me."

"There are two bedrooms. I'm in one of them. If you stay in the other, it's none of my business."

I let go an exasperated sigh and stormed out the back of the house. From the backyard I tried calling Bud's cell phone, but only got the voice mail. Next I tried Annette's house, but got her machine. I repeated this several times with the same outcome.

Despite these frustrations, the time alone allowed me to calm down. When I returned to the living room, I knew what I had to say to Rod.

He was still on the floor filling the bookcase. The cable guy had finished his work and gone.

"I'm sorry I yelled at you earlier. But we can't both stay here." I knelt down so I could face him. "You're a great guy, and I know you won't pull anything sleazy, but I don't want a housemate. I like being by myself."

Rod picked up a book, looked at the cover, then placed it on the shelf.

"Wait a minute." I reached out and took the familiar image of the Nile. "What are you doing?"

"I'm combining our libraries. See, your Agatha Christie goes before my Philip K. Dick."

I looked at the box he was unloading. It was mine. "But this was in the van."

"You said you weren't leaving so I got the dolly off the truck and unloaded the van for you." Rod gestured down the hall. "I already had my things in the guest room on the left, so I put you in the room with the quilt on the bed. I think it used to be Bud's bedroom."

I jumped up. "Why do you want me here? It makes no sense."

He pretended to look at the open boxes of books. "Because I'm crazy about you and you're crazy about me."

"I am not."

His head tilted up and we made eye contact. "Lillian Hawkins, you are so crazy about me. Deny it all you like, but we both know it's true."

I couldn't look him in the eye. My brain gave the order, but my body refused. It was a giant, screaming admission of the truth. "Oh, crap."

He stood, and before I could stop myself, we were kissing.

I heard a feminine laugh and then my uncle's voice saying, "I can't leave you two alone for five seconds."

I reluctantly pulled away. Bud stood in the doorway carrying two grocery bags. Annette stood behind him holding her daughter's hand.

"Mommy? What's funny?"

Annette suppressed a giggle. "Nothing, dear."

I took a step toward Bud. "Did you tell us each we could stay here?"

"You didn't look too broke up about it a couple seconds ago."

Rod, whose cheeks were now fire-engine red, walked across the room and gestured to the grocery bag. "Can I help with those?"

"Rod, you always show proper respect to your elders." Bud passed him one of the bags. "Let's take this on out to the kitchen.

I'm fixin' to barbecue, and I'm bettin' you don't know much 'bout how to grill up a proper piece of sirloin."

We all drifted out to the backyard, where the sun managed to drive away most of the winter chill. Bud and Rod rolled out a large square of AstroTurf, which nicely covered the dead grass, weeds, and dog poop. A barbecue appeared from under the back porch, and folding chairs were set up. Bud expertly lit the charcoal, and while it got hot, he rattled off barbecue tips like a Zen master.

Chelsea squealed with delight as Pepper paused to lick her face. All the little girl's shyness had vanished, and I wondered if the change was due to the dog, Bud, or her mother's improved mood.

Bud was putting meat on the grill and I was opening a beer when Chelsea asked, "What's wrong with Pepper?"

The animal stared intently down the driveway and made low growling noises.

"Dude," a voice said, "I'm totally telling you I smell food."

I laughed. "We're back here."

"Lilly, dude, you got food?" Freddy turned the corner, followed by Teddy. He surveyed the scene and grinned. "Beer, chips, barbecue . . . looks like you totally knew I was coming."

I glanced at Bud. "Do we have enough?"

"I got brats and chicken in the fridge." He headed for the back porch and winked at the Wonder Twins. "And if I'd known you was comin', I'd have baked that cake."

Rod came and put his arm around me. I didn't pull away. Teddy and Freddy saw and exchanged a look.

"You're welcome to stay," I said to them.

They did. A minute later Teddy froze with a beer can halfway to his lips. "Dude, what about Callum?"

"What about Callum?" I asked.

"Yes, what about me?" Callum followed Bud out the back door. Each man carried an armload of food down the back steps.

Teddy lowered his eyes like a guilty schoolboy. "We kind of left him in the van."

"You can't kind of leave someone in a van," Callum said. "You either do or don't, and in this case you did."

I managed to get over my shock and speak. "I've never seen you outside the station. Did you abandon the scanner?"

He reached the bottom of the stairs, noticed the AstroTurf, considered it for a moment, then followed Bud to the card table next to the grill. "I've never had a shooter single-handedly catch a murderer. I've never had a shooter follow that up by moving out of their apartment without a word where they were going. I've never had a shooter fail to call in after all that drama and carnage and let me know they were all right." He opened his arm and dropped his load of buns and condiments.

Bud tipped an imaginary hat at him. "Much obliged for the help."

Callum nodded, then turned back to me. "None of that has ever happened before, so I've never had to abandon the scanner."

"Dude, I told him you were cool," Freddy interjected, "but he insisted on coming over and checking."

I looked at Callum. "Really?"

His eyes moved evasively around the backyard. "I was off in an hour, anyway, and Marcie's watching the assignment desk."

"Dude," Freddy said, "he was, like, totally worried about you."

Teddy nodded and added, through a mouthful of potato chips, "Totally."

Callum frowned. "I was concerned."

"Totally concerned," Teddy countered.

"It doesn't matter." Rod handed Callum a beer. "Now that you're here you can stay and eat."

Callum glanced around the yard. He shrugged his shoulders. "Lord knows I've put in enough unpaid overtime the last couple days."

Bud patted him on the back. "That's the spirit."

"What about Trent?" I asked. "Is he going to be okay with this?"

Freddy and Teddy erupted into squeals of laughter.

Even Callum smirked. "He's out for the day. Apparently somebody dumped a bunch of garbage on his lawn last night."

"Dude, it was way better than garbage," Freddy told him. "There was like weird lawn decorations and furniture."

I couldn't bring myself to look at Bud.

"I even saw a trampoline," Teddy said. "I took pictures, but Trent got mad and said we weren't allowed to put it on the news."

"Did Trent get a description of the man who did it?"

"One of the neighbors saw them." Freddy found the chips and began munching. "They had a truck and wore ski masks."

"Them?" I asked. "There was more than one?"

Bud moved some meat around on the barbecue. "That'd be a two-man job, Little Sister." He gave Rod a sly, sideways glance.

I walked over to Rod, who'd managed to stay out of the conversation by playing with Chelsea.

"What did you do?" I whispered.

He could barely contain his laughter, but somehow managed to say, "I don't know what you're talking about. I don't even own a ski mask." He then kissed me and I forgot to be upset.

A little later Bud sent me into the house for more chips. I found them on the kitchen counter and turned to go back out. Callum stood at the back door.

"Everything okay?" I asked.

"So you and Rod, huh?"

I nodded. "Me and Rod."

Callum looked troubled. "You may have the wrong idea about him. He looks sharp and cool, but he's actually very shy."

"I know."

"Frankly, he's pretty geeky. I think sometimes girls dump him when they figure that out."

"I know."

"But he's a good guy and . . ."

I opened my arms. "And what?"

"I think you could do some damage if you treat him badly."

I shook my head. "I'm not going to treat him badly."

"You wouldn't mean to, but . . . Take for instance when he first started at KJAY. Freddy pulled a lot of stupid hazing-type pranks. I kept thinking Rod would refuse to work with him, but each day he came back thinking it would be different."

"He sees the best in people, and when something does go wrong, he believes the next time will be different," I said matter-of-factly.

Callum nodded. "Yes."

"And you think that makes him vulnerable because, of course, people rarely change and the next time is almost never different."

Callum nodded again.

"Don't worry." I stepped onto the back porch and looked down at the unlikely group assembled in Bud's backyard. "That's why I'm crazy about him."

ACKNOWLEDGMENTS

None of this would be possible without Molly Friedrich, Lucy Carson, and Paul Cirone. After being rejected by forty-seven agents, I had the unbelievable good fortune to be pulled from the slush pile at The Friedrich Agency.

I'm deeply indebted to Trish Lande Grader for taking a chance on Lilly Hawkins during the worst economy since the Great Depression.

My most heartfelt thanks go out to everyone at Touchstone and Simon & Schuster. My editor, Sulay Hernandez, has been amazing from the start. Her support and feedback was integral to shaping the final manuscript. My copy editors, Steve Boldt and Jessica Chin, saved me from my worst grammatical instincts. The production, marketing, and sales departments, as well as publisher Stacy Creamer, have all gone above and beyond.

I'd also like to thank my family and all the friends who helped me during the writing of this book. My mother, my father, Cheré Coen, Matt Harry, Hillary Huth, Tracy Imley, Jo Imhoff, Ceasonne Reiter, Peter Schuurmans, Barbara Stepansky, and Kim Zachman all graciously gave up their time to read and give advice.

I'm especially grateful to Rachel Manija Brown for reading two different versions of the manuscript and for her thoughtful feedback. It was her suggestion that led me to create the character of Rod Strong.

Finally, I'd like to thank my husband Jeff for his unwavering support.

Touchstone Reading Group Guide

A BAD DAY'S WORK

News camerawoman, Lilly Hawkins, gets the scoop on all her competitors when she is first to film the crime scene of a gruesome murder. She hurriedly returns to the office to screen her footage, only to discover that the tape is blank. When Lilly returns home, two dirty cops attack her, demanding that she produce the tape of her footage or suffer additional attacks. Working against the clock, Lilly must clear her name and solve the murder before she becomes the next victim. Along the way, Lilly receives help from a surprising source who challenges her to rethink the way she's always seen the world and herself.

For Discussion

1. At the start of the novel, what does McFarland establish about Lilly Hawkin's status at KJAY? What has happened to her? What are her challenges? Why is it important to Lilly that she acquire good footage of the Valley Farm's murder scene?

2. What do we learn about the nature of Lilly's work as a shooter? According to Lilly, there are key "Gets" to shoot in every news story. Identify some of Lilly's shooting assignments, her

intended "Gets," and her success rate. How would you rate Lilly's skills as a shooter?

3. How would you characterize Lilly? What are her strengths and her weaknesses? How are your perceptions of these altered throughout the story? Do you like Lilly? Why or why not?

4. Describe Lilly's relationships with her two potential suitors, "Handsome" and Rod Strong. What are Lilly's perceptions of each? Whom did you find most appealing? Why?

5. By the time Skinny and Belly attack Lilly in her apartment, what does Lilly believe or know about the Valley Farms murder? How does the attack impact the direction or focus of her investigation? What does she learn about the particulars of the case in her efforts to meet her attackers' 2 p.m. deadline?

6. As the novel progresses, Lilly's taped recording of the murder scene becomes extremely valuable to a number of key characters. Identify these characters and the value of the tape to each. By the story's end, what meaning does the tape provide to any or all of them?

7. Why does Lilly seek out her uncle Bud? How does his presence aid Lilly? What are they able to discover together?

8. Explore the nature of Lilly's relationship with her uncle Bud. What do they believe about each other? How do the actions of the story support or challenge their conceptions of each other?

9. Lilly gains a surprising ally in Rod Strong, who sheds light on the nature of her relationships with her colleagues at work. What does Rod reveal about Lilly's views of her colleagues? How is Lilly able to use the knowledge she gains from their interaction to assist in clearing her name? What larger lesson does she extract from the situation?

10. As Lilly progresses deeper into her investigation, a more complicated portrait of the victim, Val Boyle, emerges that contradicts the views of the police. What are the conflicting perspectives on Val? How are these conflicting perspectives highlighted in the discovery of the real murderer? How does the resolution of these conflicting portraits impact Lilly?

11. Which seemingly inconsequential events or individuals provided clues to help Lilly solve the crime?

12. Leland Warner threatens to reveal a family secret to keep her from revealing evidence that could hurt his daughter. What is the nature of his claims about Lilly's past? Is Lilly able to substantiate his claims? What does Lilly's confrontation with Leland reveal about her? Do you agree with Lilly's stance? Why or why not?

13. By the story's end, Lilly repeats a line she heard from Rod: "People aren't just one thing. You don't always know what they are going to do." What does Lilly mean to suggest with this line? What is Rod suggesting when he first says the line to Lilly? What does her repetition of this line illuminate about her character? Do you agree with her contention? Why or why not?

A Conversation with Nora McFarland

This is your first novel. What was the inspiration for *A Bad Day's Work*?

I was working as a shooter in Bakersfield and realized it would be a great set-up for a mystery, but didn't make the attempt until later when I took a job at Barnes & Noble. Meeting the authors who visited the store and working around so many books inspired me. At first I tried to write like Ross MacDonald or Sue Grafton, both of whom I've always loved, but it's just not my voice. When I try to be hardboiled it comes out pretentious. As soon as I allowed myself to be funny everything began to click.

Why did you choose to work within the mystery/suspense genre? What are its benefits and drawbacks?
Long before I attempted to write in the mystery genre I was a fan. I think it goes back to my parents showing me the film version of *Death on the Nile* when I was five. I can't imagine writing straight fiction. I'd have no idea what to do with my characters.

You have worked for a television news network. What can you tell us about the demands of putting together a compelling news story for the public?
A news story must have human elements that the audience relates to and it needs to support journalism's core mission of giving people the information that they need to be well informed taxpayers and members of the community. It also has to have great pictures because it's fundamentally a visual medium. Plus, anything about Anna Nicole Smith. I'm only half kidding. You need to balance what people want and what they need. Unfortunately, there's always an element of making sausage. You're working on deadline and probably trying to do too much with too few resources.

At the start of the novel, you note that Lilly Hawkins is a rarity, a female shooter. Is that true to life? What appeals to you about the world of a shooter?
I was the only female shooter in Bakersfield and there were many other television markets without any women photographers. It's gotten better since then, but shooting is still a male-dominated profession. It's a physically demanding job that you simply must be aggressive to be successful at. Those are traits associated more with men, but it doesn't mean women can't be great shooters or even the best.

One of the factors changing the landscape is the proliferation of One-Man-Bands. That's when a reporter shoots their own video.

In smaller television markets the economic pressures are forcing stations to eliminate photographers. One or two shooters remain on the payroll to handle live shots and maintain the equipment, but most of the photography is done by reporters. Since many of the reporters are women, this has changed the dynamic. It's also something Lilly will eventually have to deal with at KJAY.

Shooting really is a double edged sword. The very thing that makes it so attractive, the excitement and adrenaline rush of chasing a story, is what wears you down. I eventually burnt out and took a job that didn't require me to visit crime scenes in the middle of the night. Many of my fellow shooters also left the business or transitioned into different positions. It's difficult to keep that kind of pace up.

Did Lilly turn out as you originally envisioned? What do you hope readers take to heart with Lilly?
Lilly absolutely did not turn out like I originally envisioned. I had planned for her character to be someone who begins the novel with low self esteem and, because of everything she goes through, changes into someone with high self esteem. But as I wrote, I felt myself pulled in another direction. I kept creating subplots where it turned out Lilly was her own worst enemy and had fundamentally misjudged other characters and situations. Also, I felt like I'd betrayed the character by portraying her as wimpy. I did a second draft with major changes and abandoned the self-esteem idea completely. That's when Lilly came into her own.

What challenges did you encounter with writing your first novel?
The biggest challenge was not being very good at it. I was trying to run a marathon, but didn't know how to walk. I learned to write slowly over many drafts and many hours at my laptop.

***A Bad Day's Work* features a wonderful cast of characters that feel like an extended family. Was that important for you to establish**

this sense of community in the novel? Were there any real life inspirations for any of these characters?

I've always loved television shows with coworkers who behave more like a family. I watched a lot of *The Mary Tyler Moore Show*, *Bob Newhart*, and *Barney Miller* when I was a little kid. I also love the films of Wes Andersen. Each one ends with a group of conflicting personalities coming together. That sense of family and community is very satisfying for me as a reader/viewer and it's probably natural that I'd incorporate it into my writing.

Leanore Drucker is the only character with real life inspirations, even though the particulars of her situation are made-up. She's based on a well known Bakersfield historian named Vivian Tucker. She was a very special lady who passed away several years ago. I took some of her mannerisms and added some from my friend Leanore Motley and then filled in the rest of the character from my imagination. But every other character and the things that happen to them are complete fiction.

You play quite a bit with the appearance of things versus their reality. Was that a natural avenue for you to explore since the work of a shooter is so visual or is this an important theme for you as a writer?

I decided it was a great way to tie together a lot of different ideas I had floating around my first draft. The video Lilly records when doing a story is incomplete without context, just like her views of people are shallow without her actually making an effort to know them. I also tried to tie that into the love story by making one of Lilly's suitors have a cynical view of people based on stereotypes and another have an optimistic, but ultimately more nuanced view.

How does your background in cinema and television impact your work as a novelist?

Something that was hammered into us in film school is that characters need to change. They need to have an arc that you can trace and is satisfying to the viewer/reader. Almost every one of my characters ends the story in a different place from where they started. The only character that doesn't change turns out to be a big jerk.

If your work was to be translated for television, who would you like to see cast as Lilly Hawkins, Rod Strong, and Uncle Bud?
Lilly is hard for me. Michelle Williams or Reese Witherspoon would both be fantastic. Kristen Bell is one of my favorite actresses, but I love her so much as *Veronica Mars* that it's hard for me to see her as another character—especially one I created.

Ryan Reynolds would be fantastic for Rod, but I also like Jason O'Mara from the American version of *Life on Mars*. He has an inherent likeability that's perfect for Rod.

Ian McKellan is my dream Bud. I hope that doesn't sound arrogant, because he's such an amazing and distinguished actor, but it would be so much fun to watch him bring Bud to life.

This is the first of a planned trilogy. What can we expect from the next book in the series?
Lilly and Rod are covering a deadly wildfire in the mountains above Bakersfield. Residents are evacuating and thousands of firefighters are pouring in. A body is found in the local lake and authorities, already overwhelmed by the natural disaster, are quick to declare it an accidental drowning. The victim turns out to be someone Lilly has a personal connection to and she begins investigating the death as the fire escalates.

Enhance Your Book Club

1. **Explore the role of TV shooters aiming to shoot the best "Gets" for their respective television station.** Watch a news broadcast on your local station, and try to think like the shooter. What were the "Gets" for each story? Was the shooter effective? How

did you evaluate the effectiveness of a particular "Get"? Was there anything you would have done differently?

2. **Review Chimamanda Adichie: The Danger of A Single Story** at http://www.ted.com/talks/chimamanda_adichie_the_danger_of_a_single_story.html or http://www.youtube.com/watch?v=D9Ihs241zeg. In this talk, Nigerian novelist Chimamanda Adichie discusses the dangers of presenting one perspective on an issue, a country, or a group of people, much like Reverend Phillips suggests to Lilly Hawkins at the victim's house. Based on Adichie's talk and Reverend Phillips's comments to Lilly, what single stories do you detect in the media today? What do you believe is the root of these single stories? What do you believe is the effect of these single stories? How might you or others challenge single stories in the future?

3. **Appearance vs. reality in *A Bad Day's Work*.** Lilly struggles to have an accurate perception of those with whom she works as well as some of the individuals she encounters on the job. Her Uncle Bud suggests she may be incapable of reading people well. Talk about a situation where you read someone inaccurately. What cues did you use to come to your conclusion about the individual? Once you were able to determine that you were wrong, were you able to reevaluate your initial cues? Why do you believe you had such a mistaken impression? Have you been able to transfer the lessons you learned into a future situation? If yes, how? If no, why not?